If it really *is* SPECTRE we're up against, they're a hard and ruthless enemy. Also, they hate me personally. I killed their original leader, so they'll be out for blood; and when SPECTRE has a blood lust, nothing is done by halves. You can't expect it to be quick and painless with them. If they get the upper hand, SPECTRE will make sure we suffer either stark terror or what the books used to call a painful and lingering death. Cedar, if you want to get out, tell me here and now. You're a great partner and I'd like you with me. But if you can't make it . . . Well, better we should split up now.'

By John Gardner

Licence Renewed
For Special Services
Icebreaker
Role of Honour
Nobody Lives For Ever
No Deals, Mr Bond
Scorpius
Win, Lose or Die
Brokenclaw
The Man from Barbarossa
Death is Forever
Never Send Flowers
SeaFire
Cold
Licence to Kill
GoldenEye

John Gardner served with the Fleet Air Arm and Royal Marines before embarking on a long career as a thriller writer, including international bestsellers *The Nostradamus Traitor*, *The Garden of Weapons*, *Confessor* and *Maestro*. In 1981 he was invited by Glidrose Publications Ltd – now known as Ian Fleming Publications – to revive James Bond in a brand new series of novels. To find out more visit John Gardner's website at www.john-gardner.com or the Ian Fleming website at www.ianfleming.com

FOR SPECIAL SERVICES

John Gardner

An Orion paperback

First published in Great Britain in 1982
by Jonathan Cape
This paperback edition published in 2012
by Orion Books Ltd,
Orion House, 5 Upper St Martin's Lane,
London WC2H 9EA

An Hachette UK company

1 3 5 7 9 10 8 6 4 2

A CIP catalogue record for this book
is available from the British Library.

ISBN 978-1-4091-3563-0

Typeset at The Spartan Press Ltd,
Lymington, Hants

Printed and bound by CPI Group (UK) Ltd,
Croydon, CR0 4YY

The Orion Publishing Group's policy is to use papers
that are natural, renewable and recyclable products and
made from wood grown in sustainable forests. The logging
and manufacturing processes are expected to conform to
environmental regulations of the country of origin.

www.orionbooks.co.uk
www.ianfleming.com

CONTENTS

For
Desmond Elliot

ACKNOWLEDGMENTS AND AUTHOR'S NOTE

As with the first continuation James Bond novel, *Licence Renewed*, I must acknowledge grateful thanks to the literary copyright holders – Glidrose Publications – for inviting me to follow in Ian Fleming's footsteps, and attempt to bring Mr Bond into the 1980s. In particular, my personal thanks to Dennis Joss, Peter Janson-Smith and John Parkinson, for their patience and trust.

Great acknowledgments must also go to Peter Isreal, of the Putnam Publishing Group, and my personal manager, Desmond Elliot, both of whom have given me valuable assistance and support: as have Tom Maschler, Mary Banks and, particularly, Tony Colwell, who spotted a character flaw and brilliantly suggested a major plot change. I would also like to express my personal gratitude to all members of SAAB (GB) Ltd, and Saab-Scania in Sweden, for the amount of time, trouble, patience and enthusiasm they have put into proving that the James Bond Saab really does exist. In particular, I must mention – Philip Hall, John Edwards, Ian Adcock, Peter Seltzer, and Hans Thornquist.

When going through the acknowledgments for *Licence Renewed*, I realised I had omitted a most important name – the knowledgeable man who privately researched a shortlist of motor cars, which eventually led to my putting Mr Bond in a Saab; Tony Snare.

Ian Fleming, being the great craftsmen he was, always attempted – with some licence, granted to all writers of fiction – to get the nuts and bolts correct. I have tried to do the same thing, with one exception. While the NORAD Command Headquarters exists – in the Cheyenne Mountains, Colorado – I found it impossible to get an accurate description of the way into this incredible defence base. It has, therefore, been necessary for invention here. All the space satellites mentioned do exist, and it is my understanding that the race for a Particle Beam Weapon is going on at this moment.

The only exception, among the satellites, is the important one which I have designated the Space Wolf. However, I am firmly assured that the capability of these weapons does exist and that they are real, even though, at the time of writing, no country will admit to any being in orbit.

John Gardner
1982

I

THREE ZEROS

Euro air traffic Control Centre, at Maastricht on the Belgian–
Dutch border, passed British Airways Flight 12 over to London
Control, at West Drayton, just as the aircraft cleared the coast a
few miles from Ostend.

Frank Kennen had been on duty for less than ten minutes
when he accepted the flight, instructing the Boeing 747 Jumbo
to descend from 29,000 feet to 20,000. It was only one of many
aircraft showing on his radarscope – a green speck of light, with
its corresponding number, 12, together with the aircraft's altitude and heading.

All appeared normal. The flight was entering the final phase of
its long haul from Singapore via Bahrain. Kennen automatically
began to advise Heathrow approach control that Speedbird 12
was inbound.

His eyes remained on the huge radarscope. Speedbird 12 began
its descent, the altitude numbers reducing steadily on the
screen. 'Speedbird One-Two cleared to two-o; vector . . .' He
stopped in mid-sentence, only vaguely aware of Heathrow approach querying his information. What he now saw on the
scope made his stomach turn over. With dramatic suddenness,
the indicator numbers 12 – 'squawked' by the Boeing's trans-
ponder – flicked off and changed.

Now, instead of the steady green 12 beside the blip, there were
three red zeros blinking on and off rapidly.

Three red zeros are the international 'squawk' signal for hijack.

His voice calm, Frank Kennen called up the aircraft. 'Speedbird One-Two you are cleared to two-o. Did you squawk affirmative?' If there was trouble on board, the wording would sound like a routine exchange. But there was no response.

Thirty seconds passed, and Kennen repeated his question.

Still no response.

Sixty seconds.

Still no response.

Then, ninety-five seconds after the first 'squawk', the three red zeros disappeared from the screen, to be replaced by the familiar 12. In his headset, Kennen heard the captain's voice, and breathed a sigh of relief. 'Speedbird One-Two affirmative squawk. Emergency now over. Please alert Heathrow. We need ambulances and doctor. Several dead and at least one seriously injured on board. Repeat emergency over. May we proceed as instructed? Speedbird One-Two.'

The captain could well have added, 'Emergency over, thanks to Commander Bond.'

2

NINETY SECONDS

A little earlier, James Bond had been reclining, apparently relaxed and at ease, in an aisle seat on the starboard side of the Executive Class area of Flight BA 12.

In fact, Bond was far from relaxed. Behind the drowsy eyes and slumped position, his mind was in top gear, his body poised – wound tight as a spring.

Anyone looking closely would also have seen the strain behind the blue eyes. From the moment James Bond had boarded the flight in Singapore, he was ready for trouble – and even more so following the take-off at Bahrain. After all, he knew the bullion had come aboard at Bahrain. So did the four undercover Special Air Service men, also on the flight, spread tactically through the first, executive, and tourist classes.

It was not simply the tension of this particular trip that was getting to Bond, but the fact that Flight BA 12 from Singapore was his third long-haul journey, made as an anti-hijack guard, in as many weeks. The duty, shared with members of the SAS, had come following the recent appalling spate of hijackings that had taken place on aircraft from a dozen countries.

No single terrorist organisation had claimed responsibility, but the major airlines were already suffering from a shrinkage in passengers. Panic was spreading, even though companies – and, indeed, governments – had poured soothing words into the ears of the general travelling public.

In each recent case, the hijackers had been ruthless. Deaths among both passengers and crew were the norm. Some of the hijacked aircraft had been ordered to fly to remote airfields hidden in dangerous, often mountainous, European areas. There had been one case of a 747, instructed to make a descent near the Swiss Bernese Alps, on to a makeshift runway hidden away in a high valley. The result was catastrophic, ending with no recognisable bodies – not even those of the hijackers.

In some cases, after safe landings, the booty had been offloaded and taken away in small aircraft, while the original target was burned or destroyed by explosives. In every case, the slightest interference, or hesitation, had brought sudden death – to crew members, passengers, and even children.

The worst incident, to date, was the theft of easily movable jewels, worth two million sterling. Having got their hands on the metal cases containing the gems, the hijackers ordered a descent and then parachuted from the aircraft. Even as the passengers must have been breathing sighs of relief, the aeroplane had been blown from the sky by a remote control device.

Major United States carriers, and British Airways had borne the brunt of the attacks; so, following this last harrowing incident – some six weeks before – both governments had arranged for secret protection on all possible targets.

The last two trips in which Bond had participated had proved uneventful. This time he experienced that sixth sense telling him that danger was at hand.

First, on boarding at Singapore, he had spotted four possible suspects. These four men, smartly dressed, expensive, and carrying the trappings of commuting businessmen, were seated in the executive area: two on the port side of the centre section, to Bond's left; the other two forward – about five rows in front of him. All had that distinctive military bearing yet stayed quiet, as though at pains not to draw attention to themselves.

Then, at Bahrain, the trouble had come aboard – almost $2 billion worth of gold, currency and diamonds – and three young men and a girl embarked. They smelled of violence – the girl, dark-haired, good-looking, but hard as a rock; the three men, swarthy, fit, with the compact movements of trained soldiers.

On one of his seemingly casual walkabouts, Bond had marked their seat positions. Like the suspect businessmen, they sat in pairs, but behind him, in the tourist section.

Bond and the SAS men were of course armed, Bond with a new pair of throwing knives, balanced perfectly and well-honed, developed from the Sykes-Fairbairn commando dagger. One was in his favourite position, strapped to the inside of the left fore-arm, the other sheathed, horizontally, across the small of his back. He also carried the highly-restricted revolver developed by an internationally reliable firm for use during in-flight emergencies.

This weapon is a small, smooth bore .38 with cartridges containing a minimal charge. The projectile is a fragmentation bullet – lethal at a few feet only, for its velocity is spent quickly, so that the bullet disintegrates in order to avoid penetration of an airframe, or the metal skin of an aircraft.

The SAS men were similarly armed and had undergone extensive training, but Bond remained unhappy about any kind of revolver being on board. A shot too close to the sides, or a window, could still possibly cause a serious depressurisation problem. He would always stick with the knives, using the revolver only if really close up to his target, and by 'close' he meant two feet.

The giant 747 banked slightly, and Bond registered the slight change in pitch from the engines, signalling the start of their descent. Probably somewhere just off the Belgian coast, he judged, his eyes roaming around the cabin, watching and waiting.

A statuesque blonde stewardess, who had been much in evidence during the flight, was passing a pair of soft-drink cans to two of the businessmen a few rows in front of Bond. He saw her face and in a flash sensed something was wrong. Her fixed smile had gone, and she was bending unusually low, whispering to the men.

Automatically Bond glanced to his left, towards the other pair of neatly-dressed men. In the seconds that his mind had focused on the stewardess, the two other men had disappeared.

Turning his head, Bond saw one of them, carrying what looked to be a can of beer, standing behind him in the aisle near the small galley at the rear of the executive class section. By this time, the stewardess had gone into the forward galley.

As Bond started to move, everything began to happen.

The man behind him pulled the ring on his beer can, tossing it down the aisle. As it rolled, dense smoke started to fill the cabin.

The two men, forward, were now out of their seats, and Bond caught sight of the stewardess back in the aisle, this time with something in her hand. On the far side, he glimpsed the fourth businessman, also hurling a smoke canister as he began to run forward.

Bond was on his feet and turning. His nearest target – the man in the aisle behind him – hesitated for a vital second. The knife appeared in Bond's right hand as though by some practised legerdemain, held down, thumb forward, in the classic fighting pose. The hijacker did not know what hit him, only a sudden rip of pain and surprise as Bond's dagger slid home just below the heart.

The whole cabin was now full of smoke and panic. Bond shouted for passengers to remain seated. He heard similar cries from the SAS men in the tourist class, and forward, in the first and so-called 'penthouse suite'. Then there were two small explosions, recognisable as airguard revolver shots, followed by the more sinister heavy bang of a normal weapon.

Holding his breath in the choking fog of smoke, Bond headed for the executive class galley. From there he knew it would be possible to cross to the port side and negotiate the spiral stairway to the 'penthouse' and flight deck. There were still at least three hijackers left, possibly four.

On reaching the galley, he knew there were only three. The stewardess, still clutching a Model II Ingram submachine gun, in the swirl of smoke, lay sprawled on her back, her chest ripped away by a close-range shot from one of the airguard revolvers.

Still holding his breath, knife at his side, Bond sidestepped the body, oblivious to the screams and coughing of terrified passengers throughout the aircraft. Above the noise came a loud, barked order from overhead 'Orange One. Orange One', the signal, from an SAS man, that the main assault was taking place on, or near, the flight deck.

At the foot of the spiral staircase, Bond dodged another body, one of the SAS team, unconscious and with a nasty shoulder wound. Then, from the short turn in the spiral, he spotted the crouched figure of one of the businessmen raising an Ingram, shoulder stock extended.

Bond's arm curved back, and the knife flickered through the air, so razor-sharp that it slid into the man's throat from the rear like an oversized hypodermic. The hijacker did not even cry out as blood spurted in a hose-like jet from his severed carotid artery.

Crouching low, Bond clambered, cat-silent, to the body, using it as a shield to peer into the upper area of the aircraft.

The door to the flight deck was open. Just inside, one of the 'businessmen', a submachine gun in his hands, was giving instructions to the crew, while his back-up man faced outwards from the doorway, the now familiar Ingram – capable of inflicting a great deal of damage at a fire rate of 1,200 rounds per minute – swinging in a lethal arc of readiness. Behind the upper galley bulkhead, some six feet from where the hijackers stood, one of the SAS men crouched, airguard revolver clutched close to his body.

Bond looked across at the SAS man and they exchanged signals: the teams had worked together over a hard and concentrated week at Bradbury Lines, 22 SAS Regiment's base near Hereford. In very short order, both men understood what they had to do.

Bond edged to one side of the slumped man on the narrow stairway, his hand reaching for the knife sheathed to his back.

One deep breath, then the nod to the SAS man who leaped forward, firing as he went.

The hijacker guard, alerted by Bond's movement, swung his Ingram towards the stairwell as two bullets from the SAS air-guard revolver caught him in the throat. He was neither lifted nor spun by the impact. He simply toppled forward, dead before he hit the ground.

As he fell, the hijacker on the flight deck whirled around. Bond's arm moved back. The throwing knife spun, twinkling and straight as a kingfisher to carve into the hijacker's chest.

The Ingram fell to the deck. Then Bond and the SAS man, moving as one, were on the hijacker, frisking and feeling for hidden weapons or grenades. The wounded man gasped for air, his hands scrabbling for the knife, eyes rolling, and an horrific croaking rattle coming from the bloodstained lips.

'All over,' Bond shouted at the aircraft's captain, hoping that it was, indeed, all over. Almost ninety seconds had passed since the first smoke bomb exploded.

'I'll check below,' he called to the SAS man who knelt over the wounded hijacker.

Down in the main section of the aircraft, the smoke had almost cleared, and Bond grinned cheerfully at a white-faced senior stewardess. 'Get them calmed down', he told her. 'It's okay.' He patted her arm, then told her not to go near the executive class forward galley.

He went himself, pushing people away, firmly ordering passengers back to their seats. He covered the dead stewardess's body with a coat.

The two remaining SAS men had, rightly, remained in the rear of the aircraft, covering any back-up action which might have been laid on by the terrorists. Walking the length of the Boeing, James Bond had to smile to himself. The three tough-looking young men and the girl who had become his suspects when boarding at Bahrain looked even more pale and shaken than their fellow passengers.

As he mounted the spiral staircase again, the quiet tones of the purser came through the interphone system, advising passengers that they would shortly be landing at London Heathrow and apologising for what he called 'the unscheduled unpleasantness'.

The SAS officer shook his head as Bond emerged into the penthouse suite. The hijacker who had been the target for Bond's second knife was now laid out over two spare seats, his body covered with plastic sheeting. 'No way,' the SAS officer said. 'Lasted only a few minutes.'

Bond asked if the man had regained consciousness.

'Just at the end. Tried to speak.'

'Oh?'

'Couldn't make head or tail of it myself.'

Bond urged him to remember.

'Well . . . Well, he seemed to be trying to say something. It was very indistinct, though. Sounded like "inspector". He was rattling and coughing up blood, but the last part certainly sounded like that.'

James Bond became silent. He took a nearby seat for the landing. As the 747 came whining in, flaps fully extended and the spoilers lifting as the aeroplane rolled out, touching down gently on runway 28R, he pondered the hijacker's last words. No, he thought, it was too far-fetched, an obsession out of his past. *Inspector. In . . . spector.* Forget about the 'In'.

Was it possible after all this time?

He closed his eyes briefly. The long flight and the sudden, bloody action at the end must have scrambled his brains. The founder, Ernst Stavro Blofeld was dead beyond a doubt, SPECTRE as an organised unit had expired with Blofeld. But who could tell? The original organisation spanned the world and, at one time, had its fingers into practically every major crime syndicate, as well as most of the police forces, security and secret intelligence services, in the so-called civilised world.

Inspector. In . . . spector. SPECTRE, his old enemy, the Special

Executive for Counterintelligence, Terrorism, Revenge and Extortion. Was it possible that a new SPECTRE had risen, like some terrible mutated phoenix, to haunt them in the 1980s?

The 747's engines cut off. The bell-like signal told the passengers to disembark.

Yes. James Bond decided it was highly possible.

3

THE HOUSE ON THE BAYOU

It stood, decaying and corrupt, on the only firm piece of ground in the midst of swamp land. The *bayou* channelled around it, then split up to join its brothers and disappear in steamy green marshes.

The nearest town was six miles away, and the few people who lived near the edge of that great watery marsh, on the lower reaches of the Mississippi River, kept away from the soggy bank across from the house.

Very old people said some mad Englishman had built the house, in the 1820s, as a grand palace from which he would tame the swamp. But he did not get far. There was trouble with a woman – in some versions, more than one woman – and there had certainly been death, from fever and disease, also from violence. The house was surely haunted. There were unexplained noises. It was also protected by its own evil: guarded by snakes, great snakes, the like of which were not seen in other parts of the swamp. These great snakes – up to thirty and forty feet in length, some reported – kept close to the house but as the nearest store owner, Askon Delville, said, 'They don't seem to bother Criton none.'

Criton was a deaf mute. Children ran from his path, and adults did not like him. But, as the great snakes didn't bother Criton, Criton didn't bother Askon Delville none.

The deaf mute would cross on a marsh hopper, about once a week, and walk the five miles to Askon's store with a list of necessities. He would collect the goods, then walk back the five miles, get into the marsh hopper and disappear over the *bayou*.

There was a woman at the house also. People caught sight of her from time to time, and it was certain she wrote out the order that Criton carried to Askon Delville's store. She was, of course, some kind of witch, otherwise she would not be able to live in such a haunted place.

People took special care to stay away when the gatherings happened. They always knew when there was going to be one. Askon told them. He knew because of Criton's shopping list. The day of a gathering, Criton usually made two trips because there was so much extra stuff needed at the house. Then, around dusk, you really kept clear. There would be noises, automobiles, extra marsh hoppers and the house, they said, got all lit up. Sometimes there was music; and one day, about a year ago, young Freddie Nolan – who wasn't scared of anything – took his own marsh hopper out, about two miles upstream, planning to sneak up and take some pictures.

Nobody saw young Freddie Nolan again, but his marsh hopper turned up, all smashed to pieces, like some great animal – or snake – had got to it.

There was a gathering this week.

Nobody except Criton and the woman – who answered to the name Tic – and the monthly visitors knew that the inside of the house was solid as the piece of rock on which it was built. The old rotting exterior clapboard was only a shell for the real thing: stone, brick, glass and steel, not to mention a fair portion of opulence.

Eleven people had come this month: two from London, England; two from New York; one German; a Swede; a pair of Frenchmen; one from LA; a big man who came every month all the way from Cairo, Egypt; and the Leader. The Leader was called Blofeld, though in the outside world the name was very different.

They dined magnificently. Later, after the liqueurs and coffee, the whole party went into the conference room at the back of the house.

The long room was decorated in a soft lime. Heavy matching curtains covered the huge French windows which looked out on to the far side of the *bayou*. The curtains were closed by the time the company assembled, wall lights glowing, with brass-shaded strips above the four paintings which formed the only decoration – two Jackson Pollocks, a Miro and a Kline. The Kline was one of the pieces of art stolen in a recent hijack. Blofeld liked it so much that they had moved it to the house and not put it on sale.

A polished oak table occupied most of the centre of the room. It was set for eleven people, complete with blotters, drinks, pens, paper, ashtrays and agenda.

Blofeld took the place at the head of the table, while the others filed to their seats, all marked with name cards. They did not sit until the Leader had taken the chair.

'This month's agenda is short,' Blofeld began. 'Three items only: the budget; the recent débâcle on Flight BA 12; and, the operation we call HOUND. Now, Mr El Ahadi, the budget, please.'

The gentleman from Cairo rose to his feet. He was a tall, dark man, with immensely handsome features and a honeyed voice that had charmed many a young woman in its time. 'I am pleased to announce,' he said, 'that, even without the hoped-for proceeds from Flight BA 12, our bank accounts in Switzerland, London, and New York contain, respectively, 400 million dollars; fifty million pounds sterling; and 150 *billion* dollars. The total, according to our calculations, will suffice for our present purposes, and, if operations succeed according to budget – as our Leader predicts – we can expect to double the amount within one year. As agreed, all profits, over and above our initial investment, will be shared equally.' He gave his most charming smile, and the assembled company sat back, relaxed.

Blofeld's hand came down hard on the table. 'Very good.' The voice had taken on a rasping edge. 'But the failure of our assault on Flight 12 is inexcusable. Particularly after so much preparation on your part, Herr Treiben.' Blofeld shot a look of disgust at the German delegate. 'As you know, Herr Treiben, under similar circumstances, others on the executive committee of SPECTRE have paid the ultimate price.'

Treiben, plump and pink, a warlord of the West German underworld in his own right, felt the colour drain from his face.

'However,' Blofeld continued, 'we have another scapegoat. You may not know it, Treiben, but we finally caught up with your Mr de Luntz.'

'Ah?' Treiben rubbed his hands and said that he also had been looking for Mr de Luntz. All his best men had searched for de Luntz without success.

'Yes, we have found him.' Blofeld beamed, the hands coming together in a clap which sounded like a pistol shot. 'Having found him, I believe he should now join his friends.' The drapes over the large windows slid back silently. As they did so, the room lights dimmed. Outside the window, the immediate environment appeared bright as day. 'An infra-red device,' Blofeld explained, 'so that the guardians of this house will not be frightened by light. Ah, here comes your Mr de Luntz now.'

A bald, frightened-looking man in a dirty, crumpled suit was led on to the patch of ground immediately in front of the window. His hands were tied behind his back and his feet shackled, so that he shuffled under Criton's grasp. His eyes rolled wildly, as though he was desperately searching the dark for a way of escape from something not defined, but obviously terrible.

Criton led the man to a metal stake, secured only a few feet from the thick glass of the window. Inside, the observers could now see that a short length of rope hung from the restraints around de Luntz's wrists. Criton attached the rope to the stakes, turned, smiled towards the window, then stepped back out of sight.

The moment Criton was clear, there came a thud from the far

side of the window, and the captive, de Luntz, was hemmed in by a metal grille of cyclone fencing attached to a heavy framework. This grille was three-sided with a top, like a small square ice hockey goal. The open front ended almost at the edge of the water, which lapped some nine feet from the window.

'What's he done?' one of the Americans asked. It was Mascro, the white-haired avuncular man from Los Angeles.

'He was the back-up man on BA 12. He did not go to the assistance of his comrades,' Treiben sneered.

'Mr Mascro,' Blofeld raised a hand, 'de Luntz has told us exactly what happened. How the others died, and who did it. Ah, one of the guardians has spotted Mr de Luntz. I've always wanted to see if a giant python really can eat a man whole.'

Standing behind the french windows, the executive committee of SPECTRE watched with fascination and horror. The infra-red gave them a clear, daylight picture. They could also hear the unfortunate victim start to scream as he spotted the reptile squirming in from the tall reeds, near the marshy water's edge.

The python was huge, at least thirty feet in length, with a fat solid body and a massive triangular head. De Luntz, tethered to the stake, began to pull and twist, trying to drag himself clear, but the python suddenly launched forward, twining itself around the man.

The creature moved with extraordinary speed, encircling de Luntz's body like some great clinging vine. It seemed only a matter of seconds before the python's head was in line with that of its victim – the two, interlocked, swaying as if in an obscene dance of death. De Luntz's screams grew more agonised as the python brought its head level with his face, the fanged jaws snapping in excited anger. Reptile and prey looked into each other's eyes for a few seconds, and the watchers could plainly see the python's crushing grip tighten on the man's body.

Then de Luntz went limp, and the pair fell to the ground. One of the observers, safe behind the window, gasped loudly. The giant snake had unwound itself with three fast flicks of its body, and was now examining its meal. The snapping jaws first made for the securing rope, tugging it clear, then moved towards the body's feet.

'That's quite amazing.' Blofeld stood very close to the window. 'See, the snake's pushing his shoes off.'

Now, the python squirmed around so that its head was exactly aligned with the body's feet, which the reptile pushed together, before opening its jaws to an almost unbelievable width and clamping down on the corpse's ankles.

The entire process took almost an hour, yet the group inside remained fascinated, hypnotised. The python swallowed in a series of jerks, resting, immobile, after each effort, until the last vestiges of de Luntz were gone. Then the snake lay quietly, exhausted by its exertions, its long body bloated from normal shape so that the watchers could clearly discern the outlines of the squeezed human frame half way down the snake's body.

'An interesting lesson for us all.' Blofeld's hands came together again. The curtains slid back into place, and the lights came up. Reflectively, the group returned to the table, some white and visibly shaken at what they had witnessed.

The German, Treiben – who had known de Luntz well in life – was the most affected. 'You said,' he began, his voice quavering, 'you said, de Luntz spoke before. . . before . . .'

'Yes,' Blofeld nodded. 'He spoke. He sang whole arias. Pavarotti could not have done better. He even sang his own death warrant. Apparently there were people expecting us on Flight BA 12. We have yet to discover if someone talked, or whether all high-risk cargoes are now being protected.

'To begin with, the plan went with clockwork precision. The girl did a magnificent job in getting herself scheduled on that flight and smuggling the smoke canisters and weapons on board. The attack took place on time, to the second, there's no doubt about that. De Luntz, however, excused himself from taking part. He claimed to be boxed in at the rear of the plane. It seems there were five guards travelling on BA 12. From de Luntz's description they were members of the British Special Air Service.' Blofeld paused, looking at each man in turn. 'All except one.'

The men around the table waited, an air of expectancy permeating the room.

'The reorganisation of this great society, of which we are all members,' the Leader continued, 'has taken a long time. We have been in hibernation. Now the world will soon see that we are awake. In particular we will have to deal with one old enemy who was a constant thorn in the side of my illustrious predecessor. Mr de Luntz – God rest his soul – identified four of the guards on that aeroplane as possible undercover SAS men. He also made a positive identification of the fifth man – the one, I might add, who caused the most damage. I personally questioned de Luntz. Gentleman, our old enemy James Bond was on that aircraft.'

The faces around the table hardened; all turned towards Blofeld.

It was Mascro who spoke at last: 'You want me to put out a contract on him? In the old days, when your . . .'

The Leader cut him short. 'It has been tried before. No. No contracts; no specialists sent to London. I have personal scores to settle with Mr Bond. Gentlemen, I have devised a method to deal with him – call it a lure if you like. If it has worked, and I see no reason for it to fail, soon we shall have the pleasure of Mr Bond's company on this side of the Atlantic. I intend to deal with him just as that reptile dealt with the wayward de Luntz.'

Blofeld paused, looking around the table to make certain all concentration was on the subject in hand.

'Soon,' Blofeld continued, 'we shall be fully launched into the planning of what has for security reasons, at this stage, been called HOUND.'

The Leader chuckled. 'Ironic, yes? A nice touch to talk of HOUND. Hound, taken from the Christian poem "The Hound of

Heaven". The chuckle had turned into a smile. 'The Hound of Heaven, or the Hounds of Heaven, eh? Hounds; Wolves. It is good, our target being America's great threat, the Wolves of Space, already circling the globe in their packs, waiting to pounce, and tear their victims apart – and, in the midst of it, Mr Bond. This time SPECTRE will wipe Mr James Bond from the face of this planet.'

There were grim murmurs of agreement from around the table before Blofeld, glancing at a small gold wrist watch, spoke again. 'In fact, my bait should have been taken by now. Soon, gentlemen, soon we shall see James Bond face to face. And the beauty of it is that he will not know whom he is meeting, or what is really in store for him.'

4

PILLOW THOUGHTS

James Bond glanced affectionately at Ann Reilly's face, quiet and beautiful in sleep, on the pillow next to him. The sleek and shining straw-coloured hair was tousled around her oval face. For a fleeting second, she reminded Bond of Tracy – his wife of less than a few hours before Ernst Stavro Blofeld so viciously gunned her down, on the autobahn from Munich to Kufstein, as they were beginning their honeymoon.

Ann Reilly – a member of Bond's own Service, assistant to the Armourer and second-in-command of Q Branch – was known by all and sundry within the big headquarters building overlooking Regent's Park as Q'ute. An apt nickname for the elegant, tall, very efficient and liberated young lady.

After a slightly shaky start, Bond and Q'ute had become friends and what she liked to call 'occasional lovers'. This evening had been divided into two parts. First, duty – the checking and firing of Bond's new personal hand gun, the Heckler & Koch VP70, the weapon which both M and the Armourer had now decided would be carried by *all* officers of the Service.

Bond had objected. After all, he had usually been allowed to choose his own hand gun, and was more than put out when his trusted Walther PPK had been withdrawn from service in 1974. On his last mission he had been severely criticised for using an old, yet highly efficient Browning. In his own stubborn way, 007 had fought for his personal rights – an action applauded by

Q'ute, a champion of feminism which, by definition, meant she also championed certain male causes.

But if M's word was law, then the Armourer would see the ruling was carried out, and Bond had, in due course, been issued with the VP70.

While the VP70 was much larger than the Walther, Bond had to admit that the weapon posed no problem as far as concealment was concerned. It felt good, with its longer butt and good balance. It was also very accurate, and lethal – 9mm, with an eighteen-round magazine and the ability to fire semi-automatic three-shot bursts when fitted with the light shoulder stock.

There was no doubt that it was also a man-stopper of considerable power, and – in recent days – between lengthy sessions with his old friend Bill Tanner, M's Chief-of-Staff, concerning the hijack and identity of the terrorists, Bond had spent a lot of time getting to know his new pistol.

So, that evening, from five o'clock to seven-thirty, 007 was on the underground range, going through a fast-draw and firing session with the expert Q'ute.

Almost from the moment he had first found himself working with Q'ute, Bond had developed a respect for her immense professionalism. She certainly knew her job, from weaponry to the complex mysteries of electronics. But she could also hold her own as the most feminine of women.

When they finished on the range that night, Ann Reilly made it clear that, if Bond was free, she was available until the following morning.

After dining at a small Italian restaurant – the Campana in Marylebone High Street – the couple had gone back to Q'ute's apartment where they made love with a disturbing wildness, as though time was running out for both of them.

The draining of their bodies left the agile Q'ute exhausted. She fell asleep almost immediately after their last, long and tender kiss. Bond, however, stayed wide awake, his alert state of mind brought about by the mounting anxiety of the past few days, and by what he had discovered with Bill Tanner.

The BA 12 terrorists had all been traced back to a German underworld figure who also dabbled in political and economic espionage, one Kurt Walter Treiben. Even the stewardess, it was now proved, had pulled strings to be assigned to that particular flight, and though she had been with British Airways for almost three years, her background also linked her to Treiben.

The most disturbing points were the dying terrorist's words and the fact that Treiben had once been an associate of the infamous Ernst Stavro Blofeld, founder and leader of the original, multinational SPECTRE.

Further investigation increased their worries. From all the hijacks there was now positive ID on six men. Two were known hoodlums on the payroll of Michael Mascro, Los Angeles' ranking criminal; one could be linked to Kranko Stewart and Dover Richardson, New York 'fixers' and gangsters; two worked exclusively for Bjorn Junten, the Swedish-born freelance intelligence expert, whose private espionage service was always open to the highest bidder; while the sixth identified man was tied in to the Banquette brothers from Marseille – a pair of villains upon whom both the French police, and the French intelligence service (Service de Documentation Extérieure et de Contre-Espionage) had been trying to pin evidence for the past twenty years.

Like the German, Treiben, the principals in these identifications – Mascro, Stewart, Richardson, Junten and the Banquette brothers – had their own personal connections with Ernst Stavro Blofeld and SPECTRE.

There could be but one conclusion: SPECTRE was alive and operating again.

Bond quietly lit one of his special low-tar cigarettes, originally made for him by Morelands of Grosvenor Street and now produced – after much discussion and bending of rules – by H. Simmons of Burlington Arcade: the earliest known cigarette manufacturers in London. This firm even agreed to retain the distinctive three gold rings – together with their own silhouette trademark – on each of the specially produced cigarettes, and Bond felt not a little honoured that he was the only customer who could coax personalised cigarettes from Simmons.

Blowing smoke at the ceiling, conscious of Q'ute in deep and satisfied sleep beside him, Bond thought of the other women who had played such a decisive role in his Service career: Vesper Lynd, who, in death, had seemed moulded like a stone effigy; Gala Brand, now Mrs Vivian, with three kids and a nice house in Richmond (they exchanged Christmas cards but he had never seen her again after the Drax business); Honey Rider; Tiffany Case; Domino Vitale; Solitaire; Pussy Galore; the exquisite Kissy Suzuki; his latest conquest, Lavender Peacock, now managing her Scottish estate with great success. In spite of the warmth and genuine affection which flowed, even in sleep, from Ann Reilly, Bond's mind ran riot. Again and again his thoughts turned to Tracy di Vicenzo – Tracy Bond.

There had been a time when Bond's memory had been lost for a considerable period; but experts had brought him back from the darkness of unknowing, and the final moments of Ernst Stavro Blofeld now lived clearly and vividly in his mind – Blofeld in his grotesque Japanese Castle of Death, with the poisoned garden: the last battle, when Bond was ill-equipped to deal with the big man wielding his deadly samurai sword. Yet he had done it, with the greatest lust for another man's blood he had ever experienced. Even now, when he thought long of Blofeld, Bond felt an ache in his thumbs: he had choked the man to death with his bare hands.

Yes, Blofeld was dead; but SPECTRE lived on.

Bond stubbed out the cigarette, turned on his side and tried to sleep. When, at last, blessed darkness swallowed his consciousness, James Bond still did not rest. He dreamed; and his dreams were of his beloved lost Tracy.

He woke with a start. A glimmer of light showed through the

curtains. Turning to look at the Rolex on the night table, Bond saw it was almost five-forty-five.

'Late to bed, early to rise,' Q'ute giggled, her hand moving under the bedclothes to add point to her humour.

Bond gazed down at her, breaking into a winning smile. She reached up, kissed him, and they began just where they had left off the night before, until the deep-deep-deep of Bond's pocket pager interrupted them.

'Damn,' breathed Q'ute. 'Can't they ever leave you alone?'

Reaching for the telephone Bond caustically reminded her that she had personally paged him, on matters of business, three times in the past week. 'No time's the right time,' he said, smiling wearily as he dialled the headquarters' number.

'Transworld Export,' said the voice of the duty switchboard operator.

Bond identified himself. There was a pause, then Bill Tanner's voice: 'You're needed. He's been here half the night and wants to see you soonest. Something very big's afoot.'

Bond glanced back towards Q'ute. 'On my way,' he said into the instrument. Then, cradling the phone, he told her what Bill Tanner had just said.

She pushed him out of the bed, telling him to stop boasting.

Grumbling, mainly because he would get no proper breakfast, Bond shaved and dressed, while Ann Reilly made coffee.

The Saab, gleaming silver, stood outside the block of flats. It had only recently been returned to him, completely refurbished by both Saab and the security firm which provided Bond, privately, with the special technology built into the turbo-charged vehicle. In seconds, the car was picking up speed effortlessly.

There was little traffic, and it took only ten minutes of relaxed driving – the car answering Bond's feet and hands like the thoroughbred it was – to get to the tall building overlooking Regent's Park. There, Bond took the lift up to the ninth floor and walked straight to M's ante-room where Miss Moneypenny sat dejectedly at her desk.

'Morning, Penny.' Bond, though feeling jaded, put on a show for his old flirting partner's benefit.

'Maybe good for you, James. But I've been up half the night.'

'Who hasn't?' A look of sublime innocence.

Moneypenny gave a wan smile. 'According to the powder vine, James, it would be with a cute little girl from Q Branch. So, I suppose, I can just eat my heart out.'

'Penny,' Bond walked towards M's door, 'I have but one heart. It's always been yours. Nibble away at it whenever you desire.'

'In a pig's eye,' Moneypenny retorted with more than a hint of acid. 'You'd better get in there, James. He told me to fire you through his door – his words – as soon as you arrived.'

Bond winked, straightened his RN tie, and knocking at M's door, walked in.

M looked tired. It was the first thing Bond noticed. The second was the girl – short, well-proportioned, athletic, but with an undoubtedly feminine smile and dark hair cut into a mass of tight curls.

Her large brown eyes did not waver as they met Bond's gaze. There was something familiar about the eyes, as though he had seen, or met, the girl before.

'Come in, 007,' M was saying, his voice edgy. 'I don't think you've ever met this lady, but she's the daughter of an old friend of yours. Commander James Bond – Miss Cedar Leiter.'

5

CEDAR

Later Bond felt that he must have looked like a ninny, standing there in M's office, jaw dropped, staring at the girl. She was something to stare at, even dressed in the casual denim skirt and shirt. Her face, like her brown eyes, showed a tranquillity which, Bond sensed, belied a fast-working mind – accurate and deadly as the body. The girl was an expert. Indeed she should be, when one considered her father.

'Well,' was all Bond could muster.

Cedar's face blossomed into a smile that reminded him, almost painfully, of his old friend Felix. It was a devil-may-care look, one eyebrow raised as if to say, get it right or go to hell.

M grunted. 'You've not met Miss Leiter before, then, 007?' M still spoke of Bond as 007, even though the famous Double-O Section with its licence to kill had long been disbanded.

Bond had known Felix was married, but when they had worked together, his old CIA friend – later turned private investigator – had never spoken of his wife or children.

'No,' Bond replied somewhat tersely, for the full implication had just hit him. 'How is Felix?'

Cedar's eyes clouded slightly, as though she had suffered a quick physical pain. When she spoke, the voice was low, husky and without a hint of what the British think of as an American accent. Mid-Atlantic, they would call it.

'Daddy's fine. They've fixed him up with the latest thing in artificial limbs.' Her momentary sadness disappeared, and the smile returned. 'He's got an incredible new hand, says it can do anything. Spends a lot of time shooting and practising quick-draw techniques. I'm sure he'd want me to say hello.'

In a split second, Bond relived that time in his life he would rather banish into oblivion – the time when Felix had lost an arm and half a leg, as well as suffering other damage which called for years of work by plastic surgeons. James Bond often blamed himself for Felix Leiter's predicament, though they had both been after a black gangster whose sadistic madness was almost unique. Buonaparte Ignace Gallia: Mr Big. In any case, as Felix would have been the first to admit, he was lucky to be alive at all after the shark attack engineered by Mr Big; while Bond took consolation in the fact that, in the end, he had put the gangster away for good – and in the most unpleasant way possible, letting the punishment fit the crime.

Quickly, Bond came out of his reverie, catching up on Cedar Leiter's last sentence: '. . . he'd want me to say hello.' She cocked her head. 'If he knew I was here,'

M grunted once more. 'I think we'd better get down to business, 007. Miss Leiter is a sleeper, just brought to life. She arrived in the early hours.' He hesitated, with a slight frown of displeasure. 'On *my* doorstep. I've listened to what she had to tell me: Chief-of-Staff's just checking her out now, with a cipher through the US Embassy.'

Bond asked if he could sit, and received a tense nod from M.

'I've already been through it. Miss Leiter will put you in the picture,' M continued.

'Oh, please call me Cedar, sir . . .' She broke off at M's withering look, realising that she had made the gaffe of all time. M strongly disapproved of easy familiarity, particularly in Service matters.

'Start, Miss Leiter,' M snapped.

Cedar's career had begun, when she was eighteen, as a secretary in the State Department. Within a year she was approached by the Central Intelligence Agency. 'I suppose it was because of my father.' She did not smile this time. 'But I was warned that he was never to know.' She kept her job at State, but went through a comprehensive course during vacations, weekends, and on certain evenings.

'They didn't want me active. That was made clear from the start. I was to be trained and take regular refresher courses, but to keep my job at State. They specifically told me that I'd eventually be called.

'Well, the call came last week. I suppose they keep tabs on you. I was planning a short trip to Europe. As it's turned out, it's an official trip, and I've been used because I'm not what you call a "face".' Cedar meant that she was unknown to any of the world's intelligence communities. 'There's one key word that M has to relay to Langley, and a key word in response, to show I'm on the level – I guess that's what we're waiting to clear now.'

M nodded, adding that he had no doubt Miss Leiter was 'on the level', as she put it. Certainly the documents, and the request she had brought made sense.

'I'm putting you on to this, 007, as it is a question of working in harmony with Miss Leiter in the United States . . .'

'But SPE . . . ?' Bond began.

'That matter will make itself clear in a moment. I'm putting you on Special Duty. Special Services to the US Government.' M picked up several sheets of paper from his desk, and Bond could not help seeing that the first was a short, typewritten note bearing the Presidential Seal. There was no further point arguing with his chief.

'What's the story then, sir?' Bond asked.

'Briefly,' M began, 'it concerns a gentleman by the name of Markus Bismaquer.'

M glanced at the papers in his hand and rattled off the details of Bismaquer's life and background: Born 1919, New York City. Only son of mixed parentage, German and English. Both American citizens. Made his first million before the age of twenty, multi-millionaire within three years. Avoided military service

during the Second World War by nature of being classified
'undesirable' – 'He was, apparently, a firm and convinced
member of the American Nazi Party. Something he has since
tried to keep quiet, but with little success.' M made a noise
which could only be interpreted as a sign of disgust. 'Sold out
all his business interests, at great profit, in the early 1950s and
has lived like a Renaissance prince ever since. Rarely seen away
from his own principality, as it were . . .'

'His own what?' Bond frowned.

'Figure of speech, 007. Miss Leiter will explain.'

Cedar Leiter took a deep breath.

'Bismaquer owns 150 square miles of what was once desert,
about eighty miles southwest of Amarillo, Texas; and M is right
to call it his principality. He's irrigated the area, built on it, and
virtually sealed it off. No roads run into Rancho Bismaquer. You
get in by one of two ways: there's a small airstrip, and he has his
own private mono-rail system. There's a closed station fifteen
miles out of town – Amarillo, that is – and you have to be very
well connected with Mr Bismaquer to take a ride on the mono-
rail. If you're really desirable you can take your own car – they
have car transporters on the rail system, and there are roads out
at the ranch; but within the compound. It's a hell of a place –
huge house; auxiliary buildings; automobile race track; horses;
fishing; everything your heart desires.'

'You've been there?'

'No, but I've seen all the pictures – from the satellites, and the
high-fly reconnaissance. Langley has a 3-D mock-up. They
showed it to me as part of my briefing. I have photographs with
me. The whole area – all hundred and fifty square miles – is
heavily fenced off, and Bismaquer has his own security outfit.'

'So what's he done wrong?' Bond took out his gunmetal cigarette case, looking at M for approval. M just nodded and began to
load his pipe. Cedar refused a cigarette. 'What's he done wrong?
Apart from making a mint of money.'

'That's the problem.' Cedar looked uncertainly at M.

'Oh, you can go ahead, Miss Leiter. 007's got to know it all before we finish.'

'Until a few months ago it was all very vague,' Cedar continued, folding her legs under her on the leather buttoned chair. M looked towards the ceiling as though appealing to the deities for good manners, and posture, in the girl. 'Politically, Bismaquer's always been suspect, but nobody's apparently worried too much, because he stays so far from the action. There is very firm evidence that he's – how do you put it? – run with the hare and hunted with the hounds?'

Bond nodded.

'That's how Bismaquer's operated over the years – looking for an "in" – a way to be accepted for political office. Nobody's ever taken him up.' She laughed, and Bond was reminded again of Felix. 'They've taken his money, but not him. In the Watergate backlash, it came out that money from Bismaquer went into the famous slush fund. Not peanuts, either. But successive administrations have kept him at bay.'

'Reasons?'

She gave a little shrug, as though to say it was obvious. 'There is also evidence that Bismaquer has been searching for a way into *any* administration, with a view to making a takeover bid.'

It was Bond's turn to laugh. 'Take over what? The United States Government?'

'I know it must sound far-fetched, but that's exactly what the feeling has been.' Cedar looked at him coolly. 'You think some of those Arabs, and their retinues, are wealthy? Well, there are families in Texas who *do* live like royalty. There are a few – like in any country – who live with dangerous fantasy. When you combine fantasy with immense wealth . . .'

Both Bond and M nodded, taking her point.

'The Nazi ideology still in him?' Bond blew a stream of smoke towards the ceiling.

'That's what the Agency thinks.'

'But a nutter like that can't be really dangerous unless . . .'

'Unless he's *doing* something. Yes?' Cedar looked directly at Bond. 'Yes, I agree, but there *has* been trouble – or a hint of it. Bismaquer's received a large number of very odd visitors at the ranch over the last year. He's also increased security, and enlarged his staff.'

Bond sighed, looking at M for help – 'This is crazy. A fellow living out his own fantasies . . .'

'Hear her out, 007,' M said quietly.

'He's up to something, all right. The FBI, were monitoring him, checking on the visitors and the equipment that went to the ranch. They decided to pass some of their findings on to the Internal Revenue Service. They in turn came up with some possible tax dodges. That gave the IRS, and the FBI, something to work on. Last January, four agents – two from each branch – went in to try and talk with Bismaquer. They disappeared. The FBI sent in two more. They did not come back. So the cops in Amarillo called on him and carried out an investigation. Friend Bismaquer knew nothing, could tell them nothing. No evidence. So the cops came out, and the Agency sent a girl in. They did not hear from her again.

'Then, a week or so back, a body turned up in some marshland near Baton Rouge, Louisiana. It was kept quiet – not a whisper from the media. Apparently the corpse was in a bad state, but they ID'd it as the Company girl. Since then, all the bodies have turned up, near the same place. Two can't be identified, but the others have been – by their teeth mostly. Every officer who set out to nail something on Markus Bismaquer, in Texas, has turned up dead in Louisiana.'

'And that's our business?' Bond did not like the sound of it. Bismaquer seemed like a psychopathic maniac, with money to burn, a private army, and a king-sized case of *folie de grandeur*.

'Very much so.' Cedar Leiter looked at M. 'Will you show him, sir?'

M delved among the papers neatly stacked in front of him, extracted one, and passed it over to Bond.

It was a clear photostat of a torn fragment of paper, the typewritten words plainly visible. Bond's face darkened as he read:

ans should, of course, be destroyed. But he wished
   make certain you had full knowledge of our substan-
l backing, world-wide. The initial thrust will
      most telling in Europe, and the Mid-East. But,
      ntually, it will leave the United States wide
   pen. With careful manipulation we can successfu
   ivide and rule – or at least
I look forward to our next meeting.

Then the scrawled, but plainly decipherable, signature:

Blofeld

Bond felt a clawing at his intestines. 'Where . . . ?' he began.

'In the rotting lining of our CIA girl's clothes. Taken from the body,' Cedar answered, her voice level. 'The analysts at Langley think Bismaquer's working in conjunction with a terrorist organisation known as SPECTRE. I was told you are an expert, Mr Bond . . .'

'Blofeld's dead.' Bond was equally cool.

'Unless, 007,' M removed the pipe from his mouth, 'unless there was progeny? Or a brother? Or someone else? You've spent considerable time convincing me that SPECTRE's active again, and behind these wretched hijackings. Now there comes evidence that a Blofeld, of some kind, is still around and consorting with a very rich, mad Texan. That piece of paper' – he gestured towards the photostat – 'suggests that Bismaquer, and SPECTRE, are embarking on some kind of venture that may set the world ablaze. God knows, there's enough danger of that with the governments, unrest, political ineptitude, recession, and the draining of resources – on an official level. Some big freelance operation could be catastrophic; and we already know, from past experience, that SPECTRE *can* cause international problems.'

As he finished there was a tap at the door and Bill Tanner entered to M's firm 'Come'.

'Checks out, sir. Just had the Embassy signal back. They don't know what it means but said it had to be something special because it was returned with considerable priority and the Presidential cipher. Their people got a little nosey, I'm afraid.'

'Well, I hope you put their noses out of joint, Chief-of-Staff.'

Tanner smiled, giving Bond a welcome nod.

M took a draw on his pipe, tapping his teeth with the stem before continuing, 'One of the other documents, 007, is a personal letter to me from the President of the United States. In it, he says the information is, in his opinion, so sensitive that he does not want to go through normal channels: hence the use of Miss Leiter. He asks for special help. In other words he wants someone from this Service to accompany Miss Leiter to the United States and infiltrate the Bismaquer set-up. Can you suggest anyone, 007? Anyone with a good working knowledge of that pustule SPECTRE?'

'Yes.' Bond already felt the adrenalin stirring. 'Yes, of course I'll go. But I've a couple of questions for Miss Leiter. What's Bismaquer's marital status?'

'Married three times,' she answered. 'First two died. Natural causes – an automobile accident and a brain tumour. His present wife's considerably younger than him. Stunning, elegant: Nena Bismaquer, formerly Nena Clavert. French by birth. Lived in Paris, where she first met Bismaquer.'

'Can we check if that's absolutely snow white?'

M nodded, giving Tanner a quick glance – an order without words.

'And the second question?' Cedar unwound her legs.

'How did Bismaquer make his first million? I presume the rest followed by careful investment.'

'Ice cream.' Cedar grinned. 'He was the first great ice cream king. Came up with things you'd never believe. One of the big chains finally bought him out, but it's still a passion with him.

He even has a lab out at the ranch. Apparently he's determined to find a completely new, untried method of making the stuff. Always coming up with elaborate recipes and flavours.'

M cleared his throat. 'Getting close is going to be the problem, that's obvious.'

'Apart from his wife and ice cream, Bismaquer has one other weak point,' Cedar offered.

They looked at her expectantly.

'Prints. Rare prints. He has a terrific collection – or so the information goes. And it really is a weakness. I understand the top brass at Langley interrogated one of the few clean people ever to get into, and out of, Rancho Bismaquer in recent years. He was a well-known dealer in rare prints.'

'Know anything about rare prints, 007?' M looked cheerful for the first time since Bond had entered the office.

'Not at the moment, sir.' Bond lit another cigarette. 'But I've got a feeling I'm going to learn quite quickly.'

'So is Miss Leiter.' M allowed himself a rare smile as he reached for the telephone.

6

RARE PRINTS FOR SALE

James Bond was always amazed by New York. Other people said it was getting worse, going downhill fast. They talked about how dirty and dangerous it was. Yet, every time Bond was sent there on an assignment, he found New York little changed from when he first knew it. Certainly, there were more buildings, and – like every city – more places you kept away from at night. But there was no denying that, as a city, it gave him more of an emotional charge than his beloved London.

This time, though, he was not in New York City as James Bond. His passport was in the name of Professor Joseph Penbrunner, whose occupation was listed as art dealer. Cedar Leiter had also changed her name – to Mrs Joseph Penbrunner – and the couple had received attention from the media: M and his Chief-of-Staff had already seen to that.

The evening of Cedar Leiter's arrival in London, Bond had taken her from the headquarters building to a safe house in a Kensington mews, one easily observed by the team of nurse-maids assigned to them. Bill Tanner had arrived within the hour to give the pair a quick rundown on the cover chosen for them. Cedar, being unknown in the trade, needed no disguise; but Bond would have to undergo some changes in appearance, and Tanner had brought along a few ideas.

Disguise, as Bond knew well enough, was best when kept to the minimum – a change of hairstyle, some new mannerism in a walk, contact lenses, maybe the fattening of cheeks with rubber pads (a device not often used as it causes difficulty in eating and drinking), spectacles, or a different mode of dress. These were the easiest things, and, on that first night, Bond learned that he would be equipped with a greying moustache, heavy-framed glasses – with clear lenses – together with a careful thinning, and complete greying, of the hair. It was also suggested that he develop a scholarly stoop and slow walk, as well as a rather pompous style of speech.

For the next few days, Bond travelled straight to the Kensington safe house each morning to work with Cedar.

M brought in a small, humourless cipher of a man, an expert in prints, especially rare English work. His name was never mentioned. The crash course he gave Bond and Cedar made them at least superficially knowledgeable in the subject.

Within the week they learned that from the early, simple woodcuts of Caxton until the middle of the seventeenth century, there were no English printmakers of any stature. Real brilliance came from the Continent, with masters like Dürer, Lucas van Leyden, and the like. They were tutored in Holbein the Younger, the first English copper plates of John Shute, and on into Hollar, Hogarth and his contemporaries, through the so-called Romantic Tradition, up to the revival and high standards of etching, and print-making, of the nineteenth century.

On the third day, M came to Kensington, asking that their instructor concentrate on Hogarth. The reason was revealed that night, when M turned up again, with Bill Tanner and a pair of his personal watchdogs in tow.

'Well, I think we've done it,' M announced, seating himself in the most comfortable chair and wrinkling his nose in a gesture of distaste at the wallpaper. Like all Service safe houses, the place had the bare amenities of a low-rated hotel.

'Two things,' M went on. 'Nena Bismaquer née Clavert appears clean. Secondly, you, Professor Penbrunner, are not in good odour with certain people in the art world. Tomorrow the

Press could well go mad. They are, in fact, searching for you right now.'

'And what am I supposed to have done?' Bond felt distinctly wary.

'Not much.' M resumed his most professional voice. 'You've come across a set of hitherto unknown, signed Hogarth prints, not unlike "The Rake's Progress", or "The Harlot's Progress", come to that. Six in all, beautifully executed and entitled "The Lady's Progress" – causing a stir, I can tell you. They've been fully authenticated. You've been trying to keep it quiet, but the cat's out of the bag now. The story goes that you're not even putting them on offer in England but taking them to the United States. Oh, there will be questions in the House, no doubt.'

Bond chewed his lip. 'And the prints?'

'Beautiful forgeries,' said M, beaming. 'Very hard to prove otherwise, and they've cost the Service a mint. They'll be brought in tomorrow, and I'll see the Press are tipped off just before you leave for New York next week.'

'Talking about leaving . . .' Bond steered M from his chair to the privacy of another room. The job was going to be taxing enough, for they could not expect assistance from either the American or British intelligence services until the last possible moment – simply because so few would know of their presence, or their assignment.

'There's no back-up,' Bond began.

'You've done jobs without back-up before, James.' M softened, using Bond's Christian name in private.

'True. Arrangements have been made for my personal armament, I presume?'

M nodded. The VP70, ammunition, and his favourite knives were to be delivered in a briefcase – which also contained the six forged Hogarth prints – to their New York hotel. 'Q Branch've set up one or two other useful things for you. There'll be a technology session with Miss Reilly before you go.'

'Then I've got one more favour to ask.'

'Ask, and it just might be given.'

'The Silver Beast.' Bond looked straight into M's eyes, noting the flicker of doubt. 'The Silver Beast' was the nickname members of the Service had given to Bond's personal car – the Saab 900 Turbo: his own property, with the special technology built into it at his expense. Jibes about it being Bond's 'toy' received only a polite smile from 007; and he knew that Major Boothroyd, the Armourer, had constantly sniffed around the machine in an attempt to discover all its secrets: the hidden compartments, tear gas ducts, and new refinements recently built into the bullet-proofed vehicle. Even Q'ute, doubtless put up to it by Boothroyd, had tried a Mata Hari on Bond to wheedle out the secrets. At the time, 007 had merely slapped her playfully on the bottom, and said she should not meddle. Now he was about to place what could be his salvation in M's hands.

'What about the Silver Beast?'

'I need it in America, sir. I don't want to be at the mercy of public transport.'

M gave a fleeting smile. 'I can arrange for you to hire a car – with the proper left-hand drive as well.'

'That's not the same, and you know it, sir.'

'And *you* know your Saab's not a Service vehicle. Heaven knows what you've got hidden in that thing . . .'

'I'm sorry, but I need *that* car and the documentation, sir,' Bond retorted.

M thought, his brow creased. 'Have to sleep on it. Let you know tomorrow.' Sucking on his pipe, and grumbling under his breath, M left.

In fact, Bond did not fancy his chances regarding the car, even though he was going to the United States on special orders. But, the following evening, after a long and testy lecture from M on the state of the Service finances, permission was granted. The Service would, reluctantly, have the Saab taken over to the United States. 'Be there, ready and waiting for you on arrival,' M told him grumpily.

Professor and Mrs Joseph Penbrunner's arrival with their Saab had, in fact, been quite something. With his voice changed to a donnish, pompous, and rather plummy timbre, Bond neatly parried the media's questions at New York's JFK airport: the media had 'assumed' he was selling the newly-discovered Hogarth prints in America. Well, he was saying nothing yet. No, he did not have a particular buyer in mind; this was a personal visit to America. No, he did not have the prints with him, but yes, they were already, he could reveal, in New York.

Privately, the disguised Bond was pleased with the vocal tones which he had based, from long memory, on those of his old housemaster during those two unfortunate halves at Eton. The man had been a pain – in all senses – to Bond, and now he took delight in mocking him. At the same time, Bond made certain Professor and Mrs Penbrunner would hit the evening news as well as the headlines by his turning crusty and rude. The media were not really interested in art, he said, only the trouble they could stir up. 'When it all comes down to it,' he added, pulling Cedar through the throng, 'you fellows'll only be concerned with the price. Dollars, dollars and more dollars. All you're after – the price.'

'That means you *are* here to make a sale, Professor?' one of the contingent asked sharply.

'That's my business.'

At Loew's Drake Hotel on 56th and Park, the briefcase awaited them. Bond unpacked carefully, quickly separating the prints from the weaponry. The prints would go to the hotel safe. As for the hardware? Well, he would carry the VP70, while the knives went into the specially sprung compartments – made years ago by Q Branch – in his own briefcase. Bond was so engrossed in sorting out these matters, that he failed to notice the coolness which had started to build, like a weather front, around Cedar.

During the days in the Kensington safe house she had insisted on calling him plain 'Bond'. When he had politely, and with his usual charm, asked her to address him as James, Cedar flatly refused. 'I know you and my father were buddies,' she had said, not looking at him, 'but we're into a professional relationship now. I call you Bond – except in public when we're playing husband and wife. You call me Leiter.'

James Bond had laughed. 'Okay, you can keep it like that. But I'm afraid I shall go on calling you Cedar.'

On returning from depositing the prints, Bond found her standing in the middle of the room, arms folded and foot tapping – a most attractive posture, whether she intended it to be or not.

'What's up?' he asked breezily.

'What d'you think's up?'

Bond shrugged. A creature of habit, he had started to unpack in the usual way, even dumping his towelling robe on the large double bed. 'Haven't a clue.'

'That, for one,' pointing out the robe. 'We haven't even settled who's going to use the bed and who's sleeping on the couch. As far as I'm concerned, Mr James Bond, the marriage is over once we're in private.'

'Well, of course I take the couch.' Then, heading for the bathroom, Bond flung over his shoulder, 'Don't worry, Cedar, you'll be safe as a nun with me. And you can take the bed every time. I've always preferred to live rough anyway.'

He could sense her petulance behind him, but when he came out, Cedar still stood by the bed, looking almost contrite. 'I'm sorry, James. I'm really sorry to have thought that of you. My Dad was right. You're a gentleman, in the real sense of the word.'

Bond did not blush, even though 'gentleman' was scarcely a word ladies used to describe him.

'Come on, then, Cedar. Let's go out and have a good time – or at least have dinner. I know a place not far from here.'

They walked to the elegant Le Périgord, on East 52nd.

'If you want French food in this city, you do get the authentic thing here,' Bond told Cedar, not even noticing the slight tilt of her eyebrows, or the smile that crossed her face, on hearing an

Englishman telling her, American born and bred, about the best places to eat.

She admitted he was right, though, for the meal could not have been bettered – although Bond chose the simplest of dishes: *asperges de Sologne à la Blésoise* – plump and tender asparagus in a sauce of cream, lemon and orange rind, with a dash of Grand Marnier, mixed into a hollandaise base – poached fillets of sole *au champagne*; and a mouth-melting *tarte de Cambrai*, made with pears.

Sharing a bottle of Dom Pérignon '69 – which Bond pronounced 'safe' – Cedar relaxed and began to enjoy herself, experiencing as she did so a strange sensation. For though Bond did not once slip out of character as Joseph Penbrunner, she thought she could see the man behind the disguise, the man her father had spoken of so often: the blue, unforgettable eyes; the dark, clean-cut face which had always reminded her father of Hoagy Carmichael in his younger days; the hard, almost cruel mouth which could soften so unexpectedly. A magnetic attraction, that was the only phrase for what she felt, and she couldn't but wonder how many others had felt it before her.

The meal over, they walked back to the Drake, collected the room key and took the elevator up to the third floor.

The three heavily-built men in sharp, neatly-cut suits, converged on the couple as the elevator doors closed behind them. Before Bond could even reach inside his jacket to snatch at the butt of the VP70, a hand closed around his wrist, while another removed the pistol.

'We'll go quietly to the room, honh, Professor,' one of them said. 'No problems. We're just delivering an invitation from somebody who wants to see you, okay?'

7

INVITATION BY FORCE

The work Cedar and Bond had done together, at the Kensington safe house, included devising a series of signals and moves to be used in a situation such as this. Bond nodded towards the heavy who had spoken, scratched his right temple and coughed. To Cedar this meant, 'Go along with them, but watch for my lead.'

'No problems, honh?' The spokesman was the largest of the three men, a few inches taller than Bond, with the muscular frame and barrel chest of a weight-lifter. The others looked equally hard and fit. Professional hoods, Bond thought, professional and experienced.

The big man had taken the room key from Bond. Now he calmly opened their door and ushered the couple inside. A quick hard shove propelled Bond into a chair and hands which felt like twin monkey wrenches held his shoulders from behind. Cedar was treated in similar fashion.

It was a moment before Bond noticed the fourth man, standing by the window, occasionally glancing down into the street. He must have been in the room already as they entered. Bond recognised him at once as the slim athletic man with a neat military moustache, looking altogether overdressed in a maroon tuxedo, who had approached him earlier in the hotel lobby and pressed a gold-edged card into his hand. The man had introduced himself as Mike Mazzard, had said something about being at the press reception at the airport and wanted a private talk about the prints. Bond had been rather brusque and brushed aside the suggestion of a quiet drink at some casino or other, taking the man for a journalist after an exclusive interview – though he hadn't mentioned a paper. Bond hadn't even looked at the card properly but simply pushed it into his pocket saying that he wouldn't be seeing anyone until they had had a night's rest.

'So, Professor,' said the big man, who had taken a position in the centre of the room and was idly tossing the VP70 from hand to hand like a gorilla playing with a stone. 'You're carrying a piece, honh? D'ya know how to use it?'

Bond, still in character, let out a pompous splutter, meant to convey outrage. 'Of course I know how to use it,' he blustered. 'Let me tell you that in the War . . .'

'What war would that be, friend?' croaked the man holding him. 'The American Revolution?'

The three heavies brayed with laughter.

'I was an officer in the Second World War,' Bond said with dignity. 'I've seen more action than . . .'

'The Second World War was a long time ago, friend,' the big man interrupted, weighing the VP70 in his hand directly in front of Bond. 'This is a pretty lethal piece you got here. Why're you carrying it anyway?'

'Protection,' snapped Bond in his best Penbrunner manner.

'Yeah, I figured that. But protection from what?'

'Muggers. Thieves. Ruffians like you. People intending to steal from us.'

'When're you going to learn some manners, Joe Bellini?' said the cool, measured voice from the window. 'We're here with an invitation, not to put Professor Penbrunner through a third degree in his own room. Remember?'

'Steal from you? We're not here to steal from you,' the heavy man called Bellini went on with feigned politeness, his face displaying affronted innocence. 'You got some pictures, right?'

'Pictures?'

'Yeah, some kinda special pictures.'

'Prints, Joe.' The man by the window spoke in a more commanding manner.

'Yeah, prints. Thanks, Mr Mazzard. You got some prints by a guy called Ho-something.'

'Ho-*garth*, Joe,' prompted Mazzard without taking his eyes off the street below.

'I own some Hogarth prints,' Bond said firmly. 'Owning them and having them aren't quite the same thing.'

'You got them here, we happen to know,' Joe Bellini said with mock patience. 'In the hotel safe.'

Mike Mazzard, at the window, turned to face Bond, who now realised that he was by far the most dangerous of the four. He carried himself with a certain sleekness and authority.

'Let's get it straight,' he said. 'No one's going to hurt either of you. We just want you to understand the situation. We're here to represent Mr Bismaquer, who wants to see those Hogarth prints. Call it an invitation. But he doesn't figure on waiting till tomorrow for an answer. You got his card – the one I gave you in the lobby. I guess he wants to make you an offer . . .'

Joe Bellini chuckled. 'An offer he can't refuse, honh.'

Mazzard was not amused. 'Be quiet, Joe. It's a straight offer. All you have to do is call the front desk and get them to send up the prints, and then we can get it moving.'

Bond shook his head. 'Can't be done,' he said with a smile. 'I have one key. They have the other. As in a bank. The prints are in a safety deposit box,' he lied. 'No one but the duty officer and myself can get at them. Not even my wife . . .'

With relief, Bond congratulated himself on his last-minute change of mind, when he had decided that the prints would be even safer in the Saab's secret compartment, especially if they needed to leave in a hurry.

'Like Mr Mazzard says,' Joe Bellini went straight on, all politeness now gone, 'we don't want to hurt nobody. But if you don't co-operate, then Louis and the Kid here' – indicating the man holding Bond – 'can get very unpleasant with your little lady.'

Mazzard left the window, walked around Joe, who still toyed with the VP70, and halted in front of Bond.

'Professor Penbrunner. May I suggest you and Joe here take a walk downstairs, collect the prints, then we can all get to Kennedy. Mr Bismaquer has sent his own private jet to collect you, specially. He *had* hoped you'd join him for dinner. It's a little late for that now. But we can make up for lost time, and you and Mrs Penbrunner can still get a good night's rest at the ranch. You'd be more comfortable there than at this dump, I can assure you. Now, what d'you say?'

'Look here, Mazzard,' Bond spluttered. 'This is an outrage! I already told you earlier, we are not making any engagements before tomorrow. If you really represent the man – Bismaquer, did you say his name was . . . ?'

'Save it for posterity,' interrupted Bellini, 'and let's split. And don't try anything stupid.' He moved across to Cedar, and, with a casual flick of his hand, tore her dress from neck to waist, revealing the fact that she wore no brassière.

'Nice,' breathed Louis, looking down over the shoulder he still held in a firm grip. 'Very nice.'

'Cut it out,' commanded Mazzard. 'There's no call for that sort of thing. I am sorry, Professor, but you see, Mr Bismaquer isn't used to having no for an answer. Now, I'll collect your things together while you and Joe get the prints. We can be at Kennedy and away sharp if we get moving now.'

Bond nodded. 'All right,' he said quietly, disconcerted because, for a second or so, he too found it impossible to take his eyes from Cedar's partially revealed breasts. 'But my wife will need to change. We can collect the prints on the way out . . .'

'We'll get the prints *now*,' Mazzard said flatly, brooking no further argument. 'Stop waving the Professor's gun about, Joe. Put it away in the closet, you've got your own.'

Joe Bellini produced a small revolver from his coat. Having shown Bond that he was armed, he pocketed his own gun again and placed the VP70 on the bedside table.

Mazzard nodded to the Kid and the twin wrenches relaxed on Bond's shoulders. Bond moved his arms gingerly, trying to restore the circulation as quickly as possible. At the same time, he gave a small cough and flicked an imaginary thread from his lapel – the body language for Cedar to be ready. Aloud he said he would need his briefcase.

'My key's in it.' He gestured to where the case stood beside the collapsible steel and canvas luggage rack.

Mazzard picked up the briefcase, weighed it, and gave it a couple of quick upward jerks of the hand. Satisfied, he handed the briefcase over to Bond. 'Just the key, and go along with Joe.'

The case was a version of his original elaborate Swaine & Adeney bag, modified by Q'ute for 007's use on this present operation. Its main features – a more effective device based on one of the hidden compartments in the Bond original – were two spring-loaded slim compartments sewn into the inner lining on the right-hand side. At a setting of treble three on the left tumblers, and treble two on the right, the springs would operate at five-second intervals, delivering the handles of Bond's Sykes-Fairbairn knives through the bottom of the case.

As he took the briefcase on to his lap, Bond assessed the situation. They were certainly in a tight spot, for it now dawned on Bond that not only was there no option to complying over the night safety deposit box, but neither could he allow these hoods to discover the secrets of the Saab. For a fleeting moment, he considered the possibility of getting rid of Joe before they reached the car. Dealing with one in the open would be much easier than trying to tackle four in the confined room. But what then would happen to Cedar? If he raised an alarm, who could tell what they would do to her? He couldn't risk it. The alternative – turning the tables here and now on the four – seemed against all the odds. Could he rely on swift action from Cedar? A glance in her direction, a fractional meeting of the eyes, told him she was ready.

Mazzard was nearest to him and would have to go first, Bond

decided, carefully turning the left-hand tumblers to treble three, then twisting the briefcase sideways so that two slim concealed knife apertures lay directly over his right thigh. Once Mazzard was taken out, he must tackle Joe Bellini and trust to luck and surprise for the other two. It all depended on three things: his own accuracy, Cedar's readiness, and how quickly the Kid moved.

He shifted the case slightly, then turned the right-hand tumblers to treble two. There was no sound as Bond moved the case again, sliding his hand to the underside ready to receive the first knife after the initial five-second delay. He felt the handle slip down into his right hand, and, with the knowledge that he only had five seconds before the next knife would be ready, made his move.

Throwing knives are so finely balanced that even an expert has difficulty making the weapon behave as intended. An agile throw, correctly performed, should always bring the point of the blade into a forward, horizontal position as it reaches its target.

Bond wanted nobody injured unless it proved unavoidable. To do this, both his throws had to be exceptionally accurate and at least one beat off so that the heavy pommel, above the grip, would reach the point aimed at before the razored edge.

Hardly moving in his chair, Bond flexed his wrist, putting maximum force behind the first throw, then reached down just in time for the second knife to be delivered from the case.

The first knife was aimed faultlessly, the pommel catching Mazzard with a thud – slap between the eyes. He could have known nothing as his head jerked back soundlessly, the knife falling to the floor and the body following it. Cedar moved at the same moment as Bond, pushing down with her feet and, with all her weight, toppling her chair back against Louis, who was caught off-guard, diverted by Mazzard's sudden fall. Bond was aware only of the grunt and crash as he went over, propelled by Cedar and the heavy furniture.

By this time, the other knife was in Bond's hand, his body

turning minutely to position himself for Joe, whose reactions were considerably faster than 007 had anticipated. Luckily the big man only managed to move a few inches to his left, so that the pommel of the second knife landed heavily beside his right ear.

As though frozen in time, Joe Bellini stopped in his tracks, one hand half way to the pocket containing the revolver. The knife fell away awkwardly, slicing at his ear and almost severing it. He let out a strangled cry, staggered forwards and toppled across Cedar and Louis as they struggled on the floor.

The Kid moved indecisively behind Bond, who dropped the case and, putting full weight on the balls of his feet, sprang from the chair and leaped for the VP70 lying waiting on the bedside table.

He went for the weapon with a wild karate shriek, expelling the air from his lungs, covering the three paces in less than two seconds. Even as his hand grasped the pistol butt, thumb flicking at the safety catch, Bond swivelled, arms outstretched, ready to fire at the first target to spell danger.

The Kid's right hand was half way inside his jacket when Bond shouted, 'Hold it. Stop!' The Kid showed an intelligent sense of survival. He stopped, hand wavering for a second, then – eyes meeting Bond's – obeyed.

Just then Cedar broke free, leaped to her feet with startling speed and brought both hands down, in a vicious double-chop, to the sides of Louis's neck. The man grunted and slumped to the floor. Bond walked up to the Kid, smiling, reached into his jacket, removed the weapon he had been preparing to use and then administered a sharp tap behind the ear. Whereupon the Kid joined his friends in oblivion.

'Change your dress, Cedar,' Bond said quietly; then, on second thoughts, 'No, give me a hand with this lot first.'

Together they stripped the four hoods of their weapons, Cedar apparently unaware that her breasts were on full display. Bond fished into the special compartment of his briefcase and brought out a small sealed plastic box which he forced open. He drew out the chloroform pad and administered it to the four men who lay spreadeagled about the floor.

'Crude and not very effective, but it's easier than trying to get tablets down them,' Bond said. 'It's only meant for emergencies such as these. Old and tried methods are often best. At least we'll be sure of half an hour.'

They secured the hands and feet of the four men with their own belts, ties and handkerchiefs. It was then that Cedar saw what Bond's knife had done to Joe Bellini's ear – the top half-inch sliced through, leaving a bloody flap dangling and joined by only a thin strip of tissue on the outer edge. Bond fetched some ointment from the all-providing case to help staunch the blood flow. Deftly Cedar fitted the flap back in place and bound it up as best she could with lint and sticking plaster from the bathroom cupboard.

At last she realised that she was half naked and, with no embarrassment, stripped to her tight white briefs and plunged her legs into a pair of jeans, pulling on a shirt as Bond threw their things roughly into their bags. Suddenly he remembered the gold-edged card that he had thrust into his pocket at that first meeting with Mike Mazzard in the hotel lobby. He pulled it out and examined it.

On one side was a sort of crest, incorporating an elaborate letter B, with the words 'Markus Bismaquer' underneath, embellished with curving flourishes. Below that in tiny block capitals were the words: ENTREPRENEUR – AMARILLO, TEXAS. Scrawled on the back of the card in a sloping hand was a brief message:

Prof & Mrs Penbrunner –
Honor me by being my guests for a few days. Bring the Hogarths.
It will be worth your while. My Security Manager, Mike Mazzard,
will see you to my private jet at Kennedy.

M.B.

Squashed in at the bottom, written as if an afterthought, was an insistence they make it for dinner that night and a telephone number to ring should there be any problems. Bond handed the card to Cedar.

'To Amarillo, then. By car, I think,' he said curtly. 'They won't expect that. Have you got all your things?'

Bond saw a furrow of worry cross Cedar's face. 'Your reputation will go before you, James.' There was a small twinkling smile as she used his first name.

'You mean an old man like Penbrunner doing a knife-throwing act and a few karate moves?' Bond said, replacing the knives into their spring clips in the briefcase.

'Quite.'

He thought for a moment. 'Bismaquer's after us. He will know shortly that we're no pushovers. It'll be interesting to see how he reacts. Now, let's get a move on.'

'What about them? Will you call the police?'

'We don't want to start a hue and cry now. I'll leave some money and the key in an envelope in the laundry room. I noticed they leave it open. Lucky we have the sort of old-fashioned lock on this door you can't undo from the inside without a key. They won't be in a hurry to ring down to the desk, and it'll take them quite a time to pick their way out.'

Bond bent down to see if he could find another key in Mazzard's pocket and produced a skeleton that he must have got by bribing one of the chambermaids.

'Time to go,' he snapped. 'We'll take the back stairs.'

8

INTIMATIONS OF MORTALITY

They did not stop to look back across the river at that magnificent skyline twinkling with lights from the sharp outlines of skyscrapers, the vast twin towers of the World Trade Center dwarfing everything else. They needed to put distance between themselves and Bismaquer's hoods. Bond also had to have time to think. If, as they suspected, Bismaquer was part of SPECTRE, and, possibly, the new Blofeld himself, their adversary could already be one step ahead of them.

Bond had learned never to underestimate SPECTRE. Now, his duty was to out-think the enemy and his first inclination was to head for Texas and face Bismaquer – playing it dangerously, by ear. On reflection, as he slid the Saab neatly through the traffic, Bond decided it would be best to hide somewhere for a couple of days.

'If we watch each other's backs,' he told Cedar, 'and keep very low profiles, we'll soon find out if Bismaquer's really out for blood. Anyone with SPECTRE connections would have an army of underworld informers searching for us by now.'

It was Cedar who suggested Washington. 'Not the metropolitan area or Georgetown. Somewhere near by, though. There are plenty of big motels we could use, just off the main highway.'

The idea made sense. Once on the turnpike, Bond put his foot down, winding the turbo up to a safe and legal maximum, then flicking on the cruise control. They reached the District of Columbia around three in the morning, both watching for any possible tail. Bond took them around part of the Capital Beltway, then finally located the Anacostia Freeway, where they spotted an exit with a motel sign.

The place they had chosen was certainly large enough to get lost in for days – some thirty storeys high, with an underground car park where the Saab could be tucked away. They registered separately, as Ms Carol Lukas and Mr John Bergin, and were given adjoining rooms on the twentieth floor with balconies giving a view across the green belt of Anacostia Park and the river. Cedar pointed out, in the distance, the Anacostia and 11th Street bridges, with the Washington Navy Yard a smudge against the landscape.

Two days, Bond calculated. Two days lying low and keeping their eyes open. Then they could head west, and, to use his own words, drive like hell. 'With luck we should get to Amarillo within forty-eight hours. One night's stop somewhere, to conserve energy, and, by that time, we should know if Bismaquer's put a tail on us. If not . . .'

'Straight into the lion's den,' Cedar finished for him. She seemed cool enough about the prospect, though neither of them could fail to remember the fate of their colleagues – dragged dead and putrefied from the Louisiana marshes.

On Bond's balcony, as the dawn came up over distant Washington, they made plans.

'Time for a reverse in disguises,' Bond announced.

The management had them registered in new names, but had seen Bond in what he liked to call his 'Penbrunner hat'. Now he washed the grey from his hair, removed the moustache and spectacles, and – apart from the thinner hair, which would grow again quickly enough – looked almost his old self.

Cedar would be easily recognised by Bismaquer's lieutenants, so she worked for an hour or so on her own appearance – restyling her hair, darkening her eyebrows, adopting severe pebble-lens spectacles. These simple devices changed her looks completely.

The main problem, as Bond saw it, was keeping a careful watch for Bismaquer's men. 'Six hours on and six hours off. In the main lobby,' he decided. It was the only way. 'We find suitable vantage points, and just mark faces. If one, or all, of that unholy quartet turns up, then we take the necessary action. Two days, and I reckon we'll have thrown them.' They then made the final decision – to leave the motel late the following evening. Bond was to stay out of his disguise, and Cedar would change back to her normal appearance before starting the journey.

The routine began straight away. They tossed for the first watch, and Cedar lost, heading down to the lobby to keep her six-hour vigil.

Before taking a rest, Bond quickly checked his luggage, the most important piece being the briefcase. The knives were back in their slots, but he removed one, strapping it to his left forearm before going through the other items in the case: Q Branch's personal survival kit.

The upper section contained papers, a diary, and the normal accoutrements of any businessman – calculator, pens, and the like. In the lower section, which was accessible by both hinged and sliding panels, Q'ute had assembled what she called back-up material: a small, snub-nosed S & W 'Highway Patrolman' with the four-inch barrel and spare ammunition; a series of toughened steel picklocks, gathered together on a ring, which also held a slim three-inch jemmy and other miniature tools, all built to Q'ute's specifications; a pair of padded leather gloves; half a dozen detonators, kept in a compartment well-removed from a small lump of plastic explosive, and a length of fuse.

Originally Q Branch had planned to include an electronic device for detonation purposes, but at the last moment it was decided that thirty-five feet of nylon half-inch rope, together with a couple of miniaturised grappling hooks, would be more likely needs. Even though the rope was slim and easily concealed, it took up space, leaving no room for any more sophisticated climbing gear. If put to it, Bond would be using the bare minimum. Everything in the hidden compartment was protected by moulded foam rubber.

After checking the VP70 and spare magazines, 007 stretched out on the bed, quickly dropping into a deep, refreshing sleep from which he was awakened, five hours later, by the alarm call he had ordered: 'This is your three o'clock alarm call, the temperature is 67 degrees and it is a pleasant afternoon. Have a nice day . . .' Bond replied, 'Thank you,' and the voice chattered on, 'This is your three-o-one alarm call, the temperature is 67 degrees and it is a pleasant afternoon. Have a nice day . . .'

'And you,' Bond mouthed at the computerised voice.

Bond showered, shaved and changed into dark slacks and one of his favourite Sea Island cotton shirts, then slipped his feet into a pair of heavy rope-soled sandals. A short, battledress-style navy jacket hid his holster and VP70 automatic. Right on time, he took over from Cedar in the motel lobby.

They did not speak; merely a glance and nod effected the change-over. Bond soon discovered that you could view the lobby from a seat at the coffee shop counter, as well as from the bar.

On that first spell of duty – during which 007 ate a large portion of ham, two eggs sunny-side up with pan-fried potatoes, and visited the bar for a disciplined single-vodka martini – there was no sign of anyone showing photographs to the reception staff, for identification purposes; neither did any of the four heavies from New York make an appearance.

So the time passed, without a hint of any tail. Between shifts, both Bond and Cedar monitored the television newscasts. There was no story about men being found bound and gagged, at the Drake Hotel in New York; or of Professor and Mrs Penbrunner and their prints going missing.

Bismaquer was either playing a waiting game, or his henchmen were carrying out a fruitless search.

Neither Cedar nor Bond were to know that a sharp-eyed bell-boy had noted their punctual comings and goings in the hotel lobby. The bellboy waited for twenty-four hours and, instead of reporting the fact to the management, made a telephone call to New York.

During the call, he was closely questioned about the appearance of the man and woman. At the other end of the line, the man to whom he had reported sat back and thought for a while. He was one of the many agents on the payroll of a large consortium, the criminal nature of which remained unknown to him. What the private eye did know was that the consortium was on the look-out for a man and woman. The descriptions were different from those he had been given, but, with a few simple changes, this pair might well be those for whom a handsome bonus was being offered.

It took him some ten minutes to make up his mind. At last he picked up the telephone and dialled. When a voice came on the line, the private eye asked, 'Hello, is Mike there?'

'We've either thrown them,' Bond said at the motel, on the second evening, 'or they'll all be waiting for us somewhere along the route to Amarillo.'

He took a bite out of a large tuna fish sandwich, washing it down with a draught of Perrier water. Cedar had brought food up from the coffee shop after her last watch. Tuna fish sandwiches were hardly Bond's style, but they seemed to be Cedar's favourites. She was very silent, combing out her hair, returning to her normal appearance.

'Something worrying you?' Bond asked, noticing the look of concern on the girl's face, reflected in the mirror.

She took a long time to answer. Then: 'How dangerous is it going to be, James?'

So far, Cedar Leiter had shown no sign of anything but utter professionalism. 'Not losing your nerve, Cedar?' he asked.

Again a pause. 'No, not really. But I'd like to know the odds.' She turned from the mirror, crossing the room to where he sat.

'You see, James, this is all kind of unreal for me. Sure, I've been trained, well-trained, but the training always seemed, well, kind of fantastic to me. Maybe I've been behind a desk too long – and not the right desk at that.'

Bond laughed, nevertheless feeling the twitch in his own stomach, for he was not without fear when facing a threat from SPECTRE. 'Believe me, Cedar, it's often far more dangerous to stalk the corridors of power. I'm never really at my best sitting in at those endless meetings, sharing secrets with the Whitehall mandarins – in your case the people from State – or the military. Back in London, my firm all look like grey faceless men. You never know where you stand. But in the field, it's still the old story: you have to be blessed with nerve, cheek, and a lot of luck.'

He took another sip of the Perrier. 'This one is trouble, for two reasons. First, we have no proper back-up team, nobody we can turn to at the last minute.'

'And second?' the girl asked.

'That's the worse part. If it really *is* SPECTRE we're up against, they're a hard and ruthless enemy. Also, they hate me personally. I killed their original leader, so they'll be out for blood; and when SPECTRE has a blood lust, nothing is done by halves. You can't expect it to be quick and painless with them. If they get the upper hand, SPECTRE will make sure we suffer either stark terror or what the books used to call a painful and lingering death. Cedar, if you want to get out, tell me here and now. You're a great partner and I'd like you with me. But if you can't make it. . . Well, better we should split up now.'

Cedar's large brown eyes melted into a look which Bond recognised as both appealing and dangerous.

'No, I'm with you all the way, James. Sure I'm nervous, but I won't let you down. You've kept your part of the bargain.' It was her turn to laugh. 'I was worried to start with, I admit it. My Dad painted a pretty lurid picture of you – a swashbuckling

Lothario, he called you once. I guess you're still a bit of a swash-buckler. As for being a Lothario, I haven't had time . . .'

She moved closer, looping an arm around his neck. Bond took hold of her hand and gently removed the arm. His smile was touched with sadness.

'No, Cedar. And don't think I'm not both flattered and tempted. It would be tremendous. But you're the daughter of one of my best friends – and one of the bravest men I know.'

Still, in a different place and time, James Bond knew he would have taken Cedar Leiter to the bed across the room and slowly, languorously, made love to her.

'Come on, let's get going,' he said, hearing the huskiness of his own voice. 'When we get downstairs, I want you to pay the bill, while I bring the car around to the front.'

Cedar nodded, picking up the phone and alerting reception: they would be leaving in about fifteen minutes. 'Can you have our checks ready, please? And send someone up for the luggage in ten minutes.'

Bond was already completing his packing. 'You can do the map-reading, too,' he grinned. 'And what do we want a bellboy for? To take the luggage down? That's usually my partner's job.'

He ducked, just in time, as Cedar tossed a hair brush at his head.

While Bond and Cedar were thus engaged, a black limousine pulled up at the main entrance, twenty floors below. Bond, himself, could have described the occupants precisely. A dark, tanned and agile man, with a slightly hooked nose, was at the wheel. Next to him, sat a large, tall and barrel-chested figure, dressed in a dark suit and a somewhat old-fashioned, broad-brimmed fedora. In the rear lounged a man with rodent-like features, the thinness of his face out of balance with the broad shoulders and large hands. A fourth man whom Bond might have expected, with a military moustache, in ostentatiously expensive clothes, was not in the car. This was strictly Joe's business, and Mazzard could go to hell if he didn't like it. No creep could make a mug of Joe Bellini and get away with it.

'Just do your jobs,' Joe Bellini ordered. 'Louis and me'll go through the routine cop act. Okay?'

Joe and Louis got out of the car, walked into the lobby and, eyes taking in anything that moved, went up to the reception clerks, to whom they flashed leather-walleted police badges. The badges were followed by a few terse questions and the handing over of photographs for identification.

Two of the clerks immediately identified Professor and Mrs Penbrunner, adding their room numbers and the fact that they had checked in under different names.

'Is there something wrong?' one of the girls asked, looking concerned.

Bellini gave her a dazzling smile. 'Nothing serious, honey. Nobody has anything to worry about. We're just supposed to be looking after them. The Professor's an important man. We'll stay out of their way and be discreet.'

He went on to say that he had another man in the car outside and would deeply appreciate it if his boys could have the run of the place – just to check it out.

That would be perfectly okay. The receptionists would report it to the duty manager. Was there anything else they could do to be of help? Yes there was. Joe Bellini fired a dozen questions at them, and in less than five minutes had the answers he wanted.

Back in the car, Joe went through the plan once more. 'We only just made it,' he told the Kid at the wheel. 'They're leaving in the next few minutes. You got the walkie-talkie?'

His ear throbbed under the neat, fresh plaster. They had done their best with it at the hospital, but were fearful it would not heal as Joe had left it too long before getting proper attention. His hand kept going up to the wound as he detailed the Kid to watch the elevators, which luckily were grouped and could be seen easily from a hidden vantage point on the twentieth floor.

There were no back stairs, so it would be that way out or by the fire escape.

'Louis and me'll be in the maintenance complex under the building. Don't get seen and don't miss 'em. Just use the walkie-talkie. Got it?'

Joe Bellini, with Louis in attendance, clutching a high-powered walkie-talkie, again left the limo and entered the building. The Kid parked the car and followed the other two.

Having been given precise directions by staff anxious to co-operate with the police, Joe and Louis descended the four sections of concrete steps into the basement complex from which all the utilities – electricity, heating, air conditioning and the elevators – were monitored.

The engineer on duty was a smart, fresh-faced young man, who looked puzzled when the two strangers entered, and even more puzzled as he crumpled into unconsciousness, following a chop from Louis's right hand.

Bellini worked quickly, checking off the various banks of instruments and switches controlling the smooth running of the hotel's utilities, rather like the engine room of an ocean-going liner. It took him two minutes to find the section which controlled the elevators. Producing a small oblong box from his pocket, he located the sections he needed to work on, then opened the box, revealing a set of electrician's screwdrivers.

Each of the four elevators was operated by a separate bank of controls, the elevators themselves being standard, electrically-propelled cars with a supplementary system for each unit: generator; motor; final limit switches; counterweights; drum, and secondary sheaves; plus the usual safety devices, designed to cut off power and apply clawlike brakes. Each electrical component was triple-fused, so the likelihood of all the fuses failing, on one elevator, was minimal.

Carefully, Joe Bellini began to unscrew the fuse boxes for each elevator car. As he did so, Louis took a pair of heavy wire-cutters to the thick metal seals on the four levers marked 'Drum Release.

Danger,' at the top of the banks of instruments and fuses. The drum releases, unlocked the governors controlling the drums that wound, and unwound, the elevators' main cables. Unlocking a drum would immediately allow it to spin freely. Only maintenance engineers would need to release the drums in this fashion, and then, only when the car in question had been isolated and placed at the foot of the shaft, against the special buffer.

To release the drum when a car was in motion would mean certain death for any occupant were it not for the safety devices, with their back-ups.

Within six minutes, all four elevators were at grave risk. The fuse boxes were unscrewed, the fuses themselves plainly visible and accessible to Bellini, while the drum releases could be pulled at any time.

Standing back to look at their handiwork, they suddenly heard a familiar voice, clear on the walkie-talkie. 'Christ,' the Kid was whispering urgently into his unit, 'we're just in time. They've left the room. Some luggage just went down. They're coming now. It's her all right. He looks kinda different, but it's him too. It's them, Joe.'

On the twentieth floor, Cedar and Bond, briefcase in hand, sauntered towards the elevators. Large leafy plants decorated the elevator alcove. Bond, his back now to the plants, pressed the down button.

In the basement, facing the uncovered fuses Joe Bellini waited, screwdriver in hand, while Louis's right arm hovered over the four drum release levers. The third car stopped at the twentieth floor. With a smile, Bond ushered Cedar in, then followed. The doors closed noiselessly, and James Bond pressed the button for the lobby.

As he did so, the Kid's voice echoed around the maintenance room, far below. 'Car three! They got into car three!'

Joe Bellini quickly flicked every fuse out of the banks

controlling car three. As he did so, Louis hauled down on the drum release lever for the same car.

Bond smiled at Cedar. 'Here we go then. Heading West.'

'Wagons roll . . .' Cedar's words were cut short as the lights went out, and they were both thrown to one side. The elevator car lurched, then began to drop down the shaft at a sickening, gathering speed.

9

WHEN THE FUN REALLY STARTS

Cedar opened her mouth in a scream, but there was no noise, only her face contorting in terror. Bond, seeing her dimly in the gloom, did not know if the sound was blotted out by the terrible crash and banging as the elevator plummeted, swaying and smashing against the sides of the shaft.

In those seconds, though, Bond seemed to hear her – a horrible diminishing shriek of terror, as if he stood apart, still at the top of the elevator shaft. It was a strange experience, in which half of his mind remained detached.

'Hold on!' Bond's yell was drowned by the cacophonic crash of metal and wood, combined with a rushing windlike noise and pressure on his ears. When the car had started its fall he had his palm loosely on one of the hand rails which ran along three sides of the car. Pure reflex tightened his grip at the first jolt, before the long drop began.

A picture of the car, splintered, and shattered out of all recognition at the bottom of the shaft, flashed in and out of Bond's mind.

From the twentieth floor, with increasing speed, they went past the fifteenth . . . fourteenth . . . thirteenth . . . twelfth . . . eleventh . . . unaware of their position in the shaft, only knowing the final horror would soon be on them.

Then, with a series of shaking bangs, as the sides rattled against the metal runners, it happened.

Down in the maintenance complex, Bellini and Louis had

already taken to their heels. Their getaway would be simple in the panic which would follow – at any moment – when the elevator car disintegrated against the huge buffer at the bottom of its shaft. But Joe Bellini had no way of knowing that the motel elevators were built with one, old-fashioned, extra safety device which did not depend upon complicated electronics.

Two metal cables ran down the length of the shaft, their use unaffected by loss of power. These thick, hawser-like ropes were threaded loosely through the claw safety brakes under the car itself. The very action of the car overspeeding on a downward path caused the hawsers to tighten, exerting pressure inwards, with the result that two of the claws were activated, one on either side at the front of the elevator car.

In the first few seconds of the downward plunge, one of these 'last chance' automatic devices, on the right of the car, had been sheared off by the buffeting of metal against metal. The left-hand cable held, slowly pressing inwards. At last, as they streaked past the eleventh floor, the safety brake clicked, and the claw automatically shot outwards. Like a human hand desperately grasping for a last hold, the metal brake hit one of the ratchets in the guide rail, broke loose, hit a second, then a third.

Inside the car, there was a series of reverberating, jarring bumps. The whole platform tilted to the right, and each jolt seemed to slow the downward rush. Then, to the sound of tearing wood and metal, the car tipped to the right. Bond and Cedar, both trying to keep a grip on the hand rail, were conscious of part of the roof being torn away, of the ripping as they slowed; then of the final, bone-shuddering stop which broke the forward section of the floor loose.

Cedar lost her grip.

This time Bond heard the scream, and, even in the dimness, alleviated by light coming in through the splintered roof, saw Cedar sliding forward, her legs disappearing through the hole in the floor. Still gripping the rail hard with one hand, he lunged outwards and just managed to grasp her wrist insecurely with the other.

'Hang on. Try to get some kind of a hold.'

Bond thought he was speaking calmly until he heard the echo of his distraught voice. He leaned forward at full stretch, allowing his hand to loosen its grip for a second, then tighten on Cedar's wrist.

The whole car creaked under them, its floor sagging downwards like a piece of cardboard so that almost the entire length of the shaft below became visible. Slowly, giving her encouragement, goading her into trying to get her other hand on to his arm, Bond began to pull Cedar back into the car.

Though she was not heavily built, Cedar Leiter felt like a ton weight. Inch by inch, he hauled her back. Together they balanced precariously, almost on tiptoe, clinging to the hand rail.

How long the car could stay as it was, insecurely jammed in the shaft, was impossible to tell. Bond was sure of only one thing: unless some of their weight was removed, their chances diminished with every minute that passed.

'How are they going to . . . ?' Cedar began, in a small voice.

'I don't know if *they* can.'

Bond looked down. He saw that his briefcase was, miraculously, still with them, trapped behind his feet. Moving gently, pausing after each shift in position, he reached down for the case.

Even this simple action proved the urgency of their situation, for, every change of attitude caused the car to groan, rock, and creak.

Quietly he explained what he was about to do. Balancing the briefcase at an angle against the hand rail, Bond sprang the tumbler locks. Carefully he delved into the hidden compartments for the nylon rope, gloves, the set of picklocks and tools and one of the small grappling hooks.

The hooks would take immense weight. In the closed position, each of them was about seven inches long, roughly three inches from the point of the hook to the base, and a couple of inches in thickness. It was necessary to go through a three-part unlocking sequence to unspring one of them, which then shot out to form a circle of some eight claws, all running from a steel securing base.

With the gloves on, tools and pick-locks hanging from a large thong and clip on his belt, and the rope coiled over one arm, Bond closed the case. He passed it to Cedar, telling her to hang on to it at all costs, then secured the nylon rope to the grappling hook. He leaned forward, one hand still on the hand rail, to peer down through the ripped and broken floor. The sides of the shaft, with its criss-cross of metal girders, were plainly visible.

Taking the bulk of slack on the rope and coiling it into his left hand, Bond dropped the grappling hook through the gaping mouth which formed the forward end of the floor. It took three or four swings on the rope before the claw clamped into place around one of the strengthening girders some five feet below the car. Gently Bond payed the rope out, trying to gauge the exact length that would take him clear of the car and past the grappling hook.

Bond went through the scheme for Cedar, trying to give her as many tips as possible. Then, with a grin and a wink, he took hold of the rope and wound it around himself in the simple old abseil fashion – the rope merely being passed under the right arm, down his back and through the legs, being taken up again in the left hand, and coming in under the arm. There was no time for improvised safety karabiners or double rope techniques.

Slowly he allowed himself to slide forward, feeling the car move; shuddering, as his weight shifted. It was now or never. Then, as he neared the final gap, the whole car began to vibrate. There followed a rasping noise, as though the metal holding it in place would give way at any moment. Suddenly, he was clear and falling, trying to control the drop, keeping his body straight and as near to the side of the shaft as he dared. Metallic vibra-tions from the car seemed to surround him and the fall seemed to go on for ever, until the sudden jerk on the rope cut into his back, arms, and legs.

As Bond had feared, the weight of his fall pulled the nylon tight, then the tension released, and he felt himself rising again like a yo-yo. It only needed too much of a backward spring on the rope for the grapple to become unhooked.

Winded, and not quite believing it, Bond found himself hanging, swinging hard against the concrete and girdered wall. He felt his muscles howling in protest. The rope cut deeper as his wrists and hands struggled to hang on.

The small, enclosed world gradually swung into focus: dirty cement; girders, with traces of rust; oil, and, below, the dark cavern that seemed to descend into hell itself.

Bond's feet were firmly against the wall now, and he was able to look up. The car was jammed across the shaft, but for how long was anyone's guess. Already the upper section of woodwork had developed a long crack. It was only a matter of time before the whole section split. The car would then drop heavily on its side.

It would be a hideous way for them to go. But it was SPECTRE's way, Bond was certain of that. He took a deep breath and called up to Cedar.

'Be up for you in a minute.'

Kicking out from the wall, he allowed his hands to slide on the rope, bringing his feet within touching distance of the nearest girder. As the bottoms of his rope-soled shoes slammed into the metal, Bond hauled on the rope, grabbing for support from the big oily guide rail.

The latticework of girders was reasonably easy to negotiate, and Bond climbed it with speed, keeping the rope firmly around himself, until he reached the grappling hook. There he paused for breath, the car rattling in the breeze that came up the shaft's tunnel. Vaguely, among the creaking, metallic noises, he thought he could hear other sounds – shouting and steady hammering.

The sagging floor of the car was some five feet from his head. Unhooking the grapple, he climbed higher, eventually finding a suitable place among the girders to refix the hook; this time less than a foot below the car.

Turning his body so that he could lean back against the wall, Bond once more shouted to Cedar, giving orders in a voice designed to command immediate obedience.

'I'm going to throw the rope in. Tie the briefcase on, then let it down slowly. But don't lose the rope. Keep hold of it until I tell you.'

By this time he had pulled in all the slack of the rope, which had snaked down the shaft almost out of sight. Hanging on to the girders with one hand, Bond coiled several feet of rope around the other. Then, with a cry of 'Ready?' – and an answering call from Cedar – he aimed the balled rope at the flapping mouth which was all that was left of the open floor of the car.

The ball of rope went straight as an arrow. For a second or two, he saw that the length now protruding from the opening in the car was sliding back. Then it stopped, and Cedar's voice came filtering down.

'Got it.'

About a minute later the briefcase, tied now to the end of the rope, descended slowly towards him.

Cedar payed out the rope until Bond shouted for her to stop. Very carefully he reached forward, took the case, and, balancing it on the girder, untied the knot. He attached one of the metal fastenings on the briefcase to the large clip on his belt. Then he shouted to Cedar to haul in the rope and get a tight hold on it. 'Wrap it around your wrists and shoulders if you want,' he called to her. 'Then just slide out. It's around fifteen feet down to the next floor and set of doors. If we can make that, we'll have a secure ledge, and I'll try to open the damned things. Come on when you're ready.'

She came quickly. Too quickly. Bond saw her legs emerge and

the rope drop past him. Then he felt the blow as the side of her shoulder hit him.

He was conscious of the grapple taking the strain, and of the car shifting just above his head. But by that time his balance had gone, and he was suddenly scrabbling for the swinging rope in front of him.

He wrapped his hands around the nylon, and they were both swinging gently, one above the other, bouncing off the walls of the shaft.

'We're going to have to go down one above the other,' he called, short of breath. 'Just straight rope climbing stuff to the ledge on the next floor. The rope'll just about make it.'

Cedar's voice came back, breathless and excited. 'I only hope it'll hold our weight.'

'It'll do that all right. Just remember not to let go!'

'You really think I'd forget?' she shouted back, starting to move, hand over hand, the rope wrapped around her ankles as she went.

Bond followed Cedar's lead, trying to imitate her rhythm on the rope in order to reduce the swing. He had been bruised and battered enough from bumping against the girders. Finally he saw that below him Cedar had made it, and was standing on the narrow ledge, both hands still tight on the rope, her feet spread out and body leaning forward.

She was calling something up to him.

'There's someone on the other side of the doors,' he heard her shout. 'I've told them we're here.'

Nodding, Bond continued his climb down until he felt his feet touch the ledge. Even as they did so, there was a hiss and the outer doors opened. A fire chief, and three other uniformed, helmeted men stood aside, mouths agape, as Cedar and Bond stepped into the corridor.

'Ah, thank you,' Bond said as though a commissionaire had just held the door open for them. Then he staggered, feeling the strain hit him. Cedar grabbed his arm, and he took a deep breath.

The firemen and motel staff gathered around them. Bond waved away a doctor and asked that they be taken straight downstairs. 'We've got a plane to catch,' he added.

As they went, he whispered instructions to Cedar: 'Pay the bill and get what information you can. Then slip away and meet me at the Saab. We don't want too many questions, and certainly no cameras.'

When the party reached the crowded and noisy lobby, Bond was no longer with them. Even Cedar did not see him go. 'One of my disappearing tricks,' he told her later. 'Easy when you know how.'

In fact it *was* relatively easy. Bond always worked on the principle that, in a crowd that was confused and uncertain, all you had to do was to be positive: a determined move, in a definite direction, assuming the look of a man who knew precisely where he was going and why. It worked nine times out of ten.

In the underground parking lot, Bond did not go straight to the Saab, but waited, out of sight, behind another car directly opposite. It was over half an hour before Cedar appeared, running from the service elevator.

Bond emerged as soon as he saw she was alone. 'I told them I had to go the john,' she said. 'They want you as well. Questions and more questions. We'll have to move fast.'

In a matter of seconds they were in the Saab, and, a few minutes later, out and away, roaring down the Anacostia Freeway.

'You're the navigator,' Bond told her. 'We want Amarillo, Texas.'

As she directed him, Cedar gave Bond what information she had gleaned. 'Definitely our friends from New York,' she told him. 'I got their descriptions.' She went on to explain how they had come in posing as detectives, asked for directions to the maintenance complex, and how the duty man had been found unconscious. 'Apparently they'd stripped the controls for all the elevators,' she added. 'Whichever one we used, they had us.'

Bond smiled grimly. 'I told you. When SPECTRE wants you dead, they don't like doing it clean. Well, at least we know what we need to know. First Bismaquer wanted us as his house guests, then he tried to have us killed. I guess he'll have to settle for the first.'

As he said it, the delayed shock took hold. Bond felt his heart pumping and hands shaking on the wheel. He slowed slightly and, after a minute or two, the reaction passed. Taking a deep breath, he glanced at Cedar.

'We'll have to stop and buy some new luggage on the way. But at least we've got the essentials, including the prints.' The prints remained hidden in one of the many secret compartments in the Saab.

'So, my dear Cedar' – he grinned again, then relaxed and his mouth reformed into its hard, cruel line – 'so now the fun really starts.'

10

THE ROAD TO AMARILLO

They drove steadily through the night, skirting Pittsburgh around dawn, then heading west again. The Saab, set on its cruise control, gobbled up the ribbon of road, and during that first long day they stopped only for snacks and gasoline. The car, tuned to perfection before being flown to America, took to the broad four-lane highways like an unleashed jet.

Just before nightfall, they were already nearing Springfield, Missouri. Bond pulled off the highway and drove into a small motel, where they registered in separate cabins, Cedar as Mrs Penbrunner, and Bond under his own name.

Already, before the incident with the elevator, he had explained their tactics to Cedar. 'Even if Bismaquer doesn't know my true identity, I have to go in as myself.'

Cedar was concerned. 'Isn't that pushing our luck, James? You've already told me SPECTRE has a private and personal grudge against you. Why not keep the Penbrunner role going as long as possible . . .'

Bond shook his head. 'It's not going to fool them for long – even if it's done so already, which I doubt. Now, *you* are really not known. Mrs Penbrunner will probably pass, and we may just get some advantage by making them believe I'm here to look after you.'

She was still concerned about this when they reached the motel. 'You're setting yourself up as a target. Doesn't that worry you?'

'Of course,' said Bond, 'but I've done it before. Anyway, Cedar, do you really believe that the great Markus Bismaquer would go to all the trouble of having us removed, by way of an elevator shaft, if he didn't know it was me? Think about it: first the fearsome foursome turn up with an invitation: Bismaquer requests the pleasure of seeing the Hogarth prints before anyone else. Then we manage to disappear. True to form – SPECTRE's old form, that is – they winkle us out near Washington, and without the aid of any law enforcement agencies. Think about it, Cedar, and you'll see how good they are. They always were in the past. So they find us and try to give us the fast elevator trip. No niceties about the Hogarth prints. Just death, sudden, and a very nasty way to go.'

She nodded agreement. 'I suppose you're right. But it still sounds crazy – the idea of just turning up at Bismaquer's Rancho Notorious . . .'

'Tethered goats have been known to catch tigers.'

'And goats often end up sacrificial,' Cedar countered. 'With their throats cut.'

'Tough on us goats.' Bond gave a sardonic smile. 'Remember, Cedar, we go with knives as well. The fact is I have no option. Our job is to find out if Markus Bismaquer's running the show. If it really is a reconstituted SPECTRE it's most important to discover what they're up to. We're snoops, like the others. They got chopped. Why?'

The conversation went on in their rooms and in the car, when they drove into Springfield to provide themselves with new clothes, and again over a meal in a small restaurant, where Bond declared the chicken pie one of the best he had ever tasted and Cedar insisted that he try Apple Jonathan, a delicious baked concoction of green apples, cream, maple syrup and eggs.

Back at the motel, they unwrapped their parcels, filled the newly-purchased suitcases, and arranged a series of signals to be used in the event of trouble during the night.

Bond quietly checked out the motel, and its surroundings,

paying special attention to the parked cars. Satisfied, he returned to his cabin, laid out a new pair of jeans, shirt, boots, and a windbreaker. He then luxuriated under a shower – scalding hot, followed by a fine spray of ice cold water. Thus refreshed, he slid the VP70 under his pillow, placed a chair against the door, and secured the windows before getting into bed.

Almost as his head touched the pillow, he was asleep. He had long ago learned the art of resting, allowing the problems and anxieties to be swept from his mind, yet never dropping into really deep oblivion while he was on an assignment. Sleep he certainly had; but his subconscious remained active, ready to prod him into instant awareness.

The night passed without incident, and by noon the next morning they had circumvented Oklahoma City. The Saab, cool with its interior air conditioning, whined at high turbo power along the flat endless terrain of prairie and desert leading to the edge of the Great Plains and the panhandle of Texas.

Once more they stopped as little as possible, and, around nine in the evening, negotiated Amarillo, circling the city so as to enter from the west, on the assumption that any watchers would be looking out for the Saab along the eastern access roads.

Again, they chose a small, obscure motel, and as they climbed from the car, the heat hit them like a blast furnace. It was already dusk, lights were coming on, and the cicadas sang a constant aria among the trees and dry grass. Both men and women wore jeans, boots and large-brimmed stetsons. With a shock, Bond realised they had really hit the West.

The manager drawled them into an adjoining set of rooms, said there was a saloon and diner across the street – if they did not want to use the motel's coffee shop – then left them to their own devices.

'Well, Cedar,' said Bond, smiling, 'how about food?'

The food turned out to be the best bowl of chili either of them had tasted in a long time. But Cedar looked nervous as they said goodnight at her door, and Bond, sensing her anxiety, told her not to worry.

'Just remember all they taught you,' he said, 'and all we've worked out together. It'll only need one of us to get out if we strike gold. One alert – to your contacts, or mine, or both. We're equal partners in this, Cedar. Our job is to pin them down; get proof, and, if they've got some nasty work on hand, stop them. Now, remember, six o'clock in the morning.'

She bit her lip.

'Nothing wrong is there?' Bond searched for clues in her eyes.

She gave a heavy sigh. 'Of course there is, and you know it.' She smiled, reaching up to kiss his cheek. 'And you're right. Dead right. So if it can't be, then I wish my Dad was here. He'd love to be working with you again.'

'Stop getting sentimental, Cedar. You're as good as your father ever was; and I suspect you'll prove it in the next day or so. Now let's get some sleep.'

Bond stretched out on his bed fully clothed, with the automatic near at hand. He dozed, slept, and woke with an alert start, as the alarm call came through at five-thirty.

Showered, shaved, dressed, Bond was just in time to greet Cedar, who arrived at the door, bearing a flask of coffee and hot waffles with syrup on a tray. The coffee shop did a twenty-four hour service, she explained. At six o'clock promptly, perched on the bed, sipping coffee, Bond dialled the number on the card he'd been given by Mike Mazzard.

The telephone rang for almost thirty seconds. Then a male voice answered, although it took Bond a moment to realise a man was speaking, for the voice was thin, reedy, pitched very high and inclined to squeak in the upper register.

'Rancho Bismaquer.'

'Put me on to Markus Bismaquer.' No please or any of the other courtesies.

'I guess he'll still be asleep. He doesn't get up until six-thirty.'

'Then get him up. This is very important.'

A long pause. Then, 'Who wants him?'

'Just say that I represent Professor Penbrunner. I have Mrs Penbrunner with me, and I'm anxious to speak with Bismaquer.'

Another silence.

'The name was . . . ?'

'I didn't say. I'm only acting for the Professor, but if you want to tell Bismaquer, you can say my name's Bond. James Bond.'

007 was not certain, but he thought he detected a slight intake of breath at the other end. Certainly the reply came back fast as a bullet. 'I'll wake him right away, Mr Bond. If you're acting for Professor Penbrunner, I'm sure he'll want to know.'

There was a long wait, then another voice came on the line: soft, gently drawling and friendly, with a deep, pleasing chuckle.

'Markus Bismaquer.'

Bond nodded to Cedar. 'My name's Bond, Mr Bismaquer. Mrs Penbrunner's here with me. I have power of attorney for Professor Penbrunner whom, I understand, you wished to meet.'

'I did, that's right. Mr – er – Bond did you say? Yes, yes, I invited the Professor and Mrs Penbrunner to fly out here in my private jet. I guess it wasn't convenient for them. May I ask if you have the Hogarths with you?'

'Mrs Penbrunner *and* the prints. Both.'

'Ah. And power of attorney? Which means we could make a deal?'

'If that's what you really want, Mr Bismaquer.'

Bismaquer chuckled. 'If the prints are all they're cracked up to be, that's the *only* thing I want. Where are you?'

'Amarillo,' Bond replied.

'At a hotel? Let me send Walter Luxor – he's my partner – out to pick you up . . .'

'Just give me directions. I have a car, and good locational bump.'

'I see. Okay, Mr Bond . . .' The deep voice gave simple instructions for leaving Amarillo, and slightly more complicated ones from the point at which they had to leave the main highway and follow secondary roads to the mono-rail station.

'If you can be there at ten, I'll see the train is waiting for you. There's a section for automobiles. You should bring yours with you to the ranch.' Once more the chuckle. 'You'll need it to get around the place.'

'We'll be there at ten o'clock sharp.' Bond hung up and turned to Cedar. 'Well Mrs Penbrunner, he sounds very relaxed. We take the mono-rail at ten. So he's putting the ball neatly back in his own court. Sounds a very smooth gentleman.' He added that they were to be met by Bismaquer's partner, one Walter Luxor. 'Know anything about him?'

Cedar said there was a file. He appeared to be an innocent stooge, no more than a boy when Bismaquer took him into the old ice cream business. 'Been with him ever since. We don't know much more about him. Something of a glorified secretary really, though Bismaquer always calls him his partner.'

By nine-fifteen they were on the road once more. Cedar followed the instructions Bond had scribbled during the conversation with Bismaquer. Five miles out of town, they reached the turn-off. They had also collected a tail.

In the golden haze which had come with the sun, both Bond and Cedar could clearly make out the black BMW 528i riding at a comfortable distance behind them, two men unidentifiable in the front seat.

'Guard of honour?' Bond asked aloud. Silently he thought, guard of honour, or a hit team? Quietly he leaned across Cedar to press one of the square black buttons on the dashboard. A compartment slid open to reveal the large Ruger Super Blackhawk .44 Magnum he always carried in the car, part of the private, and most secret, 'gee-whizz' technology built into the vehicle without even the Armourer's knowledge.

The .44 Magnum was not just a man-stopper. Bond liked to think of it as a car-stopper if necessary. One properly placed bullet from this magnificent, single-action revolver could wreck an engine.

'Hey, that's . . . big,' breathed Cedar.

'Yes it is. A little extra protection if we need it.'

As it turned out, however, they had no use for the Blackhawk. The mono-rail station became visible at a good ten miles' distance – a low building, set behind wire fencing.

When they reached the fencing, they saw it was some twenty feet high – double-banked cyclone, with large red notices attached

DANGER. THIS FENCE AND THE FENCES AHEAD ARE DANGEROUS. TOUCHING OR TAMPERING WITH THEM WILL CAUSE INSTANT DEATH BY ELECTROCUTION.

Under this friendly warning there was a red skull, and the double lightning-flash international sign for electricity. The fence could be breached only through a pair of firmly bolted, heavy steel gates. On the far side of the gates was a small blockhouse and a large concrete area leading to what they now saw, was an oblong station building.

Two men, uniformed in fawn slacks and blue shirts bearing the insignia Bismaquer Security, appeared from the blockhouse. They carried hand guns holstered on their hips, and pump-action shotguns under their arms.

Bond let down one of the electric windows. 'We're expected. Mrs Penbrunner and Mr Bond.'

'Ten o'clock the mono's expected.' The men looked like identical twins, spawned by a pair of Epstein's larger human sculptures. Both were close to seven feet in height: big, tanned, and mean around the eyes.

Through his driving mirror, Bond could see the BMW still standing well back. Its lights winked twice, and one of the guards spat.

'Guess it's okay,' he said in a Texas drawl. Then he looked at his companion. 'Turn the juice off,' nodding towards the block-house.

'Is that for real?' asked Bond, pointing at the sign.

'Bet your ass.'

'Ever kill anyone?'

'Plenty. They got permission for it up on the ranch. Nothin' any law can do if someone gits hiself kilt. Place's lit up at night. Only take the power off when people're comin' in or out. If you want privacy here, buddy, you got it – if y'can pay fer it.'

The other man came out of the blockhouse, unlocked the heavy bolts on the gates, and the two guards swung them open.

'Quick as y'can,' shouted the one to whom Bond had been talking. 'They don't like us leavin' the juice off longer'n need be.'

With care, Bond rolled the Saab into the yard, watching as the guards closed the gates. One of them went back to the block-house. Through his mirror, Bond saw that the BMW had disappeared. A watcher, he concluded. Once the Saab was within Bismaquer's domain, the nursemaids could be quietly withdrawn. All part of the service. Typical – Bond thought – of SPECTRE's thoroughness. He pressed the button on the dashboard again. There was a hiss and the Blackhawk compartment slid back into place, just as the first guard came up to the driver's side.

'You got the steerin' on the wrong side, buddy, y'know that?'

Bond gave a polite nod. 'English car,' he explained. 'Well, not the car, but the steering.'

'Yep. I heared they drive on the wrong side over there.' The giant Texan thought for a moment. 'Jist point the nose at those doors and sit. Okay? Don't git out, or you end up dead as a frozen ox. Right?'

'Right,' agreed Bond.

Large metal doors were built into the facing end wall of the oblong building. Bond shrugged and raised his eyebrows at Cedar.

'Guess y'don't argue none,' he muttered, breaking the tension and causing Cedar to giggle.

Cedar's briefing had reflected the tight security on Rancho Bismaquer, and Bond already had some idea of what to expect if SPECTRE was involved. But the scale of this operation could only bring a sneaking admiration. No roads led into Bismaquer's large ranch, only the mono-rail protected by deadly electric fences, high as prison walls, together with automaton-like guards. Bond also wondered about the tail car, the BMW. Had they, in fact, been under discreet surveillance from the time they left Washington after the elevator incident?

Wrapped in these thoughts, Bond took out his gunmetal cigarette case, offered one to Cedar, who refused, and lit a Simmons for himself. He felt an itch of concern. It had not been there when he had begun the long trek from England; and, since then, life had been full of incident: the attempted kidnap in New York; the falling elevator; and then the long, fast drive to Texas. Now, poised on the brink of entering Bismaquer's world, Bond knew he should not dwell on the more morbid possibilities. As M would say, 'Worry *at* it, 007; don't worry *about* it.'

They did not have long to wait. Just on ten o'clock, Bond felt the car vibrate slightly. He slid his window down and heard the heavy whine of a turbine. Bismaquer's system would, of course, be a split-rail suspension: one huge rail with the train riding on it, so that it appeared the train was impaled, hanging on the rail. Yes, naturally, Bond repeated to himself: nothing but the best for Mr Markus Bismaquer.

The turbine whine grew louder. They could not see the vehicle arrive, but one of the guards walked slowly over to the doors facing them, unlocked a metal box in the wall, and pressed a button. Silently the doors slid back.

A long ramp sloped upwards. The guard waved them on, and Bond started the engine, taking the ramp in first.

They climbed a good twenty feet before the ramp flattened to become a gently-curving tunnel, like a very large version of the jetties used for boarding aircraft. In turn, this tunnel took them into the train itself.

Men in similar uniforms to the guards – but with the symbol Bismaquer Services in gold on their blue shirts – guided Bond into position. When the car was correctly parked, one of them approached and opened the door. He addressed them politely without accent: 'Mrs Penbrunner. Mr Bond. Welcome aboard. Please leave your car here, with the handbrake on.'

Another of Bismaquer's men opened the passenger door for Cedar. As it closed again, Bond – who had already put on the automatic device for securing the engine – clicked down the passenger door lock. Then he climbed out, briefcase in hand, and locked his own door.

'The keys'll be safe with me, sir.' The man stood waiting.

Bond did not smile. 'Safer with me, always,' he said. 'If you want it moved, come and get me.'

The man's face remained impassive. 'Mr Luxor's waiting for you, sir.'

Standing at the end of the vehicle compartment was a man who was especially noticeable for the rake-thinness of his body, and a face which looked like a skull over which thin, almost transparent, skin had been tightly stretched. Even the eyes were sunk back deep into their sockets. In personal appearance, Walter Luxor looked like the walking dead.

'Mrs Penbrunner. Mr Bond. Welcome.'

The voice was the same, high-pitched squeak Bond had heard on the telephone that morning. Now this mobile skeleton held out a bony hand. Bond saw Cedar wince as she shook it. A second later, Bond knew why: it was indeed like clasping the palm of a corpse – cold, limp and clammy. Press too hard, he thought, and you would end up with a handful of powdered bone.

Luxor ushered them into a beautifully-designed coach, with

upholstered leather swivel chairs; tables anchored to the floor, and an attractive hostess ready to serve drinks.

No sooner were they seated than the turbine whined, dropping in volume as they slid from the station and smoothly gathered speed.

Even at this height, Bond could see the protective, electrified cyclone fences on either side of the track. Above and beyond them the desert and plain stretched to the horizon.

The hostess came over, asking what they would like to drink. Bond asked for a very large vodka martini – shaken, not stirred – giving her the precise instructions. Cedar took sherry, as did Luxor. 'An excellent choice,' Luxor said. 'A very civilised drink, sherry.' He smiled, but there could be no humour in a face like his, only the grim joke of death.

As though to put them at ease, Walter Luxor continued talking.

'Markus only had the vehicle transporter and club coaches on the rail today. Perhaps, when you leave, he'll let you make a choice.'

'A choice of what?' Bond asked.

'Mono-rail cars.' Luxor spread out the crab-bone hands. 'Markus has had several famous replicas made to fit the system – one of his little idiosyncrasies. He even has a replica of your own Queen Victoria's special railroad car, one of the Presidential car, a perfect one of the state railroad car used by Tsar Nicholas, and a copy of the coach in which the 1914–18 war armistice was signed. That one doesn't exist at all now. Hitler made the French sign their separate peace in it; it was destroyed later.'

'I know,' Bond said abruptly. The face was bad enough, but the strangulated, high-pitched voice was almost unbearable. 'Why replicas?' he asked shortly.

'Well, that's a good question,' said Walter Luxor. 'Markus is a great collector, you know. He prefers the real thing. He tried to buy Queen Victoria's railroad coach to have it converted, but they weren't selling at the time. He did the same with the others.

No sale. If a good one comes on the market, well, he'll probably be the top bidder. He usually is. You wouldn't be here if he didn't want the Hogarth prints.'

'We nearly weren't here,' Bond observed, but Luxor chose either not to hear or to ignore the remark.

The hostess arrived with the drinks. Bond approved: it was one of the best martinis he'd had, excepting those he made for himself. Luxor talked on to Cedar, while Bond stared out of the huge window. The mono-rail must have reached a speed of well over a 150 miles per hour, yet they appeared to glide effortlessly over the plain. It was not unlike low flying, but without any buffeting or turbulence.

The journey took just over fifteen minutes. Then, gently, the speed was reduced. Bond saw three or four long sections of cyclone fence reaching away into the distance, then a high thick wall, wired at the top and reaching to at least twenty feet.

As they passed the wall, the mono-rail car slowed to a standstill. Most startling of all, the scenery changed dramatically – a fleeting glimpse of green, with trees, before they were enveloped by the curved white walls of a station.

'Would there be room in your car for me?' Luxor looked at Bond, who was repelled to find that, even when you stared hard into the sunken eyes, there was little hint of life there.

'Plenty of room,' Bond replied.

'Good. I will direct you from the station. The Bismaquer ranch is quite large, though of course you can't miss the big house. It's right near the station.'

Once down the disembarking ramp they could have been outside any small American railroad stop. Doubtless this was another part of Bismaquer's collection: a small turn-of-the-century station, probably removed from a ghost-town.

Bond glanced around. Only minutes before he had been looking at dry rock and brown, sunbaked, desert grass. Now, with the great wall sweeping away to left and right, they could have been in a different country. There were grass and trees, tarred roads leading off from the station, tree-lined avenues, and even a small bridge crossing a creek.

'Turn right,' Luxor said, 'and straight down the main drive.'

Bond heard Cedar give a startled intake of breath. Facing them, set amid lush lawns, was a huge white house. Wide steps led up to a portico where square columns rose to a flat roof. The main roof was pitched back over the rest of the house, its red tiles a splash of colour against the overall whiteness. There were dogwood trees in front of the house, flanking the drive, and Bond thought, vaguely, that he had seen it before.

'Tara,' whispered Cedar. 'It's Tara.'

'Tara?' Bond was lost.

'*Gone With the Wind*. The movie – Margaret Mitchell's book. It's the house from the movie. You know, James, Vivien Leigh, Clark Gable . . .'

'Ah,' said Bond.

'How very clever of you.' The squeak rose excitedly from Walter Luxor. 'It usually takes people longer. They think they've seen pictures of it. Markus fell in love with it when he saw the movie, so he bought the designs from MGM and built it here. Ah, here's Markus now.'

Bond had pulled the Saab up in front of the broad steps, down which a great bear of a man came, his face wreathed in smiles. The voice, in direct contrast to Luxor's was deep, gruff and embracing.

'Mrs Penbrunner! Why couldn't your husband come too? Ah, this must be Mr Bond. Come on, let's go on to the veranda and have a drink. There's plenty of time before luncheon.'

The face was pink and chubby: the face of a well-scrubbed baby, or an elderly cherub. Or, Bond speculated, a devil? Slowly he climbed out of the Saab. Bismaquer must have been in his late sixties, with wispy, soft, silver hair and clad in crumpled white suit, full of energy, laughing with childlike enthusiasm in a manner clearly designed to make people like him at first meeting. Could this be the new Blofeld? The head of the resurrected SPECTRE?

'Come, Mrs Penbrunner,' he heard Bismaquer say, '. . . come, – Mr Bond. I know we're in Texas, but I make the best mint juleps in the world. How about that? Mint juleps, Texan style!' Once more the infectious, growling laugh. 'You just fill the glass up with crushed ice, load in the gin and add a sprig of mint on top.' Bismaquer roared at his own recipe, then turned to watch Bond coming up the flat steps from the car.

Yes, Bond thought, seeing the happy gleaming eyes of this pink, white, and silver billionaire. Yes, the new Blofeld could easily be just this sort of man.

Then he saw the sliver of Walter Luxor, the skull face ghastly in the shadow pattern on the portico. Or Luxor? Living in the shade of all this wealth, with easy access to power?

Bond's real work was only just starting – with a vengeance.

11

RANCHO BISMAQUER

James Bond politely declined Markus Bismaquer's lethal mint julep, choosing instead another vodka martini.

'Of course, of course!' Bismaquer exclaimed. 'Anything you like! I never force a man to eat or drink what he doesn't want. As for women . . . Well, that's different.'

'Meaning?' Bond cut in tersely.

A white-coated servant had appeared through the main doors and stood waiting behind a large trolley-bar. But Bismaquer was content to serve his guests himself. He looked up over the bottles, hands poised, his cherubic face a mask of surprise.

'I'm sorry, Mr Bond. Did I offend you?'

Bond gave a shrug. 'You said one should never force a man to eat or drink something he does not want; then you implied it was different for women.'

Bismaquer relaxed. 'A joke, Mr Bond. Just a joke, among men of the world. Or, maybe you're not a man of the world?'

'I've been accused of it.' Bond did not let his mask slip. 'I still don't see why women should be treated differently.'

'I only meant that they have to be coaxed sometimes.' He turned to Cedar. 'Don't you sometimes like to be coaxed, Mrs Penbrunner?'

Cedar laughed. 'That depends on the coaxing.'

The high-pitched voice of Walter Luxor joined in. 'I think Markus was trying to make a joke based on the old saying that when a woman says "no" she means "maybe" . . .'

'And when she says "maybe", she means "yes",' Bismaquer chimed in.

'I see.' Bond took the proffered martini, flattening his voice to give the impression that he was a man without humour. When playing someone like Bismaquer, he calculated – all growl and laughs – it was better to take on an opposing role.

'Well, here's to us.' Bismaquer raised his glass. 'Then, perhaps, Mr Bond, we can look at the Hogarths. There's time before luncheon.'

Bond nodded silently, then observed, 'Time is money, Mr Bismaquer.'

'Oh, the hell with time,' said Bismaquer with a smile. 'I've got the money, you've got the time. Or if you don't, I'll buy it. When guests come all this way, we like to entertain them.' He paused, as though appealing to Cedar. 'You'll stay for a few days, won't you? I've even arranged for the guest cabins to be opened up.'

'A day or two won't matter, will it, James?' Cedar looked at him in a pleading manner, giving just the right emphasis.

Bond sighed, turning down the corners of his mouth. 'Well, I suppose . . .'

'Come on, James. I can always call Joseph if you want me to.'

'It's up to you,' Bond said, feigning surliness.

'Done.' Bismaquer rubbed his hands together. 'Now, could we . . . er . . . would it be possible to see the prints?'

Bond looked at Cedar. 'If that's all right with you, Mrs Penbrunner?'

Cedar smiled sweetly. 'You have the last word on that, James. My husband put it into your hands.'

Bond hesitated. 'Well, I see no harm. I think you should examine them inside the house, though, Mr Bismaquer.'

'Please,' Bismaquer appeared to hop, his large body moving from foot to foot, 'please call me Markus. You're in Texas now.'

Bond again nodded. He took out his car keys and went down the steps to the Saab.

The prints were in a special, heat-proof folder, neatly secured in a slim, false compartment under the movable shelf in the Saab's large boot. Without giving the men on the portico a chance to see the hiding place, Bond removed the folder, then locked the boot.

'Nice little car,' Bismaquer said from the portico, giving the Saab a condescending look which seemed somehow out of character.

'It'd show a clean pair of heels to most commercial cars in its class,' Bond said flatly.

'Ah.' Bismaquer gave a broad smile. An almost tangible ripple of happiness passed through the large frame. 'Well, we'll have to see about that. I've got a few cars myself, and a track. Maybe we could organise something? A local Grand Prix.'

'Why not?' Bond motioned with the folder, looking towards the house.

'Oh, yes. Yes!' Bismaquer all but trembled with excitement. 'Let's leave Mrs Penbrunner in Walter's safe hands. After luncheon, I'll see you're taken over to the guest cabins. Then we'll arrange a guided tour of Rancho Bismaquer – of which, Jim, I'm pretty proud.'

He gestured towards the tall doors, allowing Bond to pass into the huge, cool, parquet-floored hallway, with its imposing gallery staircase. Whatever else, Markus Bismaquer had a certain style.

'The print room, I think.' Bismaquer led the way down a wide, airy corridor, opening a pair of double doors at the end.

Bond almost gasped with surprise. It was not a large room, but the walls were high and screens jutted from them at intervals. Almost all the wall space was covered, and, even from the limited education he'd had in the Kensington safe house, Bond could identify some of the prints which hung there.

There were at least four very rare Holbeins; some priceless, though rather crudely coloured, playing cards; a signed Baxter colour print (which Bond's instructor had pointed out as almost unobtainable) and a set of what appeared to be original Bewicks, from the famous *General History of Quadrupeds*. Prints covered the jutting screens as well as the walls. Somewhere, from hidden speakers, baroque music filtered into the room, giving it a pleasant, peaceful atmosphere. The floor was of highly-polished wood, the only furniture high-backed chairs set at intervals and a large table in the bow of the room's one tall window at the far end. These too, Bond supposed, must have been priceless antiques.

'You'd have to call this a pretty handsome collection, wouldn't you, Jim?' Bismaquer waited patiently at the end of the room, visibly proud of his showpiece.

'People call me James,' Bond corrected him, remaining sombre. 'But, yes, I'd say these are considered, and sensible, acquisitions. Joseph Penbrunner told me you had two passions in life . . .'

'Only two?' Bismaquer raised an eyebrow, the quizzical cherubic expression looking somehow incongruous on such a large body.

'Prints and ice cream.' Bond reached the table as Bismaquer gave a bellow of laughter.

'Your Professor Penbrunner has had bad information. I have many more passions than prints and ice cream. But, I'm lucky enough to have made my pile while I was young. Walter Luxor is an experienced investment counsellor as well as a friend and colleague. The original fortune has doubled, trebled, quadrupled. In fact, the man's a genius. The more I indulge my tastes, the more my holdings multiply!'

Bismaquer gestured in the air, as though imitating the accumulation of wealth. He held out a pudgy hand, reaching for the prints. For a second, Bond wondered if the man was knowledgeable enough to spot them immediately as forgeries. But it was too late to worry about that in any case. Then, quite suddenly, Bismaquer changed the subject.

'You must, by the way, forgive Walter's strange appearance.

He looks like a dry stick, I know, like you could break him in two. But looks are deceiving. I don't suggest you try it. Really, he's strong as a horse.

'A car accident,' Bismaquer went on. 'I spent a fortune getting him rebuilt from top to bottom. His body was severely damaged, and the burns were God-awful. We got the best surgeons money can buy. They had to regraft the face almost completely. One of Walter's passions is speed. He is a *very* good driver. In fact, when we organise that little Grand Prix I spoke of, you'll be up against Walter.'

Skin grafts and an entirely new body? Bond wondered. True, Blofeld had been choked to death, but he did not know what might have happened after that. Could it possibly be that . . . ? No, better to let things take their course and learn as much as he could along the way.

'The Hogarths, please, James.'

With great care, Bond opened up the folder, taking each print with its covering tissue, and placing them in order on the table before removing the tissues.

'The Lady's Progress' was a typical Hogarthian subject. The first two prints depicted the Lady living in idle luxury. The third was her downfall, when the husband – now dead – was revealed to have had a multitude of creditors, so that she was left penniless. The final three prints showed the various stages of the Lady's disintegration, drink turning her into a common whore, so that she finally ended as a horrible image of her former self: raddled, craving, and foul, among the seventeenth-century sinks and sewers of London's poor.

Bismaquer leaned over the prints in an attitude of reverence.

'Remarkable,' he breathed. 'Quite remarkable. See that detail, James, those faces. And the urchins, there, peeping out from that window? Oh, you could spend a lifetime just looking at these! You'd find something new every day! Tell me, what's your asking price?'

But Bond would not commit himself. Professor Penbrunner

was still uncertain about selling. 'You'll be the first to admit, Markus' – he did not care for the easy familiarity – 'that it's very tricky to value items such as this. They're unique. No other set seems to have survived. But they're genuine. I have the authentication documents in my car.'

'I *must* have them,' Bismaquer said, enthralled, 'I simply *must* . . .'

'What *must* you have, Markus?' The voice – low, clear and with a tantalising trace of accent – came from the door, which neither Bismaquer nor Bond had heard open.

They both turned from the table, Bond almost doing a double-take, as Bismaquer gave a delighted growl. 'Ah! Come and meet James Bond, darling. He's here representing Professor Penbrunner. James, this is my wife, Nena.'

Bond was already prepared for Nena Bismaquer to be younger than her husband, but not this much younger. The girl – for she could at most have been in her mid-twenties – paused in the doorway, the sunlight from the great window pouring towards her like a floodlight. It was the entrance of an actress.

Dressed in exceptionally well-cut jeans and a royal blue silk shirt with a bandanna knotted at her neck, Nena Bismaquer gave Bond a smile calculated to make even the most misogynistic male buckle at the knees.

She was tall – almost matching Bond's height – with long legs and a firm, striding walk. As she crossed the room, Bond saw in an instant that Nena Bismaquer would be at home and comfortable anywhere. She had that special poise which combined all the attributes he most admired in a woman: style, grace, and the obvious ability to take on the athletic pursuits of what is known as the great outdoors.

As she came closer, he felt a charge, an unmistakable chemistry, passing between them, the charge which said she would also be more than athletic in the great indoors.

If such a thing as black fire could exist, it was there in her eyes, an ebony matching the long hair which fell to her shoulders and was pushed casually back on the left side, as though by the brush of her hand. The dark fire blazed with knowledge reaching beyond her obvious youth. Her face appeared perfectly balanced with her body – a long, slender nose and rather solemn mouth, the lower lip a fraction thicker than the upper, giving a hint of sensuality which Bond found more than engaging. Her grip, as they shook hands, was firm – a hand which could caress, or hold hard to the reins of a horse at full gallop.

'Yes, I know who Mr Bond is. I've just met Mrs Penbrunner, and it's a pleasure to meet you . . . may I call you James too?'

'Of course.'

'Well, I'm Nena; and to what extravagance are you tempting my husband, James? The Hogarth prints?'

Bismaquer allowed a rumble of laughter to come from the back of his throat and break, like a waterfall. He gave his wife a bear hug, lifting her off the ground and swinging her around like a doll. 'Oh, and who's talking about extravagance?' He shook with happy laughter – a summertime Santa Claus without the beard.

Bond could not help seeing the shadow cross Nena Bismaquer's face as her husband set her down, arms still around her, pulling her towards the table. She almost seemed to flinch at his touch.

'Just look at these, my darling! The real thing. No others like them in the world. Look at that detail – the face of that woman. Look at the men there, drunk as skunks . . .'

Bond watched as she examined the prints, one by one, the trace of a smile starting at the eyes and dropping to her lips, as a long, beautifully manicured finger pointed to the last picture. 'That one could have been drawn from life, *chéri*.' A glissando laugh, harp-like, and without malice. 'He looks just like you.'

Bismaquer gave a playful bellow of simulated rage, lifting his hands high.

'Bitch!' he crowed.

'So, how much are you asking?' said Nena Bismaquer, turning to Bond.

'There's no price tag.' He gave her a steady smile, staring unflinchingly into her eyes. For a second, he thought he detected mockery in them. 'I cannot even promise they're for sale.'

'Then why . . . ?' Her face remained calm.

'Markus invited the Professor and his wife here. He wanted to be first to look at the prints.'

'Come on, James. First to make an offer, you mean.' Bismaquer did not seem to have changed, yet there was something between husband and wife: intangible, but there.

Nena hesitated, then said lunch would be ready shortly. 'We'll take you over to the guest cabins later . . .'

'And a grand tour, how about that, my little darling?'

She paused at the door. 'Marvellous, Markus. Why not? You can charm Mrs Penbrunner, and I'll show James around. How about that?'

Bismaquer chuckled again. 'I'll have to watch you, James, if I leave you alone with my wife.' He gave his cherub beam.

Nena, though, had disappeared. Get the knife in quickly, Bond thought, and, before giving Bismaquer a chance to continue talking, he asked bluntly: 'Markus, what about your invitation to Professor Penbrunner?'

The pink and white face turned towards him, a mixture of puzzlement and innocence. 'What about it?'

'Penbrunner asked me to take it up with you. To be honest, he didn't want Cedar – Mrs Penbrunner – to come at all. It was she who insisted.'

'But, why? I don't . . .'

'The story, as I have it from both the Penbrunners, is that your invitation was delivered by force.'

'Force?'

'Threats. Guns.'

Bismaquer shook his head, puzzled. 'Threats? Guns? All I did was send the jet to New York. And I asked Walter to organise it with a firm we sometimes use – a private investigation and body-guard service. Just a plain, simple invitation; and a guard to see the prints and the Penbrunners got safely to the plane.'

'And the name of the firm?'

'The name? It's Mazzard Security. Mike Mazzard's . . .'

'A hood, Markus.'

'A hood? I wouldn't say that. He's taken care of lots of little things for us.'

'You've got your own security people, Markus. Why use a New York agency?'

'I don't think . . .' Bismaquer began. 'But God! Guns, threats? My own people? But they're local boys, I'd never use them except here. You mean, Mazzard's men actually *threatened* the Penbrunners?'

'According to Mrs Penbrunner and the Professor, Mazzard himself did the talking and three armed heavies backed him up.'

'Oh God!' His mouth dropped. 'I'll have to talk to Walter. He arranged everything. Is that *really* why the Professor wouldn't come?'

'That, and an attempt on his life. And on Mrs Penbrunner's.'

'Attempt? Jesus Christ, James! You're damned right I'll find out what happened! Maybe Mazzard misunderstood? Maybe Walter said something . . . ? God, I'm sorry. I had no idea! If we have to, we'll get Mazzard down here. You bet your ass we'll have him here before the day's over!'

It was quite a performance, Bond gave him that. Friend Bismaquer was an actor of no mean talent. He could also afford to make little mistakes about invitations, afford to deny respons-ibility. Bond would have to brief Cedar to drop in the full facts concerning the attempt in the elevator.

A gong sounded discreetly, from somewhere in the house. 'Lunch,' Bismaquer announced, visibly shaken.

Before they went into the cool, pleasing dining room, with its shaded windows, silently moving servants and colonial

American furnishings, Bond slipped out to the Saab, returning the prints to safety. The meal turned out to be animated, if wearing. Bismaquer, Bond discovered, liked holding the centre of the stage all the time, so that his *éminence grise*, Walter Luxor, and Nena Bismaquer became merely part of his court.

Their host was inordinately proud of the ranch, and they learned a great deal about Rancho Bismaquer before actually viewing it. He had purchased the large tract of land soon after making his first big killing – the sale of the ice cream business.

'The first thing we did was build the airstrip,' he told them. The airstrip had since been much enlarged. 'Had to be. Most of the water, for domestic use anyway, is flown in every two days. We have one pipeline underground, right out of Amarillo, but there've been problems with that, and we use it mainly for irrigation.'

Once work began, Bismaquer had put his priorities in the right order. A third of the land was for grazing purposes – 'Landscaped and everything. We've a fine herd out there. Unusual, but actually it pays for a lot of the fun.' The fun, as he liked to call it, was contained in the remaining hundred square miles which had also been irrigated and landscaped, with massive loads of fertile soil and fully-grown trees, either flown in or brought overland by tractor. 'You said, James, that you'd heard I had only two passions – collecting prints and ice cream. Well, there's more to it than that. I guess I'm a collector of just about everything. We've got a fine stable of cars, from ancient to modern, and some good horses too. Yes, ice cream is something I still tinker with . . .'

'There's a laboratory and small factory, right here on the ranch.' This was about the only time Luxor managed to get a word in.

'Oh that.' Bismaquer smiled. 'Well, I suppose we make a little money from that too. I still act as consultant to several companies. I like creating new flavours, new tastes for the palate. I tinker. Make the odd bulk load, then ship it off. Sometimes the companies turn it down. Too good, I guess. Don't you find people's palates are getting blander?' He did not wait for an answer, but went on to tell them about the special quarters built for the staff, which housed over two hundred men and women, and the luxury Conference Centre, which took up a couple of square miles. It was sheltered from the main tracts by a thick swathe of well-tended plants and trees: 'A jungle really, but a jungle kept in check.'

The Conference Centre was yet another source of revenue. Large companies used it, but only as often as Bismaquer chose, which was four or five times a year. 'In fact there's some conference due in a couple of days, I think. Right, Walter?'

Luxor nodded agreement.

'And there's this, of course. Tara, my very proud possession. Quite something, eh, James?'

'Fascinating.' Bond wondered what was really going on in Bismaquer's mind. How long it would take him to make an offer on the prints – if he really wanted them? After that, what plans had he for his guests? Though Bismaquer had acted in the most natural way possible, he must, by now, know who Bond was – the name itself would mean a great deal to Blofeld's successor. And what was this conference in a couple of days' time? A meeting of SPECTRE's leading lights? The Rancho Bismaquer was just right for the new leader of SPECTRE – a flamboyant world, in which fantasy could mingle neatly with the harsh realities of extortion and terrorism.

When something particularly unpleasant happened, Bismaquer could, like all good paranoids, forget about it: tinkering with new ice cream flavours, driving around his private race track, or just basking in the true Hollywood fantasy of the great screen house, Tara. Gone with the wind.

'Well, you folks'll want to freshen up,' Bismaquer said abruptly ending the meal. 'I have something to discuss with Walter – you know what I mean, James. I'll get a guide to take you over to the cabins, then we'll pick you up for the grand tour around four – say four-thirty. Is that okay?'

Both Bond and Cedar said it would be fine, and Nena spoke for the first time: 'Don't forget, Markus, I've got a prior claim on James.'

The now-familiar guffaw. 'Of course. You think I'd miss the chance of spending some time alone with our delightful Cedar? It's the two cabins you've arranged, dear, isn't it?'

Nena Bismaquer told him that was so and as they left the dining room, she brushed against Bond and said with a look which was more than a simple pleasantry, 'I look forward to showing you around the place, James. And talking to you.'

There was no mistaking it: Nena was giving him some kind of message.

Outside, a pick-up truck waited in front of the Saab, a scarlet flag flying from a rear antenna. 'The boys'll lead you to the cabins,' said Bismaquer with a beam. 'Meanwhile, don't worry, James. I'm going to get to the bottom of what you told me. Oh, and tonight I want to talk business with you. An offer for the prints. Don't think I didn't notice, by the way, how neatly you took them out again.'

'My job, Markus.' Bond thanked them for the delicious meal, and as they set off in the Saab, Cedar started to giggle. 'Wow, what a set-up!' she exclaimed.

'Set-up is the word,' Bond answered.

'You mean the invitation to stay for a couple of days?'

'That, among other things.'

'Everything to make us feel at home and put us at ease.'

'Just fine,' said Bond. 'Markus is quite the king. He was innocent as a new-born babe about the goons in New York.'

'You tackled him about that?' Cedar frowned as Bond ran through his conversation with their host.

They had gone about a mile from the house now, trailing the pick-up which moved steadily ahead of them.

'Whatever the quarters are like,' Bond warned her, 'we have to presume they're wired. The telephones too. If we want to talk, we should do it in the open.' When they were given the tour, Bond said, they should single out places to reconnoitre. 'The Conference Centre sounds like a natural. But there'll be others. Time could be shorter than we think, Cedar, and we'd better begin straightaway.'

'Like tonight?'

'Just like tonight.'

Cedar laughed again, 'I think you may find yourself otherwise occupied.'

'Meaning?'

'Meaning Nena Bismaquer. She's ready to drop her expensive shoes under your bed any time you feel like it, James.'

'Really?' Bond tried to sound innocent, but he vividly remembered Nena's look and the way she spoke to him. Being married to Markus Bismaquer would obviously have its compensations; but maybe there were things that the fantasy of the ranch and Tara could not supply. 'If you're right,' he mused aloud, 'if there's any truth in that, Cedar, I'll see we're not disturbed tonight. Heaven can wait.'

Cedar Leiter gave him a hard look. 'Maybe,' she said. 'But can Hell?'

The landscape had gone through a couple of changes already. 'Think of everything that man had ferried into this place,' said Cedar, shaking her head in amazement. They had covered about ten miles and were now climbing to a ridge crested by a thick copse of fir trees. The truck signalled a left turn, taking them along a path directly through a thicket of evergreens, then, with dramatic suddenness, into a broad clearing.

The two log cabins stood facing one another, about thirty feet apart. They were beautifully built, with small porches and neat, white paintwork.

'They're making sure,' Bond muttered.

'Sure of what?'

'That we're neutralised here. Only one entrance through the

trees. Surrounded and easy to watch. It's going to be difficult, Cedar: difficult to get out of. I'd put my last dollar on TV monitors and electronic alarms; plus a few live bodies in the trees. I'll take a look later. You armed, by the way?'

Cedar shook her head dismally, knowing Bond was right. The cabins were merely places where guests could be easily monitored.

'I've got a Smith & Wesson in the briefcase,' Bond continued. 'I'll let you have it later.'

The driver of the pick-up was leaning out of his cab.

'Take your pick, folks,' he called. 'Have a nice stay.'

'It makes a change from the motels,' Bond said happily, 'but I'd feel safer at Tara.'

Cedar grinned at him. 'Frankly, dear James,' she replied, 'I don't give a damn.'

Some twenty miles away, in a small study with lime-green walls and the bare necessities – desk, filing cabinets, and chairs – Blofeld dialled a New York number.

'Mazzard Securities,' a voice at the New York number answered.

'I want Mike. Tell him it's Leader.'

A few seconds later, Mike Mazzard was on the line.

'You'd better get down here fast,' Blofeld commanded. 'We have problems.'

'I'm already on my way,' Mazzard chuckled, 'but there're other things to deal with for the conference. I'll be there in a couple of days. Sooner if I get through.'

'As quickly as possible.' There was no doubt about the anger in Blofeld's voice. 'You've bungled enough already. And we've got Bond here like a sitting duck.'

'As soon as I can. You want everything right, don't you?'

'Just remember, Mazzard, the house on the *bayou* has very hungry guardians.'

Blofeld cradled the telephone and sat back, thinking about the next moves in SPECTRE's game. So much time and planning and then that cretin, Mazzard, had almost wrecked it. No orders had been given for Bond to die, and Mazzard was always far too trigger-happy. Eventually, Blofeld thought, something would have to be done about Mr Mike Mazzard.

HOUND. Blofeld smiled at the word. High above the earth, at this very moment, the Americans had their hounds out in force, with more in reserve. They claimed none of these weapons was in space, but this was merely a subterfuge. Within days now, SPECTRE would lay its hands on every piece of data concerning these Hounds of Heaven, the Space Wolves – and what a plan, what ingenuity, what profits! The Soviets alone would pay a fortune for the information.

From the conception of HOUND there had been the need for one major scapegoat, and, in the back of Blofeld's mind, Bond had always fitted the part. Now James Bond was in Texas – trapped, lured, snared. Ripe for the allotted role, and the ignominious death Blofeld had planned for him.

The business in Washington – though unscheduled and contrary to instructions – must have shaken the Britisher; but Blofeld had other things in mind, other activities to keep Bond off balance. Only in the end would death come to Mr James Bond.

Blofeld began to laugh aloud.

12

GUIDED TOUR

The cabins were identical except for their names – Sand Creek and Fetterman. If Bond remembered correctly, these were the names of two bloody massacres during the Indian wars of the 1860s. Sand Creek, he seemed to recall, was the scene of an act of revolting treachery, leading to the butchery of old men, women, and children. Pleasantly chosen names for guest cabins.

It was in true Blofeld fashion, though, as was the whole ranch. Neither was Bond surprised to find the interiors of the cabins as spacious and well-appointed as everything else. Each had a large sitting room with television, stereo and VTR; a bedroom which would put even the most grandiose hotels to shame; and a large bathroom, furnished with shower and sunken jacuzzi. The only difference lay in the paintings. Sand Creek sported a large reproduction of Robert Lindneux's canvas depicting the massacre, while the other cabin contained a blow-up reproduction of the *Harper's Weekly* engraving of the Fetterman battle.

There were telephones which, they soon discovered, connected with the main house and nowhere else. It would be impossible to call each other, and Bond was also disturbed to find that neither of the cabins was provided with lock or key. No privacy for these guests.

They tossed a coin for cabins, Bond getting Fetterman. He helped Cedar move her luggage into Sand Creek.

'They're not picking us up until four-thirty,' he told Cedar, 'so

I'll give you ten minutes, then we can do a short reconnaissance.'

It was essential, Bond thought while unpacking, to discover
the secrets of Rancho Bismaquer as soon as possible. At least
there was the Saab. Their equipment could stay in the locked
car and remain safe. A normal Saab was difficult enough for any
would-be thief. Bond's personalised model – with its heavy
bullet-proofing and other extras – was fitted with sensors which
activated alarms, should anyone even attempt to tamper with it.
For the time being, though, he was more concerned for their
personal safety, having no illusions about the manner in which
they had been isolated on this high, wooded knoll.

Cedar, taking her cue from Bond, was ready – in fresh jeans,
shirt, and a fringed Western jacket – within the allotted time.
Bond had also changed, and emerged in a lightweight cream suit
bought in Springfield. He was, like Cedar, wearing leather boots,
and he had altered the holster position for the VP70 – attaching
it to his belt, to the rear of his right hip.

Alone in his cabin, he had unlocked the briefcase. Now he
gave the small revolver, with ammunition, to Cedar.

'Ready for anything,' Cedar said, batting her eyelids at him.

'Let's play at being emotionally entangled,' Bond said quietly,
taking her hand as they walked towards the dirt track between
the trees.

'I don't have to play, James.' She glanced at him, gripping his
hand tightly and moving closer.

Bond once more sensed the unthinkable temptation. Cedar,
with those great saucer brown eyes, could have seduced a saint.

'Don't, sweetheart,' he murmured. 'It's hard enough already.
Your father's my oldest American friend, and you are the apple
of his eye, I've no doubt. Please don't make it more of a problem.'

She sighed. 'Oh James, you can be a fussy devil. Nobody thinks
twice about things like that any more.' She stayed silent until
they were well into the trees, then added, through gritted teeth,

'And you watch it with the Bismaquer woman. She'd eat you alive, make no mistake.'

For the sake of any real, or electronic, watchers, they made it seem like a casual stroll, but both of them stayed alert, their eyes searching everywhere. Still, they spotted no surveillance gear:

'Perhaps they keep a watch with radar – or some other system – straight from Tara,' Bond said, thinking aloud as they broke cover from the trees.

The knoll gave them a superb view across the ranch. About eight miles below and ahead stood a veritable small town of brick and adobe buildings – the living quarters, Bond supposed, for Bismaquer's retainers; while off to the right the stark blazing white of a T-shaped building glared in the sun. They could see that this large structure lay close to the protecting boundary wall and was encircled by a thick layer of greenery.

'The controlled jungle,' Bond said nodding towards the complex. 'That must be the Conference Centre. We have to get a look at that.'

'Through the jungle?' Cedar raised her eyebrows. 'I wonder what they've got hidden in all that stuff. See? There's some kind of pit on the outer edge, and fencing near the buildings.'

Bond thought of the possibilities of wild animals, reptiles, even poisonous flowers. The previous head of SPECTRE had known all about poison gardens – there had been one at the Castle of Death in Japan. There were hundreds of ways people could be kept out of, or imprisoned within, the Conference Centre's compound – not to mention the more mundane devices such as high voltage fences similar to those used to protect the mono-rail.

The view itself was certainly breathtaking, but Bond willed himself to keep things in perspective and his mind in high gear. Getting into the Conference Centre remained a most necessary objective.

There was also Bismaquer's laboratory which, they suspected, was the long building set near the ranch's main highway running below them. The laboratory looked like an easy target, though Cedar pointed out that there was a second building, like a warehouse, built behind the laboratory and partially camouflaged by trees. A wide exit road led from its rear, twisting and finally curving back to meet the main highway.

In the very far distance, covered by a bluish haze, lay grazing land; and, from their vantage point, they could make out the tiny dots of cattle. It was also apparent that the knoll was not the highest ground. To the left of the Conference Centre, Bismaquer's land sloped gently upwards to a broad plateau upon which the airstrip had been built, a plateau large enough, they both judged, to accommodate very big aircraft.

Almost as though for their benefit, there was a sudden blast of engine noise, drifting across the thirty or forty miles, and, as they watched, a Boeing 747 hurtled into the air.

'If they can take Jumbos, they'll be able to fly almost anything in and out.' Bond's eyes narrowed against the harsh, hot light. 'That's another target. Let's tick them off, Cedar: we need a good look at the Conference Building; Bismaquer's laboratory; the airfield . . .'

'And the mono-rail station at this end.' Cedar's grasp tightened on his hand. 'Just in case we have to get out that way. At least we know what we'd be up against at the other end.'

'The Dracula brothers, and a quick burn-up on the fence.' Bond's mouth tightened into a cruel smile. 'All full of joy and money, Bismaquer may well be; but the whole place stinks like a dung hill. He's got a small army on the spot, and a nice fun palace, plus the race track, wherever that may be, plus the cattle. Bismaquerland, Texas's answer to Disneyland. But do you know, Cedar, behind all the fun and frolics I can almost smell SPECTRE. This place has all the outrageous splendour that would have appealed to its late and unlamented founder, Ernst Stavro Blofeld.'

Bond wished he had some field glasses with him, or materials with which to make a map. After a while, Cedar asked if he thought they could get out.

'We only try that after we've made certain of two things, and you know it.'

She nodded, her face set hard. 'What SPECTRE's up to, if this is their base . . .'

'It's their base all right.'

'. . . and who the real culprit is.'

'Right.' Bond's face remained impassive. 'Who do you reckon? Bismaquer or Walter Luxor . . . ?'

'Or Lady Bismaquer, James.'

'Okay, or Nena Bismaquer, why not? But my money's on Markus himself. He has all the paranoid symptoms: a Chris Cringle cover, an obsession with wealth and possessions, always wanting more. I vote for him, with Walter Luxor as his chief eunuch.'

'Don't be so sure about the eunuch bit.' Cedar swallowed. 'I sat next to him at lunch. Those hands tend to wander.' She shivered at the thought. 'And I can't lock my door.'

Bond moved her away from the edge of the knoll to inspect the woods once more. 'They must have *some* kind of monitoring system,' he said after half an hour's further search had produced no clues. 'I think we try and shake any watchdogs they give us tonight, then go on a little tour of our own. Hallo . . .' He stopped still as the sound of a motor engine drifted up from the road below the knoll, and took Cedar's arm. 'That'll be the grand tour party. Don't forget, they'll split us up now, but after dinner at Tara we stick together. Right?'

'You're on, Mr Bond.' Cedar raised herself on her toes to give him a quick peck on the cheek. 'And don't forget what I said about the Dragon Lady.'

'No promises.' Bond's serious mask broke for a moment. 'My old nanny used to say that promises are like pie crust – made to be broken.'

'Oh, James . . .'

They broke cover, walking into the clearing just as Bismaquer, huge behind the wheel of an open racy-looking red Mustang GT, drove in with a flourish of dust. The Mustang screeched to a halt behind the Saab. *Circa* 1966, Bond thought, recognising the car. Probably with the 289 V-8 engine.

Nena sat next to her husband, hair wind-blown and face radiant, flushed by what had probably been a fast drive. She vaulted out of the Mustang in a graceful, single movement, her long legs clearing the door with agile ease.

'Nice little motor car,' Bond grinned. 'I wouldn't mind taking it on, if you've still got the Grand Prix in mind.'

'I can offer you competition livelier than this, James.' Bismaquer announced. 'Oh, it's on, okay. Everything's fixed. I'll show you what you'll be up against later. Are you folks all organised? Who's in which cabin? Or are you sharing?' He chuckled wickedly but without the trace of a leer.

'Cedar's in Fetterman, and I've got Sand Creek,' Bond said quickly, reversing the cabins before Cedar could blurt out the truth. If Luxor was a lecher it might be better for him to come groping after Bond in the night.

'You all set, James?' Nena Bismaquer's eyes, dancing a moment ago, suddenly turned serious as she looked into Bond's face.

'Do you want to risk the Saab?' he replied.

'She'll risk anything,' said Bismaquer, bubbling with laughter. 'Come on, Cedar. I'll show you some real driving – and quite a bit of prime Bismaquer land.'

Bond unlocked the Saab, handing Nena into the passenger seat. According to Bismaquer, the whole 'Grand Tour' took around three hours, but they would cut it short. Dinner was at seven-thirty. 'I want half an hour with you and those prints first, James. Let's meet at the track, about a quarter to seven. Nena will lead you there. Be good, and if you can't be good . . .'

Bond lost Bismaquer's last words in the deep roar of the Saab's ignition. Then, with a wave, he shut the door, and the noise softened to a rumble.

Nena Bismaquer turned towards him in her seat. 'Okay, James, I'll show you the best of Markus's pride and joy.'

'I can see it from here,' said Bond with a smile. Certainly she looked fantastic, the healthy, sun-browned complexion vying with her incredible black eyes.

She laughed, the same musical note, sliding down the scale. 'Don't you believe it. The Rancho Bismaquer's his one and only pride and joy. Come on, let me give you the tour, via the scenic route.'

They drove out, taking the road towards the small town which housed the ranch staff. There were neat lawns, a small park where children played, and Bond could see men and women going about the usual chores of any town – shopping at the large store, working in their yards, hanging out washing. The air of normality was almost sinister. Like everything else around the ranch, the town looked like a movie set.

Nena waved to people as they drove through, and Bond noticed a patrol car, with the Bismaquer Security flashes on the side.

'Highway police?' he asked.

'Certainly. Markus believes in law and order. He thinks it makes people forget they're living in an enclosed area. These people very rarely leave here, you know, James.'

Bond made no comment, just drove on, following her directions. They went out to the edge of the grazing land, then turned back, taking the airport road. It was clear Cedar and he had been right: this was no simple landing strip in the converted desert, but a full scale operational airport.

'It's called Bismaquer International, would you believe that?' Nena's tone sounded like blatant mockery.

'I'd believe it. Where next?'

She gave instructions, and soon they were coasting close to the jungle-like thicket surrounding the Conference Centre.

Bond asked if this was intended to keep people out, knowing very well, from the observations made on the knoll, that it was just that.

'Oh, keep-out, or keep-in. Keep-in really. We get the strangest people here for conferences, and they tend to get nosey. Markus enjoys his privacy. You'll see. Once he's done a deal with you, and shown off all his toys, he'll have you out and away before you know it.'

Bond slowed the car, glancing constantly at the high, impenetrable greenery. 'Looks nasty. You've got a pit around it as well. Are there dragons in there to discourage the inmates?'

'Nothing as bad as that; but you can't get through without a machete, and some skill. There's half a mile of thicket – some of it quite dangerous. And a high fence. *We* can get in, though.'

'Well, somebody has to. Presumably you provide the staff. Unless you lift them in and out by chopper?'

'Conference delegates are in fact taken in by helicopter. But here, I'll show you. You follow the green belt for about two miles more.'

'What's a lovely French girl doing in a dream world like this?' Bond said, as though to himself.

There was a moment's pause, during which 007 cursed himself, thinking he had moved too soon.

'I wonder about that myself.' Nena's voice dropped, the sparkle gone. 'All the time.' There was another silence before she said, 'Oh, it's a long, involved, and not very edifying story, James. I come out of it something of a gold-digger. Did you know that gold-diggers always get their just deserts?'

'I thought they got diamonds, mink coats, smart cars, luxury flats and – most evenings – zabaglione, crêpes suzettes, or profiteroles for their just desserts.'

'Oh, they get that too. But they pay a price. Here, straight ahead. Start slowing down.'

The road had circled almost to the high fencing and walls, on the other side of which, Bond knew, there was nothing but arid land, dry grass and rock, stretching almost as far as Amarillo.

'Pull up here,' Nena ordered.

Bond brought the Saab to a halt, then following Nena's lead, got out of the car.

She crossed to the side of the road and knelt down, as though afraid of being seen. 'I shouldn't really be giving away the family secrets.' Her smile, as she lifted her head, seemed to go like a lance to Bond's heart. This was madness, he told himself, sheer and utter. Nena Bismaquer had been unknown to him until, literally, a few hours ago; yet already he felt envy for the bear-like Markus Bismaquer. He had a surge of desire to know everything about her: her past, childhood, parents, friends, likes and dislikes, thoughts and ideas.

Warning signals rang in his head, pulling his mind back to the reality of the moment. Nena Bismaquer knelt beside what appeared to be a small, circular metal cover about a foot in diameter that looked as though it had something to do with drainage. A metal ring was recessed flush with the centre of the cover, and Nena prised it open with ease, lifting out the thick round plate as though it were light as plastic.

'See?' She showed him a U-shaped handle, lying in the revealed recess. 'Now watch.' As she pulled at the handle, a block of stone at the edge of the roadway slowly sank, as though on a hydraulic lift. The block was about five feet square. When it had dropped to around a foot below the surface, the distant hiss of hydraulics became clearly audible. The slab slid to one side, revealing a wide, tiled chamber beneath. Metal hand and foot holds ran down the wall nearest the road.

'I don't think we should go down.' A hint of nervousness came into her unusually calm voice. 'But the chamber leads to steps and a tunnel which comes out in a janitor's closet over in the main building. There's an opening and closing device down there, and another one when you get to the far end. Just one of Markus's little devices. Few people know about it. The staff we use in the Conference Centre, of course, always go in this way, about a day before a delegation arrives. Food's ferried in by helicopter; and this is always here as an emergency escape route in case of trouble.'

Her choice of words seemed odd to Bond. 'What kind of trouble?' he asked.

'I told you: we get some very strange characters among conference delegates. Markus has this thing about security. He's quite right, of course. Oh, maybe I shouldn't have shown it to you. Come on, let's get out of here.'

She reached down and pulled the lever back. The slab of stone, on its hydraulic jacks, went through the reverse procedure. When it was settled in position, Nena put the small circular cover back in place and kicked dust over it with her foot.

Back in the car, she seemed edgy. 'Where now?' Bond asked, giving the impression that the show with the hidden entrance was an interesting, but unimportant event.

She looked at her watch. They had a good three-quarters of an hour before meeting Bismaquer. 'Take the road towards the cabins.' She spoke quickly. 'I'll show you where to turn off.'

Bond pointed the Saab in the direction of the wooded knoll. Instead of taking the track up through the trees, though, she told him to skirt the knoll to the left. Ahead, Bond saw there was another track leading up the other side of the rising ground, wide enough for cars or trucks.

Half way up the far side, Nena pointed to an exit among the trees, on the right, and in a few moments they were in a small clearing: dark and surrounded by trees, with just enough room to turn the car around.

'Have you got a cigarette?' she asked after he switched off the ignition.

Bond produced his gunmetal case, lighting cigarettes for both of them. He noticed that her fingers were trembling. Nena drew hard on the cigarette, exhaling the smoke in a long stream. 'Look, James. I've been foolish. I'm sorry; I don't know why I did it, but please don't tell Markus I showed you that entrance to the Centre.' She shook her head, repeating, 'I don't know why I did it. You see, he's . . . well, he gets into a state about these things. I was carried away – a new face, someone nice, you know what I mean?' Her hand seemed to drift towards his, fingers inter-locking his fingers.

'Yes, I think I know.' The touch of her hand was like a tiny electric shock.

Quite suddenly she laughed. 'Oh dear. I'm not really very bright, am I? I could always have blackmailed you, Mr James Bond.'

'Blackmailed?' Concern, razor-sharp, sliced through Bond's nerves.

She raised her hand, lifting Bond's arm with hers, fingers tightening. 'Don't worry. Please. You don't tell Markus I gave away a state secret, and I won't mention the fact that you're a . . . Oh, what do they call it? A con merchant? A confidence artist? There's another slang name over here . . .'

'A flim-flam man?' Bond offered.

'That's good.' Again the glissando laugh. 'A good description – flim-flam.' She pronounced it deliciously as 'fleem-flem'.

'Nena, I don't know . . .'

'James.' She shook a finger at him with her free hand. 'You're in my power, my dear, and heaven knows, I need a good man in my power.'

'I still don't know what you're . . .'

She shushed him. 'Look. Markus is always the big expert. He knows about cars and horses, he certainly knows about ice cream. In fact ice cream is really the one thing he does know about. But prints? He has books, he knows what he likes, but he's no expert. I, on the other hand, am an expert. Until a few years ago, when I became Mrs Bismaquer, I studied art. In Paris, I studied since twelve years of age, and my speciality was prints. You have a set of unknown Hogarths. Unique, Markus keeps telling me. Worth a fortune.'

'Yes. And authenticated. And I haven't said they're for sale yet, Nena.'

She gave her brilliant smile. 'No, and don't think I'm unaware of that being one of the oldest tricks in the book, James. Dangle them, yes? Be uncertain about a sale? Look.' Still talking, she took his hand, locked with her own, and thrust it between her thighs. The gesture was so natural, as if she scarcely realised what she had done, but Bond felt a sudden difficulty in breathing naturally. 'Look, James. *You* know there are no new, undiscovered sets of Hogarth prints. *You* know it. *I* know it. Just as I know the ones you have are a set of very, very good fakes. They are so good that I've no doubt future generations will believe they're Hogarth originals. They'll become real Hogarths. I know how the market works. A fake work of art, if handled properly, actually becomes the real thing. Somehow you've already managed to convince some people that they're real; you have authentication, provided that's not forged too . . .'

'It's not.' Bond knew he should admit to nothing illegal. 'But what makes you so certain those are forgeries? You only had a quick look at them.'

She moved closer so that their shoulders touched, her head leaning so near that he could smell her hair – not a distilled scent, made in some expensive factory, but the real thing, human hair, cared-for, and containing its own elusive fragrance.

'I know they're forgeries, because I know the man who did them. In fact I've seen them before. He's an Englishman called – variously – Miller, or Millhouse, or maybe it's Malting?'

Nena then proceeded to give Bond an accurate and detailed description of the little expert who had so diligently put Cedar, and himself, through their paces at the Kensington safe house.

Blast, Bond thought to himself. M had been uncharacteristically careless. On the other hand, his chief was a sly old fox, quite capable of preparing a trail for SPECTRE to follow, regardless of the danger to Bond.

'Well, Nena, it's all news to me,' he bluffed, hoping that no sign of the shock showed in his face or eyes.

When she spoke next, Nena's voice gave the impression that she too was short of breath.

James. I'm not going to say anything. Just, please, don't tell him about the tunnel. I really should not have shown that to you; and . . . Oh, James, sometimes he terrifies me . . .' Her hand untwined from his, her arms reaching up as she pulled his lips down on to her own.

There was a moment, just after their lips touched, when Bond thought he heard the distant voice of Cedar telling him, 'She'd eat you alive, make no mistake.'

James Bond, however, had reached the stage when he would gladly have been eaten alive by the amazing Nena Bismaquer. In all his not inconsiderable experience, he could not remember ever having been kissed like this. It began as a caressing touch, as their lips met, then a tingling sensation – her mouth in constant motion – as they opened their mouths as one, the tips of their tongues touching, then retreating, and touching again: like two animals exploring one another; until, at last, both capitulated willingly. Gradually, the kiss became almost everything the whole act of sex should be: the lips, mouths, and tongues ceased to have separate identities – becoming one, reaching out, exploring: extending into a passion of their own.

Bond unconsciously reached for her body, but Nena's hand caught his wrist, holding him away until, breathless, they slowly surrendered each other's mouths.

James,' she spoke almost in a whisper. 'I thought the art of kissing was dead.'

'Well, it seems to be alive, well, and living in a Saab motor car in the middle of a ranch in Texas.' It was not meant to be flippant; and the way Bond spoke it did not come out that way.

She glanced at her watch. 'Oh, dear James, we'll have to go soon.' Her eyes shifted from him briefly. 'I have to ask one thing.' She looked away from him, staring out through the windshield. 'You and Mrs Penbrunner – Cedar . . . ?'

'Yes?'

'Are you? . . . Well, is there . . . ?'

'Are we lovers?' Bond helped her.

'Yes. I think, around here they would ask – are you a scene?'

'No. Very definitely no. Cedar's husband happens to be one of my best and closest friends. But, Nena, this is crazy. Markus . . .'

'Would kill you.' She sounded very calm about it. 'Or have you killed. Maybe he'll kill you anyway, James. I was going to warn you, whatever. Now I'm doing it against my will, because I'd like nothing better than for you to stay here forever. But I'd rather have you here alive. Darling James. Let me give you advice: go. Go as soon as you can. Take Markus for what you can get, but do it tonight, and then leave as quickly as possible. There's evil here. More evil than you could dream of.'

'Evil?'

'I can't tell you about it. To be honest, I don't know that much myself, but what I do know terrifies me. Markus may seem a nice buffoon – a rich, boisterous, amusing and generous teddy bear. But the bear has claws, James, terrible claws, and powers that reach out far beyond this ranch. Far beyond America in fact.'

'You mean he's some kind of criminal?'

'It's not that simple.' She shook her head. 'I can't explain. Can I, perhaps, come to you – tonight? No, I can't tonight. There's no way. If you're still here tomorrow – though if you take my advice, you'll be gone – but, if you're here, can I come to you?'

'Please.' Bond could find no eloquent words. Nena seemed at the edge of some precipice, lying, hidden, within her.

'We must go. He'll be all smiles even if we're late, but I'll go through hell afterwards.'

Silently Bond wiped his mouth, while Nena made use of the vanity mirror to brush off her lips and run a comb through her hair. As they drove off, Bond asked if she could explain her part in things. 'Just the bare facts.'

She spoke quickly, between giving him directions. Nena Clavert, as she had been, was an orphan living in Paris, with a passion for art. An uncle had helped with her education, but by the time she reached the age of twenty he was a sick man. She worked as a part-time waitress and continued her studies, living off a pittance. In the end, she began to think there was only one way: 'I seriously considered becoming a whore. It's melodramatic and laughable now. Yet then it seemed to be the only reasonable answer. Jobs were scarce and I needed money: enough to be comfortable, to learn, and to paint.'

Then the rich American, Bismaquer, had turned up. 'He courted me like you read about in books – generous presents, clothes, the best places to eat. And he didn't touch me, didn't lay a finger on me: the perfect gentleman.'

Finally, Bismaquer had asked her to be his wife. She was worried because of the great difference in their ages; but he'd said it mattered not at all to him. If he got too old and useless, she could lead her own life.

'It wasn't until he brought me here that I found the real man behind that generous nature. Yes, there's a criminal – a terrible – connection. But there are other things too: his violent temper, which only those close to him see. And his predilections, of course . . .'

'Sexual?'

'He's amazing for a man of his age, I have to admit it. But, he's sexually . . . what do you say, James? . . . ambivalent? Why do you think he has that terrible death's head, Walter Luxor, here all the time? It's not just the cleverness with money. He's . . . well . . . he and Luxor . . .'

Her voice trailed off, then regained its habitual calm.

'Sometimes he doesn't come near me for months. Then it all changes. Oh, he can plough a long furrow when he wishes . . . You turn right here,' she ordered. 'I must stop talking, or he'll see I'm in a state. Don't give him a hint, James. Not a hint.'

They followed a minor road, taking them around the back of

the smooth lawns surrounding Tara, then through a belt of trees, high and thick, which explained why Cedar and Bond could not see the racing circuit from their vantage point on the knoll.

The trees screened everything – a device Bismaquer employed throughout the ranch's entire layout. This time they hid a huge oval circuit, wide enough to take three or four cars. The bends at the end nearest to the house were gentle curves, but half way down the far side there was a nasty chicane, followed by a crucifying right-angle turn, while the next bend – at the distant end of the rough oval – was almost a Z in shape.

The track must have been all of eight miles in full circuit, and Bond picked out its hazards, the very real danger points, with a practised eye.

On the far side stood a banked wooden grandstand; below there were pits and garages. The red Mustang was just arriving under the grandstand, the skeleton figure of Luxor standing ready to greet Bismaquer and Cedar.

Bond took the Saab right around the access road which ran parallel to the circuit. As he and Nena approached, Bismaquer and Cedar became plainly visible, standing next to a car that was silver in colour, like Bond's Saab, with Walter Luxor now at the wheel.

'Be terribly careful, James.' Nena seemed to have regained her self-control. 'Once behind the wheel, Walter's a dangerous man to play around with. He's an expert, he knows this track like his own hand, and he can clock up incredible speeds. What's worse, since his own accident he's felt no fear – neither for himself nor any opponent.'

'I'm not bad myself.' Bond said, hearing the anger he felt towards Bismaquer and Luxor etched deeply into his voice. 'If they're set on this race, I think I can teach Walter Luxor a thing or two, especially if they match me properly. I'll only drive against my own class . . .' He stopped as they came up to the group and identified the other silver car. 'And it looks as though they're giving me a reasonable chance, with room to spare.' He

braked the Saab to a halt, opened the door and went around to
help Nena Bismaquer from her seat as Markus came over, slapping him on the back, emitting another of the now infuriating
guffaws.

'Did you enjoy it? Isn't it great? You see why I'm so proud of
Rancho Bismaquer?'

'It's quite a place. Makes any one of England's home counties
seem like a small farm.' Bond smiled, looking across to Cedar:
'Eh, Cedar? Isn't it tremendous?'

'Something else,' she answered. Nobody but Bond could have
understood the tinge of irony; and only Bond noticed the dagger
looks aimed directly at Nena Bismaquer.

'Tomorrow,' Bismaquer said loudly, with a flourish towards
the parked silver car. 'Do you think you're well-matched, James?
Walter'll drive against you. Tomorrow morning, I think. How
about it?'

Bond looked towards Luxor, who sat at the wheel of the
Mustang variant – the Shelby-American GT 350. This had been
a most popular high-performance competition car in the late
1960s: with a lightened body, free-flow exhaust, and the 289 V-8
engine.

'It's souped up a little, of course,' Bismaquer chuckled. 'And
it's all of thirteen years old. But I guess it'll give you a run on this
track, even with that turbo of yours. You on, James?'

Bond reached out a hand. 'Of course I'm on. Should be fun.'

Bismaquer turned his head, calling back to Luxor. 'Tomorrow,
Walter. About ten in the morning, before it gets too hot. Eight
laps. Okay, James?'

'Ten, if you like.' If it was bravado they wanted, then he was
game.

'Good. We'll invite some of the boys. Nothing they like
better'n a good road race.' Then, with a quick change of tone,
Bismaquer turned to Nena. 'Let's get back then. I have one or
two things to do tonight, and I've got to talk with young James,

here, before dinner. I expect the ladies'll want to freshen up a little as well.'

Nena gave Bond an unperturbed smile. 'Thank you for putting up with my lecture on the wonders of Rancho Bismaquer, James. I enjoyed showing you around.'

'My pleasure.' Bond opened the door for Cedar, who called her thanks in turn to Bismaquer. Engines fired, and Bismaquer led the way back to Tara, his wife at his side.

'Thank you very much for putting up with my lecture, James,' Cedar mimicked. 'Oh, my pleasure, Nena; my pleasure. You're a creep, James Bond.'

'Possibly.' Bond spoke sharply. 'But I've learned a great deal. For instance, Nena Bismaquer may be the only friend we have here. Also, we can take our time over the Conference Centre. There's a way in, directly off the road. No problem. I think tonight's activities have to be confined to that laboratory and the building behind it. Did you enjoy Bismaquer's company?'

Cedar, momentarily silenced by Bond's news, appeared to be counting to herself. 'One hundred . . .' she finished. 'To be honest with you, Bond, I wouldn't trust any of them; and if it wasn't for that predatory Nena woman, I'd put Bismaquer down as a faggot.'

'Right first time,' Bond said.

'Lawks-a-mercy.' Cedar gave a satisfied smirk as they turned into Tara's main drive. 'I'se sick, Mizz Scarlet, I'se sick.'

James Bond sat, a large vodka martini in his hand, facing Markus Bismaquer on the veranda. Walter Luxor hovered in the background.

'Now come on, James.' Bismaquer had – for the moment – put his hearty personality aside. 'The prints are either for sale or they're not. I want a straight yes or no. We've fenced around, and now I'm ready to make you an offer.'

Bond took a sip of his drink, placed the glass on a side table, and lit another cigarette. 'All right, Markus. As you say, the fencing's over. I have very precise instructions. The prints *are* for sale . . .'

Bismaquer let out a sigh of relief.

'. . . They're for sale by auction, in New York, in one week's time.'

'I'm not going in for any auction . . .' Bismaquer began. He stopped as Bond held up a hand.

'They're for sale at public auction in New York, in one week's time, unless I'm offered a certain price before that. Further, my instructions are that there is a very firm reserve on the whole set; and I am not to disclose that reserve to any prospective buyer.'

'Well . . .' Bismaquer began again. 'I'll offer you . . .'

'Wait,' Bond cut in. 'I have to warn you further that the first bid for the prints, outside the auction, will be the only one taken. Which means, Markus, that if you come in below the secret reserve, you lose for all time. My principal will instruct the auctioneer to accept no bids from a person or persons connected with anyone who has already made a private bid. In other words, you have to be very careful.'

For the first time that day, Bond thought he could detect a trace of malevolence in Bismaquer's face.

James,' he began, finally, 'can I ask two questions?'

'You can ask. I shall answer at my discretion.'

'Okay. Okay.' Bismaquer appeared to be rattled. 'The first one's easy. Every man, in my experience, has a price. I presume you're corruptible?'

Bond shook his head. 'No, in this matter, nobody can bribe me. Mrs Penbrunner's on the premises. In any case, I'm under a legal obligation. What's the second question?'

'Is the reserve based on a true value?'

'There is no true value. The prints are unique. But, to give you hope, the reserve is based on a price calculated to be the mean between a minimum and maximum that would be achieved at an open auction. I don't understand computers myself, but that's how they arrived at the figure.'

The cicadas had opened up their chirping music all around. Dusk was starting to close in and, far away, the moon began to show, big and yellow, against a clear darkening sky. In the silence, Bond heard Bismaquer cough.

'Okay, James, I'll take a shot at it. One million dollars.'

Bond had in fact been playing it by ear, with no figure in mind. Now he smiled inwardly as he spoke: 'Right on target, Markus. They're yours. What do you propose? Do I call the Professor? Do we shake on it, or what?'

'Oh, you've sure given me a hard time, James, my friend, I think we have to take it a step further. Tell me, could you scrape together a million bucks? I mean now, this minute?'

'Who, me personally?'

'It's you I'm asking.'

'Not now this minute. But in a day or so, yes. Yes, I could.'

'Are you a gambling man?'

'It has been known to happen.' Bond thought of the many chemmy tables, poker games, casinos, and private clubs in which he had played.

'Okay. I'm going to give you the biggest chance you've ever had. Tomorrow you're going out there to race against Walter. A late 1960s car against your fast turbo. I've offered one million dollars for those prints. If you beat Walter on the track, I'll gladly pay the million and add another million for your pains.'

'That's very generous . . .'

But Bond stopped as Bismaquer held up his hand.

'Whoa there, boy. I haven't finished. I've offered a million. If Walter beats you out there, you get nothing for your pains; I get the prints, and you do my paying for me.'

It was a subtle scheme – a gamble based on the knowledge Markus Bismaquer had of Luxor, the Shelby-American GT, and the track, but a gamble none the less. Except, Bond knew, if Bismaquer was the new Blofeld – or even if Luxor were – nobody was going to get anything for the prints. Bismaquer was playing with him, counting on Bond going for the bait and, in all probability, killing himself out on the hot circuit with its dangerous bends.

Whereas, if he refused . . . ?

Giving Bismaquer his most charming smile, Bond reached out in the gathering darkness to grasp the big man's hand.

'Done,' said James Bond, knowing the word might well be his own death warrant.

13

TOUR DE FORCE

'What the hell can we do now?' Cedar said, cheerfully waving farewell to the Bismaquers and Walter Luxor from the Saab.

'Sit still, fasten your seat belt, and prepare for some turbulence.' Bond hardly moved his lips. Loudly he shouted to Bismaquer, who stood at the portico, 'See you in the morning. At the circuit. Ten o'clock sharp.'

Bismaquer nodded and waved them on. The pick-up, in front, slowly started to guide them down the drive.

After coffee and brandy, Bismaquer and Luxor had made their apologies. 'When you own a spread like this,' Markus Bismaquer had said, 'there is paperwork which just has to get done, and tonight's the night. Anyhow, you two must be ready for bed. Get a good night's sleep, James. You've got the race tomorrow.'

Bond had agreed, saying they could easily get back to the cabins without a guide. But the pick-up was there, ready and waiting, and nothing by way of persuasion would change Bismaquer's mind.

So guide they had, a fact which greatly reduced their chances of playing at being lost and carrying out a full-scale reconnaissance of the ranch.

Bond brought the Saab close to the tail of the pick-up, crowding the driver, as they turned on to the main arterial highway which crossed the ranch. They could, of course, follow him, go back to the cabins and then take their chances on the open roads in the Saab, But there was little doubt in Bond's mind that the guide with the pick-up would stay for stake-out duty.

'He'll probably drop us off and then get lost somewhere in the trees, where he can keep an eye on us. After what we saw, or didn't see, this afternoon, my impression is that Bismaquer prefers human surveillance to electronics. He's got a lot of people working for him, even his own highway patrol.'

Cedar made a movement in the darkness. 'So we're boxed in?'

'Up to a point. Time's short, though. We need a look at that laboratory, and I wouldn't mind showing you exactly how to get into the Conference Centre. Correction – how *I* get into the Centre. Is your seat belt fastened tightly?'

She grunted a yes.

'Okay. What I've heard today clears my conscience.' Bond smiled to himself. 'I don't mind hurting a few people.'

They turned off the highway, heading towards the knoll – about four miles to go. Get him in the trees, thought Bond, reaching down to press another of the buttons on the dashboard which released the Nitefinder glasses he always carried.

The glasses consisted of an oblong control box, one end padded, and shaped to the head.

The brightness and focus control were on the right side, while from the front there protruded two lenses, like a pair of small binoculars. Using one hand, he strapped the system to his head, switching on as he did so.

Bond had done many hours' training driving in pitch darkness, using only the Nitefinders, which he had also worn once operationally. They gave an almost clear picture in darkness, enough for the driver to see clearly up to a hundred yards.

The adjustments made, Bond brought the Saab very close to the pick-up's tail. They were now about a mile from the knoll. Flatly he told Cedar what he was going to do.

'It's going to get very dark in a minute. Then there'll be some action; then a lot of light. With luck, he'll go off the road without doing too much damage to the truck. We need that for ourselves.'

They had almost reached the trees now. 'Okay. Hold on.' Bond flicked the Saab's lights off – with the switch peculiar to his car – and saw, through the Nitefinders, the pick-up wobble slightly on the road. For a second, the driver might well see the Saab's shape, but he would be puzzled, and the darkness behind him might throw him off balance.

Bond did not stay behind for long. Pulling out, he smoothly depressed the accelerator. The rev counter needle rose fast, crossing the 3,000 limit and bringing the turbo charger into play.

The Saab shot forward, turbo building into the satisfying whine, as they overtook the pick-up. Bond crowded the driver so that, in the darkness, he was forced to pull over. He must have seen the shape pass him, then caught the Saab full in his head-lights before it disappeared into the black zone, leaving no tail lights in its wake.

'He'll be putting on speed now, trying to catch us,' Bond said. 'Hold tight.' Without slowing noticeably, he stood on the brakes, changing down and wrenching at the wheel. The Saab went into a neatly controlled skid, and Bond, changing down for a second time, turned the car right around so that it now faced back along the road.

'Should be on us any minute.' He sounded cool, like an experienced fighter pilot leading a section into attack. One hand dropped to the small button, set just behind the gear lever. The pick-up's lights were coming now, closing fast. In a second the Saab would be clearly visible to the driver.

Still in the zone of darkness, Bond pressed the button. Another of his personalised pieces of equipment came into play. The Saab's front number plate flipped up, and, at the same time, an aircraft light, fitted behind the number plate and below the bumper, blazed out – a great cone of white, dazzling light.

The pick-up was caught full in the beam, and Bond could

imagine the driver wrestling with the wheel, throwing up one hand to cover his eyes, feet fighting the brake and clutch.

The truck slewed to one side, bounced against a tree, then, out of control, turned sideways on. The driver was free of the light's blinding glare, but too late. The pick-up slid across the road, swinging violently as the skidding wheels pushed the vehicle into a spin. The rear wheels hit the track side, and, with a sudden wrench, the small pick-up seemed to hurl itself against the trees before coming to a grinding stop.

'Hell,' Bond shouted, ripping the Nitefinder set from his head. 'Stay where you are,' he yelled at Cedar, as he grabbed his flashlight, slid the VP70 automatic from its holster, and jumping from the Saab, raced to the van.

The pick-up lay at an angle against the trees, one side severely dented. There was no sign of broken glass. The driver was another matter, lying back in the small cab, his head lolling in a manner Bond knew only too well. The force of impact had whiplashed the man's head, breaking his neck.

Dragging the door open, Bond felt for the driver's pulse. He must have died instantaneously, without knowing what had happened. For a brief moment, James Bond felt a twinge of regret. He had not wished to kill the man: a few cuts and bruises would have easily sufficed.

The dead driver was in Bismaquer Security livery, and as Bond heaved the body from the truck, his mental reservations were tempered by the fact that a large Smith & Wesson .44 Magnum – the Model 29, Bond thought – hung, holstered, on his hip. In all probability he had been right: the security man was a watchdog as well as a guide.

Bond pushed the body off the track, into the grass among the trees, tracing the area with his flashlight to make sure he could find it again. Once the corpse was well-hidden, he removed the Smith & Wesson, returned to the pick-up, and tried the engine. It started immediately and, with a little scraping as he backed away from the trees, seemed to be in reasonable running order.

The tank was three-quarters full, and the other gauges showed normal. Bond drove the pick-up alongside the Saab, keeping his eyes averted from the explosion of bright light, which burned like a magnesium burst from the front of the silver Turbo.

'Think you can manage the pick-up?' he asked Cedar, who was out of the Saab almost before Bond switched off.

She did not even bother to reply, but simply climbed in, ready to take over. Bond said he would follow her up the hill and instructed her to stop at the cabins.

Once back in the Saab, he lowered the number plate, extinguishing the aircraft light, switched on the headlights, and started the engine. Cedar began to move the pick-up slowly up the track. With a swift, neatly executed three-point turn, the Saab followed in her wake, and, without further incident, they arrived back at the cabins.

There Bond explained exactly what he intended to do and what routes they would take. The Saab was to be left in its usual place, locked and with the alarm sensors set. The reconnaissance would be carried out in the pick-up.

'People are less likely to stop us with Bismaquer's livery blazed all over it.' Bond patted the dented pick-up.

They planned to move quickly down towards the Conference Centre area so that Cedar could learn to operate the tunnel mechanism, then drive around the mono-rail station, and, lastly, back to the laboratory area.

'We should leave the pick-up out of sight somewhere near by and go in on foot,' Bond warned her. 'Then, when we get back here, I think our poor friend down the road'll have to be involved in another accident – going downhill.'

He set the sensors on the Saab alarm system, locked the car, and was just about to get behind the wheel of the pick-up – the guard's Smith & Wesson in his hand – when another thought struck him.

'Cedar, to make absolutely certain, it may be a good idea if we dummy up our beds a bit. Who knows what Bismaquer, or Luxor, have in mind for us? You know how to?'

Cedar acidly replied that she had been dummying up beds since she was a teenager, turned on her heel, and strode off to Sand Creek. Bond lit a cigarette, and sauntered, unhurried into Fetterman. It took very little time to stuff pillows into shape under the thin sheets. In the darkness, the lump in the bed could certainly be that of a sleeping figure.

Cedar was already standing by the pick-up, waiting, when Bond returned. He carried his Heckler & Koch VP70 on the back of his hip and placed the security man's Smith & Wesson on the floor of the pick-up. Cedar still had the spare revolver, and Bond had not forgotten to equip himself with Q Branch's ring of pick-locks and tools, as well as the flashlight from the Saab.

They coasted down the hill, sidelights on, and engine just turning over – an eerie sensation. They could hear only the faint sound of the wheels against the track, the rustle of the air-stream around them, and the light breeze through the silent archway of fir trees.

Bond slowly let out the clutch as they reached the subsidiary road. By now the moon had fully risen. They could easily have driven by its light, but that would only have caused suspicion, so Bond put the headlights on, turning right on to the highway for the fifteen miles or so which took them to the edge of the main wall and the jungle surrounding the Conference Centre.

It required only a few minutes to locate, and demonstrate, the hydraulically-operated entrance to the tunnel, and they were soon back on the road, staying near to the outer perimeter of the ranch on what would, in the normal world, be secondary roads.

'I'm intrigued by the conference,' Bond said, driving with more than usual care. 'When the delegates begin to arrive, I want to take a quick look-see for myself. If SPECTRE has any large-scale operation planned, this would be an ideal place for the briefing.'

'They start arriving tomorrow night,' Cedar told him, unable to disguise a certain amount of amusement.

'Oh?'

'Your friend Nena told me. In the powder room, as she so politely calls it, before dinner. The first batch arrive by air to-morrow evening – I mean *this* evening' – it having already passed midnight.

'Well, if we're all still in one piece, I think I'll sit in on one of their discussions.'

The mono-rail station was deserted, though the train, with the vehicle ramp in place, appeared to be permanently at the ready. No guards or Bismaquer patrol cars were in evidence. Bond turned the pick-up onto the road, and took them well past the fencing surrounding the lawns of Tara. Lights still blazed from the big house. Having covered the couple of miles to the trees which screened the long building behind the labor-atory, Bond and Cedar could see that people were at work inside. The rear section appeared to be deserted, but the small building was lit up like a Christmas tree.

They left the pick-up among the trees, some forty feet from the larger building, which, on closer examination, seemed to be a warehouse. The gable end was made up of high sliding doors. Windows, securely barred, ran along the side of the warehouse, but even at close quarters it was impossible to see inside in the darkness.

They moved forward, keeping low. Bond strained his eyes in the moonlit night, alert to the possibility of security guards, while, reassured, he noted that Cedar was watching the rear, the snub-nosed revolver in her hand.

There was a gap between the smaller laboratory building and the warehouse. Glancing between them Bond saw the two were connected, probably by a narrow passage. Then they arrived at the first windows of the laboratory. The light, very bright, cast a block beam on to the grass, reaching almost as far as the trees.

Straightening up, one on either side of the window, Cedar and Bond peered in.

Several women tended machinery, each of them dressed in white overalls, their hair completely swathed in turbans, hands in tight rubber gloves. On their feet they wore the kind of short boots, usually seen in hospital operating theatres. The women worked with quiet, practised expertise, hardly exchanging a word.

'An ice cream plant,' Cedar whispered. 'I got taken to one as a kid. See, the pasteuriser at the far end? That's where the mixings go: the milk, cream, sugar and flavouring.'

Using dumb show and essential words, Cedar pointed out the standard parts of factory-made ice cream. Bond frowned, a little surprised at her knowledge of how the mix was heated in the pasteuriser, to kill bacteria, before being filtered on to the homogenising vat. From there, he could clearly see the array of cold pipes for mushing and chilling the mix, and the vast stainless steel holding tank, which controlled the flow into the freezer. Then there were the units which blocked the ice cream, before an endless belt took the finished blocks into a metal-doored hardening room. From the window it looked exceptionally efficient.

Bond tipped his head, motioning Cedar forward. Crouching near the wall, he whispered, 'You seem to know it all. How professional is that system?'

'Very. They're even using real cream and milk, by the look of it. No chemicals.'

'All this from a school trip to a factory?'

Cedar grinned. 'I like ice cream,' she hissed. 'It's interesting. But that's a professional set-up in there. Small, but professional.'

'Could they turn out enough to market the stuff?'

She nodded, adding, 'In a small way, yes. But it's probably for local consumption.'

Bond caught hold of Cedar's hand, tugging her in the direction of the next section. The windows were smaller, and this time they found themselves looking into a large laboratory. Glass tubing, vats and intricate electronics were laid out on almost a grand scale.

The laboratory was empty, except for a Bismaquer Security guard standing in front of a door on the far side.

'Hell.' Bond put his lips near to Cedar's ear. 'If anything's happening, it's through there. We'll have to cut back and go around to the other side.'

'Let's have the pick-locks.' Cedar touched his hand. 'I'll see if I can look into that warehouse, while you try the windows around the corner.'

They retraced their steps, back along the wall, Bond handing over the pick-lock kit as they reached the sliding doors at the gable end. He left Cedar to wrestle with them while he crept forward, trying to gauge the exact position of the windows to the room off the main laboratory. After two errors, he discovered the right one. Peering in, from the left-hand corner, he saw Bismaquer and Walter Luxor pacing a small, bare, cell-like chamber. On closer inspection, he could clearly see that the room was in fact a cell – a padded cell. There were two soft chairs anchored to the centre of the floor, both occupied by Bismaquer employees in uniforms. An animated conversation was taking place, between these two seated men, Bismaquer and Luxor.

Bond, still crouching low, put his ear hard against the window and could just make out what was being said. Bismaquer had ceased to punctuate his conversation with the jolly laughter. Now, he seemed very serious indeed, his large body less relaxed, his gestures economic.

'So, Tommy,' he was saying to one of the seated men, 'so you'll give me the keys to your house, let me drive over and take your wife by force, right?'

The man called Tommy chuckled. 'Anything you say, chief. You just go right ahead.' His speech was distinct, unslurred, and he appeared to be absolutely in command of himself.

The other man joined in: 'Anything to make anybody happy.

Take my keys too. No problem. Take the car. I just like seeing people enjoy themselves. Me? I do what I'm told.' This one also gave a perfectly natural impression of someone meaning what he said, under no stress or influence.

'Do you want to continue working here?' It was Luxor asking.

'Why not?' came the reply from the second man.

'I'd sure hate to leave. It's great here,' the one called Tommy added.

'Listen to me, Tommy.' Bismaquer had walked across the room and stood near the window. But for the protective screening and glass, Bond could have touched him. 'Would you worry a lot if, after I've raped your wife, I killed her too?'

'Be my guest, Mr Bismaquer. Anything you want. Here, I'll give you the keys. I told you.'

Luxor had joined his chief. Even though he spoke quietly, Bond heard every word. 'Ten hours, Markus. Ten hours, and they're still both affected.'

'Amazing. Better than we ever expected.' Bismaquer raised his voice: 'Tommy, you love your wife. I attended your wedding. You're a nice couple. Why would you allow me to do such a terrible thing?'

'Because you out-rank me, Mr Bismaquer. You give the orders, I obey. That's the way it works.'

'Would you question Mr Bismaquer's orders?' Luxor asked, the squeaky voice rising.

'Why should I? Like I just said, that's the way it works. Like in the army. You take orders from the senior man, and you obey them.'

'Without question?' Luxor pushed.

'Sure.'

'Sure.' The other man nodded. 'That's how it works.'

By the window, Bismaquer muttered something Bond couldn't make out and shook his head, as though in disbelief.

Luxor turned, and, for a second, Bond thought the walking death's head would see him through the glass.

'Uncanny maybe, Markus. But a real breakthrough. We've done it, my friend. Think of the results.'

Bismaquer frowned, and Bond caught his tone. The voice was cold, bleak as a blizzard. 'I *am* thinking of the results . . .' The rest was lost to Bond, who ducked down, having heard enough, and started to go back, padding softly along the wall. Then he stopped, stock still, and pressed hard against the wall. Someone was moving in his direction and, out of reflex habit, Bond found the large VP70 in his hand.

Seconds later he relaxed. The figure, coming with exceptional speed, was Cedar.

'Let's go. Fast.' She was almost out of breath. 'I nearly got spotted by a security guard. That warehouse – they've enough ice cream in freezing units to supply the whole state of Texas for a month.'

By the time they got back to the pick-up, Bond's mind was working overtime. He started the engine, then waited for a few moments before he let out the clutch and pulled away slowly. The roads were empty. 'So they're stockpiling ice cream,' he said as they reached the turn-off from the highway.

'I'll say.' Cedar had recovered her breath. 'The warehouse is divided up into huge refrigerators. I'd looked into three of them. Then this guard came in. Thank God I hadn't gotten one of the doors open – they're heavy as sin – and I'd mostly closed the main doors, leaving just enough space for a quick getaway.'

Bond asked if she was absolutely sure she had not been seen.

'Absolutely. He'd have been after me like a bullet. I just stayed flat against one of these damned great cold stores. He came part way into the warehouse, then went back . . . back towards the laboratory section.'

'Good. You want to hear the bad news now?' As they reached the knoll, beginning to climb the sloping track to the cabins, Bond finished telling her what he had seen, and heard, at the window of the padded cell.

'So, they've got a couple of very normal-seeming guys in there, willing to obey even the most unlikely orders – like getting their wives raped and murdered?' Cedar shivered.

It was not strange, Bond thought, for her to sound incredulous. 'That's about it. *Very* normal guys. There was no way of telling, from what I could see, but Bismaquer and Luxor must've been feeding them something. They said the effect had lasted for ten hours, and, when you take the padded cell into account, there's little doubt those two men are human guinea pigs.'

'Hopped up to the eyeballs.'

'Yes. The worrying thing is that they didn't look, or sound it. They were taking orders, and complying, that's all. But orders that went against all reason or conscience. Why, Cedar? Making people into unknowing hitmen, or something like that? Why?'

'How?' she volleyed back. 'Why're you stopping?'

Bond said she was to stay in the cab. 'We have to take the driver up the hill, I'm afraid. I'll put him in the back. No need for you to do any of this.'

Cedar said it was most gallant of him, but corpses did not worry her. Nevertheless, she stayed in the pick-up while Bond dragged the dead driver to the truck and dumped the body in the back, then returned to cover up any marks among the trees.

'If they've developed a drug that shows no outward effects . . .' Cedar began when Bond returned.

'Yes.' He continued to drive up the hill. 'Yes.' It was already making a little sense. 'No side effects. No staggering, or slurring. People functioning normally . . .'

'Except in one sense.' Cedar took up a mutual train of thought. 'They'll obey orders which, in usual circumstances, would either be questioned, or acted against . . .'

'It's a weapon in a thousand,' Bond said. Then, as they reached the cabins, he asked, 'The ice cream? You think that could be the delivery system?'

'They've got enough of the lousy stuff.'

'I thought you liked ice cream.'

'I'm going off it very quickly.'

They climbed out, and this time Cedar helped with the grisly job of putting the dead driver in the cab behind the wheel. Bond checked that they had left nothing of their own in the pick-up, then returned the revolver to the driver's holster. Cedar even insisted on squeezing in, next to Bond, as he started the engine and, leaning over the body, drove the pick-up slowly back down the hill.

When they reached the top of the steepest slope, he stopped, applied the handbrake, and helped Cedar out. The engine was running smoothly and the wheels turned slightly off-centre. With a nod to Cedar, indicating that she should get out of the way, Bond leaned through the driver's side window and released the handbrake.

He was carried for a few yards before jumping clear. Then, picking himself up, Bond watched the truck gathering speed, slewing from one side of the road to the other.

Fascinated by the outcome, he hardly noticed Cedar alongside him, linking an arm through his.

The pick-up's lights showed its progress, wild and careering, as it hurtled down the slope. Then they heard the first crunch as the truck hit the trees. Its lights seemed to dance their beams into the air, then down, in a rolling, Catherine-wheel effect – their movement accompanied by an attendant clattering and grating as the vehicle began to fall apart.

It took about twenty seconds. Then the whoosh, followed by a crump as the truck finally piled up, its tank catching fire in the impact.

'The trees look like they're alive,' murmured Cedar.

'Ancient peoples held them to be very much alive and sacred,' Bond said. He also felt there was something old and terrifying about the strange shadows and odd movement created by the fire. 'Modern people too – some of them. Trees are living things. I know what you mean.'

'We'd better go.' Cedar slipped her arm free and turned abruptly on her heel, as though not able to watch the wreck any longer. 'The whole place'll see that fire. We'll have visitors before you know it.'

Bond caught up with her, striding towards the clearing and the cabins.

'We've got a lot to think about,' she said, as they reached the door of Sand Creek.

'A great deal, Cedar. Makes me wonder if we shouldn't turn and run for it now, give the authorities what we have and see if they'll come in force.'

As he said it, Bond knew this was not the way.

'It wouldn't worry me if we got out here and now.' Cedar gave him a kiss on the cheek, then tried to move in closer, but Bond gently held her off. She gave a long sigh. 'I know. I know, James. Just like I know you won't really leave this place until we have concrete evidence, with all the ends tied up.'

Bond said that was really the way of it. 'Okay.' Cedar shrugged. 'As long as you have the Dragon Lady tied into it as well. That would make me really happy. Goodnight, James. Sleep well.'

Bond started to walk past the Saab, back towards Fetterman. His hand was on the door knob when Cedar began screaming from the other cabin.

14

REPELLENT INSECTS

The VP70 automatic was in Bond's hand as he reached the door of Cedar's cabin, seconds after the first scream.

His right leg came up in a vicious kick, smashing the handle and almost ripping the door back from its hinges. Bond jumped into the doorway, then to one side, the VP70 in the double-hand grip and the word 'Freeze' already on his lips.

But there was only Cedar, standing in the bedroom doorway, shrinking back in revulsion, her body shaking with fear.

Bond crossed the living room. He grasped her shoulder, ready to fire at anything – animal, reptile, or man – inside the bedroom.

Then, he also took an involuntary step back. The room was alive with them – large, dark, creeping, and malevolent ants. They covered the floor, walls, ceiling. The bed itself had turned black, a constantly moving sea of the creatures.

There were hundreds of them, the smallest a good inch in length, squirming together, fighting to get to the bed where the dummy was now a dark seething lump.

Bond slammed the door, behind them, then looked to see how much space remained between it and the floor.

'Harvesters, I think, Cedar. Harvester ants. Out of their environment and looking for food.'

If they were Harvesters, Bond thought, they had not come in by accident. Harvesters live in arid areas and store seeds for food.

They could never have drifted in from the desert – at least not in such large numbers.

The other fact he hesitated to mention was that one sting from a Harvester ant could be painful, it could even in the right circumstances be lethal. But hundreds – maybe a few thousand – of the large insects, out of their natural environment, excited, possibly searching for food, was another matter. Several stings from enraged Harvester ants would be deadly.

'There's only one way to deal with them.' Bond bundled Cedar out of the cabin, swiftly looking behind him to make certain none of the ants had advanced into the living room. He closed the door behind him.

Bond hurried the girl across to his own cabin, one arm around her. Once inside he told her to stay in the main room – 'And keep down. Right?' – while he dashed to the bedroom for the briefcase.

Flicking the tumbler locks, Bond opened up the case, then slid and lifted the false bottom to reach what he needed: a small detonator and a couple of inches of fast-burning fuse. Quickly he inserted the fuse into the little metal core of the detonator, and, breaking all the rules, crimped the detonator to the fuse with his teeth. His old instructors would have winced. 'You can lose your teeth and kissing equipment that way, Mr Bond,' they used to tell him.

Reaching deeper into the briefcase, Bond retrieved one of the bags which contained plastic explosive. He tore off a small section and rolled the plasticine-like material until he had something roughly the size and shape of a golf ball.

Keeping fuse and detonator well away from the plastic, Bond ran out of the room again. With a further caution to Cedar to stay where she was, he raced full-tilt out of the cabin towards the Saab. Working with speed, he unlocked the alarm sensors, then the boot, which he searched rapidly.

He found the spare container immediately. For years now, Bond had rarely travelled without at least a couple of spare gallons of petrol in a plastic container, held in place in the large boot by restraining webbing.

At the door of Sand Creek, Bond unscrewed the container's cap, and moulded the plastic ball around the lip. Still keeping detonator and fuse well clear, he paused at the bedroom before pushing the detonator hard into the plastic. The only problem now was to light the fuse without igniting the petrol fumes.

Gently, Bond opened the bedroom door, his flesh creeping at the sight of an entire room moving, in obscene waves, with the fat crawling insects. Placing the container just inside the door, he took out his Dunhill lighter. He held it low, well clear of the vaporising petrol, and thumbed the wheel. The flame appeared. Quickly Bond applied it to the fuse, which spluttered immediately.

Closing the door softly to prevent the home-made bomb from being knocked over, Bond walked slowly out of the cabin. Walk, never run, they taught you: running increased the possibility of falling near a planted charge.

He had just reached the door of Fetterman when the crude device blew with a hollow roar. The explosive shot the petrol up in a fireball, straight through the cabin roof, a hand of brilliant flame clawing at the air, then fanning out inside so that the interior of Sand Creek became an inferno within seconds.

The door of Fetterman was wrenched open. For a moment, Bond thought it was blast effect, as the knob was pulled from his hand. But he saw Cedar standing there, rooted to the spot. Bond pushed her inside, sent her sprawling, and landed on top of her. Outside, flaming and smoking débris arched and showered across the clearing.

'Just keep down, like I told you, Cedar.' Bond realised he was pinning the girl down, lying almost astride her.

'If you stay like this, James, I'd be glad to.' Even in the aftermath of shock – first the ants, and then the sudden blast from the bomb – Cedar managed to laugh.

Quickly Bond rolled away. 'Just keep down,' he ordered, then headed for the door again.

Bits of burning débris littered the area. With admirable thought for priorities, Bond quickly checked that no heavy pieces of wood, or burning material, had slammed into the Saab. Next, he turned to the cabin called Fetterman, circling it, making absolutely certain that no secondary fire had started there.

It was only then that two vital facts came into sharp focus. The first Bond had already realised: such a large colony of Harvester ants could not possibly have got into the cabin by accident. But the second was even more revealing: the ants were, of course, meant to sting and kill, and the target was Bond himself. Had he not told Bismaquer that he was staying in Sand Creek, and precisely to protect Cedar, whom he had considered the more vulnerable?

Already he could hear the sound of motors: vehicles were approaching below them. When help – if you could call it that – arrived, one of two things would happen: Bismaquer and his henchmen, finding both Bond and Cedar unharmed, would either try to dispense some fast, rough justice, or they would take advantage of the situation and split them up, moving either Bond or Cedar from the cabins to Tara. Whatever happened, it was unlikely they would be given the opportunity to be alone together during the next day or so. Some quick planning had to be done and now, before anyone came near.

Swiftly, Bond made his way to the cabin, where Cedar sat with a stiff drink in her hand. 'My clothes,' she said woefully, before Bond had a chance to speak. 'Everything we bought. Up in smoke. James, I haven't even got a pair of panties left.'

Bond could not resist the obvious: 'Don't worry, my dear, I'm sure Nena Bismaquer will fit you out.'

Cedar started to retort, but Bond silenced her with a quick word. If they were separated, he said, there would have to be some means of communication. Handing over the one spare key to the Saab, he told her where the car would be hidden if he suddenly went to ground. She would have to devise some means of getting away from wherever she was lodged.

'If you're right, and the delegates for this conference start arriving tonight, I shall try to get into the Conference Centre in the early hours of tomorrow morning.' Bond hesitated, suddenly recalling the assignation he had made with Nena Bismaquer for what was now tonight. 'Midnight,' he said, 'midnight *tomorrow*. If I'm not there, make it the following night. If the car's gone, you'll know I had to leave you in the lurch; but Cedar, that'll be a last resort, and I'll be back – probably with a horde of FBI, CIA and State Troopers. So just stay put.'

Bond was still making Cedar repeat details of the car's hiding place, and their meeting arrangements when two pick-up trucks and a car hurtled into the clearing.

'Hey . . . Hey there! James, Cedar . . . are you okay.' Bismaquer's voice boomed from outside, to an undercurrent of shouts and orders.

Bond went to the door. 'We're taking cover in here. This is no way to treat your guests, Bismaquer.'

'What?'

Bismaquer appeared in all his bulk, a few feet from the door. Behind him, Bond caught sight of Nena's face and thought he detected a look of relief when she saw he was safe.

'What in hell happened here?'

Bismaquer waved towards the smouldering skeleton that had once been Sand Creek cabin. People milled around the ruins, and Bond noticed that Bismaquer's men had come prepared, for one of the pick-ups was fitted with a large tank of pressurised foam. Already a group in Bismaquer's livery had started to smother the embers.

'There were . . .' Cedar began.

'There were a few bugs around,' said Bond, casually leaning against the door jamb, 'so I came out to the car, in which I always carry a small first aid kit. I wanted some insect repellent.

Cedar heard me and thought I was an intruder.' He laughed. 'Funny really. I must explain – when we told you earlier that I was in Sand Creek and Cedar in Fetterman, we'd got them muddled. In fact, it was the other way round. But when we got back tonight, Cedar decided she preferred Fetterman after all. She didn't like the picture in Sand Creek. We were tired and, apparently, both sleep in the raw, so we didn't bother to move our things. Thought we'd change over properly in the morning. All Cedar's stuff was in there.' He nodded towards the ruins. 'My stuff's intact, but Cedar's only got the clothes she's standing . . .'

'The prints?' Bismaquer interrupted. 'Are they okay? You didn't have . . . ?'

'The prints are fine, I promise you.'

'Thank the good Lord for that.'

'Markus,' Bond snapped sharply. 'You sound like an alcoholic in a shipwreck— "Is the brandy safe?" instead of "How many have we saved?" '

'Yes.' Nena moved close to the group by the door. 'You really are callous, Markus. James could've been killed.'

'Very nearly was. What do you use for cooking in these cabins? Bottled gas?'

'As a matter of fact . . .' Bismaquer began.

'Well, some idiot must have left a faulty cylinder. I lit a cigarette; left it on an ashtray in the bedroom. I only got as far as the car, then, whomp, up it went.'

'Oh, James, I wouldn't have had this happen . . . It's terrible!' Nena was looking at him in a way that brought back the smell of her hair and the shared kiss among the dense trees. Bond found it genuinely difficult to tear his eyes away. Then he realised that another car was coming up the slope.

Bond took a step towards Bismaquer. 'While we're at it, Markus,' he assumed an aggressive tone, 'what about those damned bugs?'

'The bugs?' Bismaquer looked around him, as though about to be attacked by a plague of hornets.

'Yes, the bugs. Big, black nasty creatures – like huge ants.'

'Oh my God.' Bismaquer took a pace back. 'Not Harvesters?'

'I think so.' Bond started to pour on the anger. 'Do you get a lot of those around here, Markus? If so, why didn't you warn us? Can't Harvesters . . . ?'

'They can kill you, yes.' For a second, as he said it, Bismaquer seemed to have shed any fear.

'Well? Do you often get them?'

Bismaquer did not meet Bond's eyes. 'Sometimes. Not many though.'

'There were hundreds. We could've both been stung to death. I think you're taking it a shade casually, Markus.'

Whatever Bismaquer might have replied was cut off by the brisk arrival of the other car. Luxor was at the wheel, with two security men in attendance. They had hardly stopped – in a braking cloud of dust – when Luxor shouted for Bismaquer.

Bismaquer went over a shade too fast for Bond's peace of mind. Was Luxor in command, he wondered? The two were in close conversation, the gash in Luxor's skull head moving in rapid monologue.

'Will you be okay here, tonight, James?' Nena had come into the cabin.

'We can both stay here,' Cedar chimed in. 'We'll toss for the sofa.'

'I wouldn't hear of it, my dear.' Nena smiled sweetly. 'You'll have the guest room at Tara. And we'll do something about clothes for you first thing. If I get your sizes, one of my more intelligent girls can make a trip into town. I'd lend you some of mine, but I fear they'd be too long, and maybe a little tight for you.'

'You're so kind,' mouthed Cedar so that they could hardly hear her.

Nena turned, as Bismaquer approached them. 'Cedar's coming back to the house for the night, Markus.'

'Good.' He spoke almost as an aside. 'James, something else

has happened. Unpleasant as hell. The guy who brought you up here, the one you followed – the one in the pick-up . . .'

'Yes?'

'What happened when he left you?'

Bond shrugged, frowning. 'What do you mean? He waved us goodnight and off he went.'

'Did you hear anything after?'

Bond thought for a minute. 'No. We went into my cabin, put on some music, and had a drink. That was when we decided to change cabins. Cedar said she liked this one better than Sand Creek. I think it was the picture that did it. I know what she means – a lot of white men riding around killing off boys, women, and children. But why the questions, Markus?'

Bismaquer scowled. 'Your guide was a hell of a good man . . .'

'Fisher?' asked Nena, with a trace of anxiety.

Bismaquer nodded. 'Yep. One of the best we had.'

'What happened?' Nena Bismaquer was now definitely alarmed and could not hide it.

Markus took a deep breath. 'It seems he blew it tonight. Trouble with Fisher was that he – well, he liked the juice from time to time.'

'Partial to a few glasses when the mood took him. I know the syndrome.' Bond sounded unconcerned.

'I may as well tell you. Fisher's job was to – how do I put it? – well, to look after you. His instructions were to stay in the trees, make sure there were no problems; like animals. There are a few around.'

'Like Harvester ants?' Bond asked.

'Animals,' Bismaquer repeated.

'And he went for a drink instead?' Cedar prompted.

Bismaquer shook his head. 'Not the first drink, anyway. He'd probably already had a few. Maybe he was going for more.'

'Was?' from Nena.

'The pick-up went off the road. It's burned out in the trees at the bottom of the hill. We were in such a hurry getting up here, we didn't spot it. Walter did.'

'And Fisher?' Nena's mouth was half open.

'Sorry, honey. I know you liked him around the place. Fisher got burned.'

'Oh my God. You mean . . . ?'

'As a doornail. Most unpleasant.' Bismaquer looked from Bond to Cedar, and back again. 'You sure you heard nothing?'

'Not a thing.'

'Nothing at all.'

'Poor Fisher.' Nena turned away, her face creased. 'His wife . . .'

'It would be best if you broke it to her, my dear,' Bismaquer said peremptorily, turning away.

'Of course, Markus. First, we'll settle Cedar at Tara.' Nena moved towards her husband. 'Then,' a small sigh, 'then I'll go and break the news to Lottie Fisher.'

'Good. Yes.' Bismaquer's mind was clearly elsewhere. 'You'll be okay, then, James?'

Bond said he would be fine, then, smiling asked if the Grand Prix was still on. 'I mean after all this?'

In the light from the cabin and the headlights, he might have imagined a cloud crossing Markus Bismaquer's face, before the bear of a man spoke. 'Oh yes, James. This has been unfortunate, sure, but the Grand Prix's definitely on. Ten in the morning. Walter's looking forward to it I am sure.'

'I'll see you there, then. At the track. 'Night, Cedar. Sleep well, and don't worry about any of this.'

'Oh, *this* is the last thing I'll worry about.' Cedar flashed him a false smile. 'Good night, James.'

'And *I'll* see you tomorrow as well, James.' Nena looked him full in the face. This time it was no trick of light among the trees: the fire lay buried deep in the dark pools of her eyes, and the smile promised wonders for the following night.

When they had all left the clearing, Bond checked that the

Saab was secure, then went back into the cabin. He blocked the door with a chair and scoured the window crevices for possible entrance points. A second dose of Harvester ants, while he slept, would be a little hard to bear.

It took a further ten minutes to repack the briefcase, after which he stretched out on the bed, fully clothed, with the Heckler & Koch automatic within easy reach.

Nena had spoken of evil. Bond could feel it now, as though Rancho Bismaquer was alive with malevolence. Earlier, he had caught a trace of SPECTRE in this place: now the scent was very strong. He had tangled with them before and his instincts were finely-tuned to them, and their first leader, Ernst Stavro Blofeld. Even now, alone in this cabin on a wooded knoll, set, para-doxically, in the middle of desert, the distinct smell of Blofeld came wafting back from the hell to which Bond had sent him, during that final encounter in Japan.

One of these men was somehow connected with his old enemy. Which one? Luxor or Bismaquer? He could not tell, but he knew he would discover the truth soon enough.

He thought of the delegation, arriving in just over twelve hours, of the sinister play he had watched being enacted in the padded cell off the laboratory, next to the ice cream plant. A kind of hypnotic drug, he presumed – a 'happy pill' that removed all moral scruples, leaving the victim outwardly nor-mal but pliable beyond belief.

He looked at his watch. It was almost five in the morning and would soon be getting light. Within twenty-four hours he had to go to ground – literally: into the tunnel to the Conference Centre. In the darkness, Bond smiled, thinking of the irony if it turned out to be just another mundane and boring business conference, all above board. Yet his training and experience with SPECTRE told him this would not be so.

15

GRAND PRIX

The sun climbed into a diamond-clear sky, and you could already feel the dormant heat of the day. Within an hour or so it would become scorching: a day for staying in the cool and sipping iced drinks, for lazing and passing the time with a good conversationalist – preferably female, Bond thought.

He had not slept for long. An hour had been spent going over the Saab. These people had tricks up their sleeves, but so did 007's Saab Turbo, though he could leave nothing to chance. The Saab had to be perfect. Then even allowing for a highly souped-up engine, Bond was confident that the Shelby-American, driven by Walter Luxor, would stand little real chance.

With the turbo-charger in full operation, a normal Saab 900 can reach a cruising speed of 125 mph with ease. Restrictions forbid commercial models to exceed this maximum, and the turbo-charger itself normally limits performance to within the 125 mph range. But increase the fuel-line pressure to wind up the boost, add in the special rally conversion kit, and you get really high performance.

Bond, in fact, knew of police forces in the world which used Saab Turbos with these very variations. 'What's the use of a turbo to us, if we can't catch a commercial turbo?' one senior police officer had said to him.

Bond had himself already clocked over 180 mph on an open track, after his car was fitted with the new water-injection system, and there was no reason why he should not do it today.

He did not fear the possibility of a blow-out or even of a well-placed bullet in a tyre, for his personalized car ran on Michelin Autoporteur tyres, lookalikes of the TRX tyres, which are standard. The Autoporteurs are possessed of properties spoken about only in hushed tones within the motor industry.

No problems, Bond thought as, with air conditioning at full blast, he eased the Silver Beast along the side road which ran by the outside of the circuit. Markus Bismaquer was plainly visible, with Nena and Cedar, in front of the grandstand, which already seemed to be three-quarters full. Bismaquer's staff had obviously turned out – or been dragooned into being spectators for this special occasion.

Bond pulled the Saab into the slip road leading to the pits, coming to a standstill beside Bismaquer's group. There was no sign of Walter Luxor and the Shelby-American.

'James, you look quite the part.'

Nena Bismaquer's smile was so natural and all-embracing that Bond could not resist giving her a kiss on the cheek, something which he normally deplored. Then he realised that Cedar Leiter was giving him a hard look.

'Morning, Cedar,' he said cheerfully, kissing her on both cheeks. 'Twice for luck.'

For comfort, Bond wore a light blue and red track suit – bought with the other items in Springfield – and little else. Even with the air conditioning, he knew it would get hot out there behind the wheel, especially if Walter Luxor pressed him.

'James, I hope you slept the sleep of the just,' Bismaquer roared with his accustomed mirth, slapping Bond on the back just hard enough to make the skin tingle.

'Oh yes. Like the proverbial log.' Bond looked straight into Bismaquer's face. Gone was any sign of the previous night's strain.

'Do you want a few practice runs, James, before we start? It looks easy from here, but I can promise you that the chicane and the zig-zag on the far side are real bitches. I know, I built it.'

'Okay, I'll take her around a couple of times to get the feel.' Bond nodded towards the petrol pumps. 'Then can I fill up, deal with my oil, and all that?'

'We've got a whole crew for you, James.' Bismaquer pointed to five of his men, dressed in overalls. 'The real thing. You want to get your spare wheel out, in case you need a change? We've got everything at your disposal.'

'I'll manage. Ten laps, wasn't it?'

'Yes. And don't forget, the crew's there if you need help. We have track marshals standing by, in case anything big goes wrong.'

Did Bond detect something in Bismaquer's voice? A hint? Some sense of expecting something to go wrong? Well, they'd just have to wait and see. In the end it would be the best driver, and not the best car, that would be first across the finishing line.

Bond waved to the group, winked at Cedar and climbed back into the Saab. He pulled on his gloves and adjusted the Polaroid sun glasses.

Easing on to the grid, Bond took a final swift look at the instruments. Twice around for luck, he thought. A slowish first run – around seventy where possible – and a faster second, taking the Saab up to near a hundred, but not going higher. Keep the trumps up your sleeve. He smiled, slipping the gear lever into first, releasing the hand brake, and pulling away. He gathered speed, going through the gears, taking her to fourth as the speedometer hit fifty and giving the car a fraction more power to knock the revs over the 3,000 mark; then bringing in the turbo – a comforting whine – hitting seventy miles per hour right on the button.

On the first run, Bond did not go right through the gears into fifth. He kept the engine in check, getting the feel of the track at the relatively low speed.

From the grid to the chicane there was a good two and a half miles of straight track, but once you hit the chicane, both car and driver knew about it. From a distance the track looked as though it merely narrowed, then went through a graceful, though tight, elongated S shape. It was not until the Saab came out into the last curve of the S that Bond realised the chicane ended with a nasty, sudden, sharp lump, like a small humped-back bridge.

The bends proved to be no problem, even at sixty mph, calling for only a quick movement of the wheel – left, right, left, right. The Saab's curved spoiler, and its weight, held the machine to the track like glue. It was only when he hit the hump that Bond realised the danger.

At sixty, the car lifted off the ground for a second, as it crested during the final easy curve. For a moment, all four wheels were in the air, and it needed considerable concentration not to go off-line as the spinning tyres touched down, screeching against the metalled surface.

Bond exhaled, releasing all the breath from his lungs, realising the dangers the hump might create at real speed. He held the car out of the turn and into another mile of straight track, before the more obvious, vicious, right-angle bend.

He held her at seventy, leaving the change down until almost the last moment, going into the right-hander in third but keeping the power on to make certain there was no tendency to slide outwards. Again, the Saab did her stuff. Bond always likened cornering at speed, in this machine, to being held to the road by some invisible hand. When the pressure was really on, you could feel the rear pushed down by the speed of airflow caught in the curved spoiler.

He came out of the bend with the clock still smack on seventy miles per hour. There was half a mile of straight in which, when flat out, he could again build up speed. Resisting temptation, Bond kept her to the seventy, going up to fourth and hitting the nasty Z-bend with a change down to second, at which the speed dropped drastically to fifty.

The Z was, indeed, nasty. By rights, it crossed Bond's mind, he should have allowed himself more time to practise. You really had to haul the wheel around; and, even at this speed, it was not possible to get her up again into fourth, and a steady acceleration to the seventy mark, until the last sharp point in the Z was behind you. That would need watching.

The rest was easy: three miles or so of straight track, followed by a very gentle right-hander; another mile and a half, then the second right-hand bend, and so into the final mile, back to the grid.

The last bend, Bond quickly discovered, was a shade deceptive, the curve suddenly sharpening as you went in. But all in all, he could cope with that. On the first run, he changed down to third as the angle steepened, piling on the revs, going up again as soon as the track straightened to show a long ribbon in front of him, past the stands, and with the three flat miles to run before the chicane.

A mile from the stands, Bond slid into fifth gear and began to pile on some speed for the second run. He touched the hundred, as he saw the raked grandstand blur past: and held it until half a mile from the chicane.

He went into the gentle turns at ninety, slowing to seventy on the final curve and hitting the hump – for which he was now ready – with the needle still hovering just below the seventy mark. The Saab took off from the top of the hump, arrow straight, with Bond waiting for the thump as all four wheels hit the track. They landed as one, Bond easing the wheel to correct any slewing.

Gently, building up to the hundred, Bond moved to his right to give himself plenty of room on the turn. It would be make or break, he decided. Hit the nasty, hard right-angle at around eighty and stay there, leaning the car as far to the right as she would go, trusting the weight, tyres, and spoiler, to keep him under control.

The figures on his head-up display – and the needle – did not drop a fraction: dead on the eighty for the whole turn, though

Bond found himself leaning his body to the right, as if to compensate, and the wheels started to drift fractionally to the left.

He could do it. The right-angle could be negotiated – if positioned correctly to the right – at eighty miles per hour and, possibly, even a hundred.

This was not so easy on the Z bend. Here you had to change down; accelerator; brake; accelerator; and again, then out the other side and pile on the horses.

The Saab took the first of the final two bends at ninety, with no trouble, dropping, with a change down, at the steepening curve on the second.

He came into the last straight still at ninety, allowing the speed to drop away steadily until the stand and pits seemed to drift towards him. Forty; thirty; twenty . . . slowing to a stop.

Through the windscreen he saw Bismaquer's face, a small crease of concern between the eyes. Walter Luxor, who had now appeared, fully dressed in racing overalls, decorated with the Bismaquer insignia, took no notice. He busied himself with the silver Shelby-American, which was getting a final going over from his crew.

Bond stayed in his seat for a moment, watching the vehicle that had been matched against his own, trying to recall all he knew about the car.

The original competition Ford Mustang had been exceptionally successful in its day: first and second in the 1964 Tour de France touring car class, where its many variations showed fine performances. The GT 350, as Shelby-America's derivation of the Mustang was designated, had sleek body lines of the old fastback variety, the most obvious outward alterations being a large air scoop on top of the bonnet, and rear-wheel air scoops. The earlier versions usually had fibreglass construction around the bonnet and there were a multitude of possible combinations of engine and transmission, together with the necessary special-handling package to stop the alarming roll experienced on cornering with the stock Mustang suspension.

From what he could recall, Bond thought the car lighter than its parent Mustangs but capable of speeds well in excess of the 130 mark. The one he looked at now, through the Saab's windscreen, seemed at first sight to be an original. But, the closer he viewed the car, the more uncertain Bond became. The bodywork had a very solid look to it – an indefinable depth. Steel, he thought. Like a Shelby-American, but only in its lines. The tyres, he could see, were heavy-duty, and Bond would have bet now that he was much more than evenly matched. Certainly the design had to be a stress factor at very high speeds; but it would have been nice to look under that bonnet. Bismaquer, being the man he was, would be unlikely to match a standard, souped-up car like this against a Saab Turbo. Whatever engine they had hidden away, it would almost certainly be, like Bond's, turbocharged.

Sliding from the driving seat, Bond walked quickly towards the car, calling out within a couple of paces of the machine to attract Luxor's attention.

Bismaquer moved with unexpected agility in an attempt to cut Bond off from getting too close – a move which finally succeeded, but not before Bond managed to get a hand on the bonnet. It was stressed steel all right. The feel was there under his palm. From the one quick downward push Bond managed, the suspension also seemed very firm.

'Good luck, Walter . . .' Bond began, as Bismaquer cut him away from the Shelby-American. 'I only wanted to wish Walter good luck,' said Bond with a scowl, as though offended, feeling Bismaquer's large hand around his arm literally pulling him away.

'Walter doesn't like to be distracted before a race, James,' Bismaquer growled. 'He's an old professional, remember . . .'

'And this is a friendly race, with an important side bet between us, Markus.' Bond sounded cool, though concern had already begun to nag at the back of his mind.

Bismaquer probably had a car capable of a higher performance, but he could not know about the water injection, or the increased boost, on the Saab. Bond was in no doubt, though, about Luxor. He was up against a man who really knew racing, and – in addition – a man who knew the Bismaquer track backwards.

'Okay, Markus. You tell your professional from me that I hope the best man wins. That's all. Now, can I juice up the Saab?'

Bismaquer looked at him blankly. There was something dreadfully sinister about the gaze, for the eyes were blank and the mouth sullenly slack – no hint, or trace, of the expansive buffoon. Bond recognised the look with a certain coldness in the pit of his stomach.

It was the expression he had seen many times, the dead expression of a professional hit man. A contract killer, about to do his job.

As suddenly as the look came, it vanished, and Bismaquer smiled, his whole face lighting up.

'My boys'll do it all for you, James.'

'No thank you.' Bond preferred to see to everything himself – gas, oil, hydraulics, coolant.

The final check took around twenty minutes, after which Bond walked over to Bismaquer who chatted amiably with Nena and Cedar.

'I'm ready,' Bond announced, allowing his gaze to take in all three of them.

There was a pause, then Bismaquer nodded. 'If you'd like to come and draw for positions on the grid . . .'

'Oh' – Bond laughed – 'let's keep it friendly. Surely we can just toss for it here. I'm sure Walter won't mind, you . . .'

'James,' Bismaquer said softly. Did Bond detect menace? Or was he merely edgy, jumping at verbal shadows? 'James. You must understand about Walter. He takes this very seriously. I'll see if he's ready.'

Left alone with the women, Bond did not even attempt small talk. 'I'll say farewell now, ladies,' he said allowing his lips to break into a winning smile. 'See you after the race.'

'For God's sake, Bond, be careful.' Cedar walked with him for a moment, speaking low. 'The bastards are out to get you. Don't take any risks. It's not worth it. Please.'

'Don't worry.' Bond waved cheerfully, turning to see Bismaquer approaching with Walter Luxor.

Luxor was most correct. They shook hands, said may the best man win, and tossed for the starting position on the grid. Bond lost. Luxor took the inside, right-hand, lane.

Bismaquer intoned solemnly, 'This will be a race of a full ten laps of the circuit. Your lap numbers will be held up in the pits as you pass. Walter's in red; James, yours in blue. I am acting as chief marshal, and you will obey my instructions. You will drive down to your positions on the grid, then shut down your engines. I shall place myself on the starter's rostrum – over there – and raise the flag. You will both indicate that you have an unrestricted view of me by giving a thumbs-up sign. I shall then wave the flag in a circular motion, and you will start engines. After that I shall raise the flag, count down from ten to zero, and drop the flag. You may then drive. The flag will not come down again until the winning car passes the rostrum, at the end of the tenth lap. Is that clear?'

Bond slowly steered the Saab to his place on the grid. There had been little time to think of tactics, and his mind now raced ahead. He had no real idea of the standard he faced, so his first job would be to gauge the performance of both his rival driver and the car.

He hoped the impression given, during the two laps' trial run, was that he had pushed the Saab to a point near its limit. Tactics had to be right now, or he would stand no chance.

As he placed the Saab on its mark, Bond made the final decision. He would let Luxor have his head for at least the first five laps. This would give him valuable experience of the circuit at various speeds, and let him see whether Luxor was capable, as he suspected, of blocking any attempt to overtake by using really dangerous manoeuvres.

Providing Bond could match Luxor's skill, and the Saab was powerful enough to stay close, he would begin to make his bid at the beginning of the sixth lap. Then, once ahead, Bond could unleash the reserve power and make a run for home. If he drove with a little dash, but within the safety limits of both car and circuit, there was the distinct possibility that he could out-distance Luxor by at least half a lap. That should be his place no later than lap eight.

Bismaquer was looking at him. Bond raised his thumb, and the flag twirled. Luxor's engine fired with a roar, denoting more power than would usually be under the bonnet of a Shelby-American.

The Saab grumbled quietly, and Bond glanced around, noting the distance between the two cars and, at the same moment, catching Luxor's sunken eyes. They seemed to bore into him with an expression of intense hatred.

Bond faced forward and signalled to Bismaquer.

The flag went up. Bond slid into first, released the hand brake, and hovered his right foot over the accelerator.

The flag came down.

The so-called Shelby-American shook its tail as it streaked away from the grid. With such a fast start, Luxor was out to thrash him completely. As Bond started to build up power, he realised that Bismaquer's driver intended to put a lot of distance between them, in the shortest possible time. He kicked down hard on the accelerator, bringing the turbo in quickly, watching the speed rise.

Already, Luxor must have been averaging a hundred on the straight before the chicane. Bond kept piling on the pressure, hearing the turbo whine like a jet engine as he thrust the gears into fifth, passing the 120 mark, which brought him close up behind the sloping fastback of Luxor's car.

It was a matter of feet now, and Bond was forced to decelerate and change down to hold the hundred, riding directly behind Luxor. He saw the brake lights flicker, as they came up to the chicane. Bond changed down again rather than use his brakes, easing the car through the sashay of the chicane, the speedometer showing around seventy as Luxor appeared to become airborne over the hump at the end.

Bond hit the hump at just under seventy miles per hour, leaving his hands loose on the wheel, until he felt the solid jar as the Saab came into contact with the track again. Then he changed up, his foot toeing the accelerator.

Around the full hundred appeared to be Luxor's safe limit, and Bond followed him through the right-angle turn without letting up on speed. He allowed the Saab to drift in the Shelby-American's wake to the right, then hard right, feeling the rear tyres protest as they kept their grip. Ten of those, and the rubber would really start to burn off, Bond thought. By the time the knowledge had been assimilated, they were at the Z bend.

Here, Luxor had his own technique – using the brakes constantly on the hairpins of the zigs and zags of the bend, but putting on power, even during the short runs between.

Through, and into the next straight. Bond realised they must have taken the Z at a minimum of seventy, rising to eighty. Luxor was undoubtedly not only a confident, technical expert, but a man with steel nerves. Yet, on this long straight, he hardly took the little silver car above the hundred.

Before they reached the first of the two final bends, Bond decided that Luxor cruised at around one hundred miles per hour, with a possible forty, maybe fifty, in reserve for the straights when he needed it.

It was good technique. The circuit called for accuracy in speed, and hard work as well as concentration. Out-think him, Bond whispered to himself. If he read it correctly, Luxor was going to keep up the pace until the last three, possibly four, laps and then – sure that Bond was both tired and running the Saab flat out – he would push down and surge ahead, using his maximum speed.

They flashed past the stands. Bond, at a glance, saw that the head-up display speedometer was showing a fraction above a hundred. Luxor had drawn slightly ahead.

Maybe it was time to change tactics, not wait until later in the race. Stick with him for this one anyway; then decide when to make the first pass.

By the time they had negotiated the second lap and were screaming past the stands again, Bond was sweating, working hard, still loath to use brakes, keeping a check on speed with gears and accelerator.

This would be the ideal place, he decided, as they whined on towards the chicane. When they ended the third lap he would have a go.

The Saab was less than six feet behind the square tail of Luxor's car as they came out of the final turn on lap three. Now, he thought, watching Luxor drift slightly to the left. Not really enough room, but, if he obeyed the rules, Luxor would have to let Bond through.

A fraction of pressure on the wheel and the Saab slid to the right, coming very close to the Shelby-American. Further to the right. Bond saw the edge of the track too close to his front in-side wheel, but he pressed on, up into fifth gear and a hard kick down. The turbo reacted, and he felt the push of power, like a jet engine. The Saab's nose was reaching out, half way down Luxor's chassis, unmistakably clearing to overtake.

Then, with a jarring horror, Bond saw Luxor veer over at an angle, cutting across to stop him, increasing speed so that Bond almost had to stand on the brakes to avoid slamming into the other car's side. In a fraction of a second, the Saab was behind again, losing ground. Bastard, Bond snarled to himself. He changed down, dropping speed to negotiate the chicane. Once through, he put his foot down again, closing so that they went into the right-angle bend almost locked together.

This time, Bond felt considerable drift, the Saab sliding over to the left during the final moments of the turn. He glanced at the head-up digital figures of the speedometer and was not surprised. They registered 105; and, by the time he was aware of the speed building to 125, the zig-zag of the Z bend was on them.

Try him on the far straight, Bond thought. Force the bastard off the road if need be; the Saab had the weight to do it.

They came out of the Z bend, Luxor still accelerating and Bond determined not to lose an inch, trying to position for a breakthrough.

Then it happened.

He knew he would be able to prove nothing later. The blame would be put firmly on an overheated turbo, or some other excuse. At the time, however, he saw both the manoeuvre and the action quite plainly.

Luxor accelerated slightly, moving ahead by a few feet – three or four at the most. As Bond curled his own toes on the Saab's accelerator, he saw distinctly the small object drop away from Luxor's rear bumper. For a fraction of a second, he thought Luxor was in trouble: that stress was causing a break-up of some rear component. But the whooshing noise under the Saab made the truth plain enough.

Luxor had jettisoned some form of incendiary device, set to ignite as it hit the track.

All Bond was aware of after that was a sheet of flame surrounding the car, engulfing him, and then rapidly dying away.

They were about midway to the penultimate bend, and James Bond at first thought the bid had failed. The enveloping flame could only have been there for a second, and he had probably outrun it at this speed. Then he experienced a sense of shock as the fire warning buzzed and the red light began to blink on the dashboard.

One of the last things Bond had fitted to the Saab was the relatively new on-board, fire detection and extinguisher system, marketed and developed by Graviner. Fixed-temperature detectors – set high, and at a very fine pitch for the Saab – monitored the engine and underside of the car, especially those areas adjacent to the fuel tank. The guts of the system were situated deep within the Saab's large boot. In a protected bed sat a seam-less chrome and steel container, filled, under pressure, with the most efficient of extinguishants, Halon 1211. From the con-tainer, spray pipes ran to the engine compartment and around the car, particularly along the underside.

The extinguisher automatically fired when the detectors sig-nalled a fire warning; while the whole system could also be activated manually from a thump button on the dashboard. The light and buzzer warnings were also automatically operated the moment heat set off the sensors.

In the present case, fire had engulfed the car, catching the underside, thereby activating the system without further help from Bond.

Literally within seconds, ten kilogrammes of Halon 1211 en-gulfed the Saab, sweeping from underside to engine com-partment, extinguishing the fire immediately and leaving no damage in its wake, for the properties of Halon are non-damaging to engine components, electrical wiring, or humans. It is also non-corrosive and, once the fire had been extinguished, the evaporation rate is so fast that no residue remains.

Bond, very much aware of what was going on, changed down, braked, and took the last two bends at a moderate sixty-five. It was only when he was into the long straight – past the stand – knowing that he was entering the fifth lap, that Bond opened up the car again, relieved to feel no change in engine response.

Luxor, however, was well away – a good two miles ahead, just entering the chicane. Deep within his head, where anger boiled, Bond willed coolness. Luxor had deliberately attempted to burn him to death on the track – expecting the incendiary device to blow the Saab's petrol tank and probably the turbo-charger at the same time.

Settling himself firmly, Bond did not let his eyes waver from the road ahead. His hands ran through the gears as he increased power, roaring along the straight towards the chicane. His speed rose to over the hundred until the little green digital figures on the head-up display steadied at 130.

Bond changed down, but still took the chicane at his highest speed yet. The Saab rose like an aircraft, rotating on take-off, then bounced on its rear end first, almost out of control. Bond wrestled with the wheel. The screen of trees off the edge of the track slewed into vision. He heard the tyres protest until he brought the car back on line, pouring on a little more speed, then slowing as the Z bend approached.

From then onwards, it was a question of using speed on the straights, without trying to push the Saab to its full stretch, in order to gain on Luxor, who was going all out now, clinging to his lead.

It took another two laps before the Saab came within striking distance of its adversary. Then, nose to bumper, they crossed the line once more – into the eighth lap. Bond searched for his chance, jinking and pushing hard, while Luxor piled on more and more power.

Walter Luxor was rattled, Bond decided. The more he pushed, the more Luxor began taking chances. His driving was still immaculate, countering every move Bond made, but speed appeared to be his blind spot. He risked going through the chicane, the right-angle and Z bends, with the narrowest of safety limits.

Lap nine. Only one to follow, then it would be all over. For the penultimate time, the stands blurred past them. Bond realised he was involuntarily gritting his teeth. Whatever the consequences, there had to be some way of overtaking Luxor.

The idea germinated fast. One hope in a thousand; a risk which could end in disaster. They slid through the chicane, Luxor slowing this time as he hit the hump. Perhaps the driver's nerves were, at last, getting ragged. Now the killing, dangerous, right-angle bend.

Luxor lined himself up, keeping far to the right – his wheels almost touching the grass at the track's edge – in order to take the punishing bend at one hundred. Bond, three feet or so behind him, was himself pushing almost a hundred.

Luxor went into the turn, holding to the right, fighting the strain, to stay close to the verge for as long as possible, before pressure and speed forced the car over to the left. He reached the maximum point of turn and the car, under the stress of angle, speed, and torque, started to slide outwards. A touch on the brakes slowed him fractionally.

It was the moment Bond had been waiting for: that second before Luxor was dragged to the left and forced to slow. Bond took his final opportunity.

Instead of following directly in Luxor's slipstream, the Saab suddenly went out of line, flicking to the left. Bond checked the turn on the wheel, feeling the stress hauling the Saab even further to the left than he intended, correcting with the wheel, steering right, and knowing that, if the wheels locked, he would be in a spin and off the road.

The Saab was drifting. Then, for a second, a space appeared – clear road on the bend to Luxor's left. In a moment, Luxor's car would itself be dragged into that clear area, just as it had been each time they took the right-angle bend. In that fraction of time, Bond felt the Saab steady. He kicked on the accelerator, sensing the Saab's spoiler push the rear down on to the road. His own body was forced back in the driving seat as full power took hold.

Almost aloud, Bond prayed that the Turbo's constantly-increasing forward speed would overcome any further slide to the left and that he could still hold the Saab into the turn without touching the verge. The turbo-charger whined, rising to a pitch of noise which should, by rights, have ended in some kind of explosion.

Then, quite suddenly, it was over. The Saab shot through on the outside of the sliding Shelby-American, the numbers on the head-up display just below the 140 line. Bond straightened the wheels and poured power through the engine.

The front of Luxor's car must have just missed grazing the Saab's rear as Bond overtook. For a moment, the low body and windscreen of the other car appeared to fill the Saab's rear-view mirror. Then it dropped back a few feet. As they slowed to go into the Z bend, Luxor managed to stay close, as though attached by a cable. But as Bond cleared the final hairpin, he slammed through the gears, up to the fifth, his right foot smoothly depressing the accelerator.

With a clear road ahead at last, the Saab leaped forward. He touched 150 on the far straight, slowed for the two corners, and, at the start of the last lap, took the car right through its paces. At one point – before the chicane – the numbers hit the magic figure of 175, then a little higher on the final far straight. Luxor was now well behind by three or four miles.

It was only when Bond brought the car towards the last two bends, that he began to gear down, allowing the speed to drop away. Then he took an extra lap, at a relatively gentle pace, allowing the engine to settle and himself to readjust. He had seen Bismaquer's face, dark and angry, as he brought down the chequered flag, proclaiming Bond the winner.

Yet, when the Saab finally coasted into the pits, with the grandstand crowd applauding even though their man had lost, Bismaquer seemed to have regained his temper.

'A fair race, James. A fair and exciting race. That car of yours sure knows how to move.'

Bond, dripping with sweat, did not answer immediately but turned to watch Walter Luxor – the skull face more menacing than usual – coast in behind him.

'I don't know how fair, Markus,' Bond said at last. 'If that's really a converted Shelby-American, I'll eat my track suit. As for the firework display . . .'

'Yes, what happened there?' Bismaquer's pink, scrubbed face was a mask of innocence.

'I think Walter must've been having a quick cigarette and

dropped a match. Look forward to my bonus, Markus. A great race. Now, if you'll excuse me . . .'

He turned and walked back towards the Saab, which would certainly need his attention. But Bismaquer was at his heels.

'We'll settle all debts tonight, James – the money, I mean. And I'll take the prints. But then, I'm afraid my hospitality has got to end. Dinner tonight – seven o'clock for seven-thirty, then we can clear up the business before we eat? Okay?'

'Fine.'

'I'm sorry, but I have to ask you to leave in the morning. You see, we have this conference . . . the first people are arriving tonight . . .'

'I thought you kept clear of conferences?' Bond was already half way into the Saab, pulling on the bonnet release.

Bismaquer hesitated, then laughed – not the booming guffaw, but a deep nervous rumble. 'Yes. Yes, that's true. I can't stand conferences. Can't really stand crowds any more. I guess that was what finally convinced me I should throw in the towel in politics. Did you know I had political ambitions at one time?'

'No, but I can believe it,' Bond lied.

'I usually keep well clear of the conferences here.' Bismaquer appeared to be searching for words. 'You see,' he went on, 'well, these people coming tonight are all automotive engineers. Walter is an expert.' His face shaped a slow, rather sly, grin. 'I guess you know that by now. You realise he built that Shelby replica with his own hands?'

'Extras and all?' Bond's eyebrows tilted.

Bismaquer boomed out a laugh, as if it was all a good joke. Either of us could have died out there because of that car, Bond reflected; yet Bismaquer thinks it's funny.

The bear-like man hardly paused for breath. 'Well, these people being engineers and . . . Well, Walter's addressing them tomorrow morning: some very advanced talk on mechanics, I don't know what. Like a fool – and to make him happy – I promised to be there too . . . So there won't be much time for me to play host to Cedar and you.'

Bond nodded. 'Okay. We'll be away in the morning, Markus.' Then he turned back to the car.

'Help yourself from the barbecue,' Bismaquer called back over his shoulder.

Bond wondered when the action would start, as he watched the big man walk away, flat-footed and heavy. Either Bismaquer was going to let them get off the ranch and then have them picked up outside, or he would see to it here, on the premises. If the latter, then everything could be blown. He needed to talk to Nena, among other things, and then go to ground in the Conference Centre, his last hope of gaining hard information. If Bismaquer pounced first the whole mission would be lost.

From the start, Bond had been certain the spectacular, and lethal, hijacks were part of a resurrected SPECTRE's plan: a money-raising operation for something much bigger. All he had felt, and seen, since arriving in the United States – and particularly at Rancho Bismaquer – pointed towards a SPECTRE-directed coup of very large proportions. The hub lay here, as did Ernst Stavro Blofeld's successor.

Now, after Bismaquer's words, he knew that it would be necessary to drop out of sight at any moment, even if it meant leaving Cedar to face the music. Luxor or Bismaquer? he wondered. Which was the new Blofeld? Which of them held the key?

Bond's concern mounted as he worked on the Saab, then backed it towards the petrol pumps. He would at least have a full tank, with an oil and coolant top-up if warranted.

Luxor had not even bothered to come over and shake hands or congratulate him on the win. Worse, Cedar had disappeared without exchanging a word with him, hustled away, with Nena, by the security staff.

After the adrenalin-pumping danger of the race, James Bond now felt a reaction which came near to depression. Bismaquer could not be seen anywhere, and only a couple of chefs tended the deserted barbecue. Bond went over and helped himself to a massive steak, bread and coffee. At least he would not go hungry.

He dealt with the Saab quickly, glancing up to the stands which were being cleared. The only thing possible was to watch his own back, return to the cabin, then leave quickly and hide and wait until the night. Then down to Tara for dinner, armed to the teeth, strong in the hope that Bismaquer would not give an order for him to be snatched – with Cedar – before he could go to ground and get some real answers.

As the Saab drew away from the pits, a man with a neat military moustache and dressed in a white silk jacket watched from high in the grandstand. The car purred out of sight, heading for the rising, wooded ground.

Mike Mazzard smiled and left the stand.

16

NENA

Even at eleven-thirty, the night seemed to have lost little heat from the day.

Bond, clad now in dark slacks, a black turtle-neck and short jacket – to hide the holstered VP70 – lay among the trees, covered by branches and odd ferns already gathered during the afternoon.

Around him the noises of night animals, combined with the chirruping cicadas, had become a natural background. His hearing was acute enough to break through the series of calls and songs, and would pick up any human sound, should it come near.

In some senses, the events of the day had been anti-climactic. Bond, on getting back to the cabin, had taken a quick shower, changed, and made certain all was ready for a fast getaway. He had laid out clothes for dinner that night and packed everything else, even the reassembled briefcase, which he locked away in the Saab.

All he carried was the set of pick-locks and tools, together with the Heckler & Koch, plus spare magazines. He went through the routine quickly, leaving himself in the clothes he now wore, except for a black shirt, for the day, instead of the turtle-neck, which, he considered, would be more suitable later that night.

His hiding place was constructed with equal haste, among the trees in a corner of the clearing, affording good sight-lines of the track, cabin and Saab. There Bond stayed until dusk, leaving soon after six, to change into the lightweight suit, decent shoes and tie, before driving down to Tara.

Bismaquer was his usual jovial self, dispensing drinks on the veranda. Cedar looked cool in dark blue skirt and blouse, while Nena sparkled, her dark eyes twinkling, that glissando laugh like music to Bond's ears.

Almost as soon as he arrived, Nena asked what he was drinking, allowing their eyes to meet, and, in that meeting, signalling she had not forgotten their tryst.

Cedar remained calm, but she too seemed to be flashing signals at Bond, as though they needed to talk.

The only off-key note came from Walter Luxor, who sat sullen, hardly speaking to anyone. A bad loser, Bond thought, and a man with more important things on his mind than the small talk which seemed to roll naturally from Markus Bismaquer.

After one drink, Bismaquer suggested that, if Bond had brought the prints, they conclude their business. 'I'm a man of my word, James,' he chuckled. 'Even though, like any other man, I don't like having to part with money.'

Bond went down the steps to the Saab, retrieved the prints, and followed Bismaquer into the house. They went straight to the print room, where, with no fuss, Bond handed over the prints in exchange for a small briefcase which Bismaquer opened. 'Count it if you want to,' he growled pleasantly. 'Only you'll miss dinner if you do. The whole amount's in there. One million for Professor Penbrunner, and another for yourself.'

'I believe you.' Bond closed the case. 'Nice to do business, Markus. If I have anything else . . .'

'I'm sure you'll be of use to me again, James.' Bismaquer gave him a quick, almost suspicious look. 'In fact, I'm positive about it. Now, if you don't mind returning to the others, I'll put these away. I have a horror of anybody else knowing where I keep my really rare treasures.'

Bond hefted the briefcase. 'And this needs locking up, safe and sound. Thank you, Markus.'

On reaching the portico again, Bond found it empty but for Cedar.

'Nena Bismaquer's talking to the cook, and the death's head just wandered off,' Cedar told him quickly.

Bond was already half way down the steps. He called back quietly: 'Come and help me put this away.'

She joined him at the back of the car, and immediately Bond detected the vibrations of fear emanating from her, like an animal.

'They've got something really heavy going on, James. Christ, you had me worried in that race.'

'I wasn't exactly happy myself, Cedar. But listen to me.' He told her, in a few words, that – providing they were both left alone when dinner was over – he would be returning to the cabin. 'I'm going to do exactly as we planned, only Bismaquer's given us marching orders for tomorrow morning. I suspect they plan to let us get clear and then really nail us, but I could be quite wrong. There's a chance they'll snatch both of us here, tonight, on the ranch. Do you still have that weapon?'

She gave a little nod, whispering that it was strapped to the inside of her thigh and that it was damned uncomfortable too.

'Right.' Bond, put the briefcase in the boot, slammed it shut and twisted the key. 'As soon as you can, after dinner. I want you to get out. Don't come anywhere near the knoll or the cabins, but around dawn try and make your way to the place I told you about, where I'm going to stash the Saab. Steal a car, walk, do it any way you can. But get out. Don't get too near the Saab, just hide and watch. Meeting and pickup times as we arranged.'

'Okay. There're things to tell you, though, James.'

'Quickly then.'

'They know exactly who, and what we are,' she began. 'And Mike Mazzard arrived last night.'

'And the other three hoods?'

'I don't know, but Mazzard got hell from Luxor, for not being able to control his men. Apparently they were acting without orders in Washington. No harm was to come to you, James. I'm not so sure about myself – they called me Cedar Leiter, by the way – but they want you alive.'

'The car race . . . ?'

'Was to keep you off-balance. And the Harvester ants as well. They *knew* you weren't going to be in that cabin. The ants were definitely meant for me. Apparently you're fireproof. You should have heard Luxor. He really let Mazzard have it. That's all for sure, James. I heard everything. Orders are that you're to be kept on tap but not killed.'

'Well . . .'

'That's not all. Something's happened over at the warehouse.'

Bond made questioning noises.

'I saw by accident. A refrigerated truck came out of the trees, at the back of the warehouse, late this afternoon; and there are at least two more down there. The first truck was heading towards the airfield. They're moving that ice cream.'

Bond's brow was lined in thought. 'I wish we knew more,' he murmured. 'Perhaps I will by tomorrow night. Be very careful, though; if it's some criminal – or terrorist – activity and we've vanished, they'll be digging the place up to find us. I . . .' He stopped, conscious that somebody had come on to the portico.

A second later, Nena Bismaquer spoke: James? Cedar? Didn't anyone call you? Dinner's served.'

They went back up the steps, and Cedar entered the house first, leaving Bond to shepherd Nena through the great high doors. She let Cedar get well ahead, then turned, saying softly to Bond, 'James. I'll be with you as soon as I can after dinner. Please be careful. It's very dangerous. We have to talk.'

Bond merely bowed his head to signal he understood. The black eyes gave him a pleading look, quite out of character with the sophisticated, very beautiful French woman who walked on with poise towards the dining room.

So now Bond waited in his hiding place in the trees. For Nena? Almost certainly, he thought. Though it could well be something else. During dinner there had been some tension, and Bismaquer had undergone a sudden change of character on two occasions, once in the way he spoke to the servants, and once to Nena. Perhaps the strain was starting to tell. From what Bond and Cedar had observed, something was about to happen. If Bismaquer was, indeed, the new Blofeld, the mask could be about to crack.

Was it significant, Bond wondered, lying in the dark, that Walter Luxor had not dined with them? According to Bismaquer, the skeleton of a man was busy preparing his speech for the next day.

Luxor or Bismaquer? Bond still wondered, his eyes – now accustomed to the darkness – watching for the slightest movement.

He glanced at his watch. The dial glowed clearly. Eleven thirty-five; and, at that moment, he heard the distant sound of a motor.

Bond turned his head, trying to gauge direction. The sound was approaching from below. A small car, he judged, as he distinctly heard the gear change and the engine alter as it began its climb up the long track through the trees.

About five minutes later the headlights shafted into the clearing, followed by the little car itself, a small black sports which Bond could not immediately identify.

The car pulled up directly behind the Saab. Shutting it in, Bond thought to himself. If he wanted to get out quickly, he would have to clear the open space in a fast turn.

The driver killed the engine and lights. Through the night air, Bond heard the rustle of silk. He could just make out Nena Bismaquer, standing beside the car, then her voice, calling quietly, 'James? James, are you there?'

Softly, Bond surfaced. He crossed the clearing, one hand ready near the holstered VP70. She did not hear him until he was almost behind her.

'Oh my God. Oh James, don't do things like that.' Nena, quivering, clung to him.

'You told me to take care,' Bond said smiling down at her.

Nena Bismaquer was still dressed as she had been at dinner in a pleated silk dress patterned in white and black, very simple but revealing her particular style and personality. Simple, maybe, Bond thought, his hand touching the smooth and provocative material, but he would bet a month's salary on this little creation costing a fortune.

'Can we go inside, James? Please.' Her lips were close to his. Once more, Bond smelled her particular scent, the clean, fresh hair, though now it was mingled with something very expensive: the touch of a distillation, probably unique, and made especially for Markus Bismaquer's wife. For a moment, Bond felt a tiny pang of jealousy. Then she urged him again. 'Please, James. Inside, please.'

Bond took a step forward, letting Nena enter the cabin first. Then he switched on the light. Almost as the cabin door closed behind them, she was in his arms, trembling, then pulling away. 'I should not have come.' Her voice took on the same breathless quality he had heard in the Saab when they first kissed.

'Why then?' Bond wrapped his arms around her, feeling her turn towards him, pressing her limbs close to his.

'Why do you think?' She lifted her face and kissed him on the lips, pulling back again quickly. 'No. Not yet, anyway. I don't know what's going on, James. All I can tell you is that Markus and Walter are both out for blood. They're doing something really dangerous, James. That's all I know, all I can tell you. Both of them, they hide everything from me. Men came last night, men from the East, from New York. I heard some of the conversation. Walter said that, if he didn't win on the race track today . . .'

'You looked relaxed enough at the track . . .'

'There was no way to warn you, James. You could see. I was surrounded by Markus's men. You have to get away, James.'

'Markus has asked us to go in the morning.'

'Yes. Yes, I know . . . but . . .' She clung closer. 'But they'll be waiting, I know that. There are a lot of new people around, and I think they have the ranch surrounded – dogs, half-tracks? Is that right, half-tracks?'

'They'd be useful in desert conditions, yes.' Bond did not say that he thought as much. Bismaquer was acting as a sheep dog, moving them out and into the arms of waiting killers.

'Listen, Nena.' He held her away, by the shoulders roused by her presence, the smooth skin against his hands and the feel of the silk. 'Listen hard. Cedar is going. I am going. We're both vanishing. Not tomorrow, as Markus wants, but tonight – or in the early hours. I know something's up, so we're going to earth here, on the ranch, until one of us can get clear . . .'

'If it's you, James, don't take chances. From what I've heard they really have got the place surrounded. Is it the money, perhaps? I don't know.'

In the short silence that followed, there came the roar of a heavy aircraft flying low over the ranch.

Nena looked towards the cabin's rafters. 'That'll be part of the delegation coming in. Two separate flights tonight. Either that, or one of Markus's freighters . . .'

'Freighters?'

She gave a small, nervous laugh. 'Oh, his damned ice cream. He's in the middle of something criminal, horrible – I know that – but he can't leave the ice cream alone. He's got yet another new flavour, and he's sold it to some distributor somewhere. Tons of it. They're shipping it out tonight.'

Ice cream going to some distributor, Bond thought. Would it be straight, or spiked with whatever dreadful drug Luxor and Bismaquer had concocted? The stuff he'd seen in action, turning men into pliable, pleasant monsters who would obey, even to the selling of their wives and loved ones.

'Where are you going to hide?' she asked.

'No.' Bond was sharp. 'Better you should not know anything,

then they can't get at you as well. We'll just disappear. Hang on, Nena. Just hang on and wait. Someone will come, I'll see to that. Then the whole thing'll be over.'

'Shall I see you again?'

'Of course.'

He felt her hand drop to his thigh. 'I haven't long.' She moved very close now, whispering in his ear. 'James, just in case something happens . . .' She did not need to finish the sentence.

Gently, Bond led her in the direction of the bedroom, crossing to the bed and turning on the night-table lamp.

'No, my darling James. No lights. In the dark.'

'That's a little old-fashioned . . .'

'For my sake. No lights.'

He nodded, switched off the lamp, and climbed out of his clothes, hearing the noise of her dress sliding over her head.

Naked and lying on the bed, Bond was about to place the automatic within reach when a sudden instinct took his hand up to the lamp again. 'Sorry, Nena. I've got to have some light.'

She gave a little cry as the lamp came on, revealing her slim and lithe sun-brown figure, with those magnificent long legs. She was dressed only in silk bra and panties. She was in the act of unclipping her bra.

'James. I asked you . . .' She stopped, realising that her voice had turned harsh, like a whip-lash.

Bond apologised: 'I'm sorry. Jittery, Nena, that's all. I don't think we should be in the dark. You look so lovely, so why the modesty?'

Her face crumpled as she came slowly towards the bed. 'You would have found out. Just as Markus found out. Everybody. It can't be helped. James, I'm not a whole woman. I didn't want you to see me. It's always been like this. I . . . I . . . I feel deformed, and I don't like people . . .'

He pulled her down on to the bed, a hand searching for her. Nena's mouth opened, locking against his, and they were off again into a whirlpool of emotions, their mouths acting out the desires of their bodies.

Presently she pulled away. 'The light, James. Can we have it . . . ?'

'Show me.' Bond was determined. 'Whatever it is, there can't be any harm in seeing . . .'

She slid sideways on to him, her hands going to the clasp on her bra. Bond noticed that she could not look him in the eyes. 'I was born like this, James. I'm sorry. Some people – like Markus – find it revolting.'

Sliding her bra away she revealed the truth. The left side of her chest was smooth and flat as that of a young boy, perfectly formed but no female breast. On the right side, the firm, beautiful curve of one glorious breast – full and golden.

Strangely, perhaps because her one breast was so wonderful, an exact half-globe with a proportioned brown and pink nipple erect, the oddity appeared especially erotic to Bond.

He pulled her close, one hand cupping her. 'Dear, lovely Nena. You *are* unique. You're beautiful. There's nothing revolting about you. Certainly you're *not* half woman. Let me show you that.'

Slowly, punctuating his actions with kisses, Bond completed undressing her, and she wrapped herself around him, so that, for an hour or so, the evil which surrounded them in this strange, man-made desert island melted away – taking them into other worlds and to higher peaks, shrinking, eventually, to two human beings, turned by the magic of the love act into one.

Nena left around four in the morning, with constant kisses and worried admonitions for Bond to be on his guard. 'I *shall* see you again, James? Tell me I shall see you again.'

Bond kissed her hard on the mouth and told her they would certainly be together again.

'If,' she told him finally, as they got to her car, 'if anything does go wrong, James, rely on me. If it happens here, I'll do my best to help. I love . . .'

Bond stopped her with a last kiss. 'It's too easy to say.' He smiled in the darkness. 'Just think of what we've had, and hope for more.'

He stood near the Saab, in the clearing, watching the little car's lights disappear into the trees. Then, refreshed and cleansed by the loving contact of another person, Bond gathered his things together, climbed into the Saab and drove away, using only the parking lights. He took the route down the track, then the road bordering the knoll, climbing up the far side to the hidden layby where he had sat, with Nena, hearing her story of poverty in Paris and the dream of wealth turned sour with Bismaquer.

Having concealed the car as well as possible, he set out for the last long walk that would take him to the Conference Centre.

There was not much time left before dawn – less than two hours, he supposed – so Bond, still lightly dressed, carrying only the Heckler & Koch automatic, spare ammunition, and the ring with its picklocks and tools, adopted the old commando speed-marching technique of alternate fast walking and running.

The trek was longer than even he had gauged, and the darkness of night had already given way to that grey half-light before dawn by the time he reached the manhole cover on the edge of jungle. The metal cover came away easily, and Bond threw the big handle underneath, watching, and willing, the large slab of stone to move faster on its hydraulic jacks.

Once the entrance was clear, he replaced the metal cover and climbed down inside the tiled chamber, looking around for the mechanism which Nena had assured him was there to seal the stone from the inside. He was a good twelve feet underground and could see the entrance to the tunnel itself, lit by small blue bulbs which glowed into the distance.

The mechanism was there, near the final rung of metal holds. Pulling the lever below ground brought the hydraulic sound even closer, so that the whole tunnel seemed to reverberate as the stone slab lifted itself back into place. The faint light which had filtered in through the opening was now obliterated, and Bond was bathed in the low, eerie blue light which did not even reflect off the white tiles.

The tunnel was curved at the top, to a height of about eight feet, and wide enough for a man of Bond's size to stretch out his arms and just touch the walls with his fingertips.

From the initial chamber, one could walk straight through the tunnel archway, and Bond had not gone far when he noticed the ground begin to slope downwards slightly. There was no sound, and no dank chill, as he had expected. The rope-soled shoes, which he had chosen to wear for comfort, made little noise; yet he still took the precaution of stopping, every minute or so, listening for any sounds coming either from ahead or behind. If the complex was already in use, there was always the possibility of Bismaquer's people using this entrance to move freely between the ranch and the centre.

Bond encountered nobody in what he judged to be a mile-long walk. After sloping down and then seeming to flatten out for a few hundred yards, the ground rose again more steeply on the far side. After the speed march from the knoll, Bond could feel a dull ache in his thigh muscles.

He plodded on, as silently as before. Soon the path began to rise even more steeply and to turn in a gentle curve. Then, with hardly any warning, the whole tunnel widened and the end was in sight: another arched entrance to a chamber, this one larger than the entrance from the road.

Facing Bond was a smooth, tiled wall. He turned to examine the entire chamber, remembering Nena had told him there was a mechanism at this end too, which led to a janitor's closet. She had given him no details, however, of the device. All Bond could see in the blue light were the smooth tiled walls. No boxes, metal covers or switches.

Logic told him that the wall facing him as he came into the chamber was the most likely exit point. Furthermore, if the door was at the rear of a closet, the handle would be situated in line with a man's hand.

Starting with the centre of the wall, Bond began to examine the individual tiles, one by one, working along the rows, methodically. He pushed and probed each tile in turn, until, after fifteen minutes or so, he found the right spot. The tile slid back on a small metal runner, operating like a model of a push-up garage door. Behind it was a perfectly normal door knob.

Gently, he tried the knob. Part of the tiling moved and, as Bond pulled back, a whole section was revealed as a hinged door. The door moved noiselessly, with great ease. On the far side was a plaster wall, complete with shelving angled to the left, so that the door could carry parts of the shelves back with it.

Bond stepped out, holding the door back until he had checked the handle on the other side which was hidden out of sight, directly under one of the shelves. Only then did he allow the door behind him to close.

The closet afforded little room – just enough for a man of reasonable build to hide behind its normal door, about a pace and a half from the rows of shelves.

Once the secret door was closed, Bond had to wait for a moment so that his eyes could adjust to the darkness before edging towards the main closet door.

Again he found himself turning the handle gently and, this time, pushing the door outwards.

After the blue light and silence of the tunnel, it was startling to hear noise. Men's and women's voices echoed from above and to the side. The passageway in which Bond stood, by the closet door, was flooded with light. A window, almost adjacent, showed him that dawn had broken, and sunlight poured in.

The whole journey down from the knoll and the long walk through the tunnel had taken him much longer than he imagined. Glancing at his watch, Bond saw it was almost seven-thirty. At least that would reduce the waiting time. But where to wait? How could he infiltrate the conference without being noticed?

Leaving the closet door open for a quick getaway, Bond took a few steps into the passage. The voices were very loud and seemed close at hand, possibly just around the angle at the end of the passage some twenty feet away. The sounds reminded him of something, and it took a moment to sort out the various combinations in his head – the lively chatter, the clink of china. He was somewhere near to a communal dining room.

From the window, Bond could see out across a wide lawn, in the centre of which a large H had been inlaid in white stone. In the far distance was a tall wire fence, then a wall above which the greenery of jungle showed clearly. He was looking out directly on to the helipad.

Turning back towards the closet, Bond spotted a pair of double doors, each with a panel of thick clear glass in the upper half. Neat gold script told him that the doors led to the Conference Hall. He crossed the passage to peer through the glass panel, immediately moving to one side, out of sight.

The quick look had revealed a plush hall, like a modern and most exclusive theatre. Row upon row of tip-back, well-padded chairs ran in a wide crescent, aisles cutting through them like a sunburst. At the front of the seats was a wide stage, already prepared with a long table, behind which stood a dozen chairs. In front of the table a microphone appeared to be guarding a large lectern, while behind, like a backdrop, hung a cinema screen.

The conference hall was not empty. At least a dozen of Bismaquer's security men were passing through it – a couple of them with dogs and some armed with explosives-detection devices and anti-bugging sniffers. They were obviously screening the hall before use. Before Walter Luxor's paper to the automotive engineers? Bond wondered. Or was it really Markus Bismaquer who was going to address the meeting?

Alert now, Bond realised that some of the Bismaquer security people were quite near the conference hall doors. Silently, he moved back inside the janitor's closet, the Heckler & Koch automatic steady in his hand with the safety catch off. The security men could well pass this way; on the other hand, other Bismaquer aides might even now be using the tunnel.

No sooner was he inside the closet, the door not quite closed, than there came the sound of the security men emerging into the passage. Voices were quite clear, only a few feet away.

'Okay?' a man said.

'They all say it's clear, Mack,' came from a second voice.

Then a third: 'You went right under that damned stage, didn't you, Joe?'

'Right under, right through the access flap down there on the left. Took my flashlight too. It's clean as a new bar of soap down there. 'Cept for the dirt and spiders and all.'

There was a chorus of laughter, and Bond guessed the inspection was now finished.

'What time they coming over?' someone asked.

'The ladies and gentlemen have to be in their seats, ready and waiting, by eight forty-five. That's the order. Eight forty-five sharp.'

'Well, we all got plenty of time then. Let's get some chow ourselves.'

'Is Blofeld coming over?' It was the man called Joe who asked, and Bond felt the hair on his neck bristling with anticipation.

'Guess so. Won't do the talking though. Never does.'

'No. Too bad. Okay, fellas, let's tell the folks where they've got to be, and when . . .'

The voices receded, the clarity blurring, then vanished altogether. Bond heard boots clicking down the passage. The cleaning squad had gone.

Bond did not have to think about his next move. He stepped from the closet, gun still in hand, glancing up and down the passage. It was clear. A few seconds later he was inside the conference hall and running down one of the aisles, making for what the man called Joe had described as 'the access flap' on the left of the stage.

Within five seconds he had found it, an ordinary hinged flap with a recessed brass ring to lift it. Bond had the flap up, and had crawled under the stage, within sixty-five seconds of leaving the janitor's closet.

All he had to do now was wait. At eight forty-five the delegates would start coming in. Then, soon after that, Blofeld would arrive. Not the Blofeld he had killed, but the new Blofeld. The name was in the open now, and soon, James Bond knew, he would be able to identify the man from his two suspects. Would it be Luxor or Bismaquer himself? He knew whom his money would ride on.

17

HEAVENLY WOLF

Lying, silent, in the dark under the conference hall stage, Bond pondered again the question of Blofeld – the original man, the first leader of SPECTRE. Was his successor – the here-and-now leader – a relative? In organisations like this, a chain of command would not necessarily demand kinship. Yet, having known and fought Ernst Stavro Blofeld, Bond knew there had been a streak of dynastic ambition in him. The king is dead; long live the king.

When Blofeld had died at Bond's hands, some provision must have been made for a future leader, even if that person did not immediately appear – and there had certainly been a lengthy period before SPECTRE rose again.

Bond considered the arrogance, cunning, and madness of the original Blofeld – the shadowy figure he had first glimpsed, through reports, who worked behind the cover of *Fraternité Internationale de la Résistance Contre l'Oppression*, in Paris, on the Boulevard Haussmann.

A man of many faces, yes. Disguise, with Blofeld, had been a way of life, and with those various faces came the same sense of purpose: complete ruthlessness and determination.

Bond thought of the known lineage: half Polish, half Greek; born in Gdynia, and a wizard with money. If the new Blofeld was related, then Bond still had scores to settle. The death of his beloved wife, of but a few hours, was already avenged. Ernst Stavro Blofeld had paid the ultimate penalty for that. But now

Bond again made a silent vow: anyone remotely connected with the original Blofeld would also pay. The light of his own happiness had been extinguished without compassion. Why, then, should he show compassion now?

He felt his own fatigue begin to swamp him and he thought of Nena. If anyone commanded compassion, it was this gorgeous lady – undeniably mistreated by her husband and put psychologically off-balance by a deformity which made her feel only part woman. This was nonsense of course, as Bond had proved to her. Poor wretched woman. When this was over, he thought, Nena would need some very special care. A picture of her, naked on his bed, came vividly into his mind, and it was with this image before him that Bond drifted into sleep.

He woke with a start. Noise around him – the babble of conversation. Shaking sleep from him like a dog, Bond stretched his limbs and settled down to listen. Out there a large audience – male and female – was already gathered. He looked at his Rolex, gleaming in the darkness. It was almost nine o'clock.

A minute or so later, the murmur of the audience subsided. Applause took its place, rising to a thunder as Bond heard feet, heavy, on the stage itself; above him.

Slowly the applause diminished. There were some coughs, a clearing of throats, and then a voice – not Bismaquer's as he had expected; but the thin reed of Walter Luxor. There was a difference, though. As Luxor spoke, so the odd high notes altered. The dreadfully disfigured man appeared to find a new confidence, testing his vocal cords until he caught the acoustics of the hall, at which the voice dropped down the scale.

'Ladies and gentlemen. Fellow members of the Executive Council of SPECTRE. World Section Heads of our organisation. Welcome.' Luxor paused. 'As you see, our Leader – Blofeld – is among us, but has asked me to speak to you. It is I who have been at the centre of planning for the operation which, until now, we have spoken of simply as HOUND

'Let us dispense with the preliminaries as quickly as possible.

Time is short. We have known from the outset that, when the moment came, it would come quickly, leaving little time for manoeuvre. That moment is at hand.

'To set your minds at rest, you should first know two things. The very large sum of money earned from those daring, and, I must say, imaginative series of airplane operations, has proved to be ample for our purposes.

'Secondly, we have had a client for the major objective of our present operation for some time now. If all goes well, the profit from HOUND will not only fill SPECTRE's coffers but give each and every member of our organisation a handsome return on investment.'

Bond heard an outbreak of applause, which died as quickly as it began. Then Luxor seemed to be shuffling and rearranging his papers. Bond heard him clear his throat and begin again.

'I do not wish to make this into a marathon briefing. However, there are certain strategic and tactical points which must first be made clear to each of you. This is necessary so that a full understanding of the military and political situations can be grasped.

'The world, as we all know, appears to be permanently on the brink of chaos. There are the usual wars, terrorism, skirmishes and rumours of war. People are afraid. It should be quite plain to us all that many of their fears are fomented, and manipulated, by the military men and politicians of the so-called superpowers.

'We see marches, demonstrations, and pressure groups building, particularly within the powerful Western countries. These action groups are motivated by fear: fear of a nuclear holocaust. So, as we hear and see, people take to the streets in an attempt to halt what they see as a nuclear arms race.

'We, of course – like the great military strategists – know that the whole of a conventional nuclear arms race is a piece of neat misdirection. Agitators, foolish and ill-informed people, see only a nuclear threat.' He gave a tiny, dismissive cackle of laughter. 'What they do not see is that the bogeymen – the neutron bombs, Cruise missiles, intercontinental ballistic missiles – are merely makeshift weapons, temporary means of attack and defence. The same applies to the coast-to-coast tracking systems, and the idiocies that are proclaimed about the airborne early warning systems, such as the AWACS Sentry aircraft. All these things are like slingshots, to be used as stop-gaps until the real armament is unleashed.

'The problem is fear – fear that homes, countries, lives, are at stake. Those who take to the streets and demonstrate can think only in terms of war here, on this planet. They do not see that, in a matter of a very few years now, the ICBMs and the Cruise missiles will be negated, outdated, useless. The so-called arms race is purposely being allowed to dominate the public mind, while the superpowers pursue the real arms race: the race to provide the true weapons of attack and defence – most of which will not be used here on this planet, Earth, at all.'

There was a shuffling among the audience, before Luxor continued.

'What I am telling you is already common knowledge among the world's leading scientists and military experts. The arms race is now *not* directed towards the stockpiling and tactical deployment of nuclear or neutron weapons, though that is exactly what both Soviet and American propaganda would like people to believe.

'No.' Luxor thumped his lectern, sending vibrations through the joists and boards above Bond's head. 'No. The arms race is really concerned with one thing – the perfection of an ultimate weapon which will render all existing nuclear weapons utterly impotent.' Luxor gave his reedy laugh again. 'Yes, ladies and gentlemen, this is the mad scientist's dream, the substance of science fiction for years past. But now the fiction has become *fact*.'

Bond held his breath, already knowing what was to come. Luxor would, he was certain, talk about the ultrasecret Particle Beam Weapon.

'Until recently,' Luxor went on, 'the Soviet Union was undoubtedly ahead in its programme for the development of what is known as a Particle Beam Weapon, a charged particle device, very similar to a laser, combined with microwave propagators. Development of such a weapon is indeed well on the way to finalisation, and this weapon can, and will, act as a shield – an invisible barrier – to ward off any possibility of nuclear attack.

'As I have said, the Particle Beam Weapon was thought to be more advanced in the Soviet Union than in the United States. We now know that *both* superpowers have reached roughly the same point in development. Within a few years – a very few years – the balance of power could swing dramatically in one direction; or become absolute on both sides. For the Particle Beam is designed to effectively neutralise any of the existing nuclear delivery systems.

'The superpowers can escalate millions of Cruise missiles, ICBMs, or rocket-delivered neutron bombs. Much good will it do them. Therefore they are *not* stockpiling these arms. The Particle Beam – once operational – will prevent any country from launching a conventional nuclear attack. Particle Beam means absolute neutralisation. Stalemate. Billions of dollars' worth of scrap metal, sitting in silos all over the globe. If one superpower wins the Particle Beam race, then that power holds the entire world in thrall.

'The arms race hinges on this super weapon of defence; time is at stake, and any nuclear action must be held off until the race is won. In turn, this means we must fully understand what nuclear action really means; and, to see this, we have to look, not at those dreaded missiles and bombs, but at the strategic devices which make their use possible.'

Bond shifted uneasily. He knew that all Luxor was saying made complete sense, even though, for a non-scientist, it did sound like highflown fiction. Bond had the advantage of having already been briefed, along with other Service officers. He had spent hours poring over pages of technical data, and reading long, if simplified, reports on the Particle Beam Weapon. As Luxor said, it *was* a fact, and both the United States and the Soviet Union were now neck and neck in this, the most important arms race in history.

Luxor now started to talk about the current, highly-advanced satellites actually in space, orbiting, or stationary, operational and fully active: that whole series of hardware which made an immediate nuclear confrontation and conflagration possible.

'It is really a question of old military strategy,' he continued. 'History can always teach mankind. The problem is that to learn from history – particularly in military matters – man must adapt. For instance, World War Two began as a failure for the greater part of Europe because the military thinking of the so-called Allies, was based on the strategy of former wars. But the world had changed, and with those changes a new strategy became necessary.

'Now, at this crucial point in history, we have to think, strategically, in a very different environment. An American Senator once said, "He who controls space, controls the world." There is also an old military maxim which says you must always control the high ground. Both these statements are true. Now, the high ground is space; and space controls the nuclear potential of nations until the Particle Beam race is won or lost.

'So, members of SPECTRE, it is our task to provide our present clients with the means to control space until that race is won.'

Luxor continued, giving a great deal of information about the present satellites in use – the reconnaissance satellites: Reconsats and electronic ferrets; Big Bird and Key Hole II; the radar satellites, such as the White Cloud system; the Block 5D-2 military weather satellites which carry banks of solar cells, giving each satellite a greater longevity, plus a broad, and very accurate, coverage of world weather conditions.

Bond's anxiety increased. The facts – simple and incomplete – concerning these satellites, were easily obtainable, but Walter

Luxor showed a knowledge far and above any published data. The information he now passed on to the SPECTRE audience was of the most highly classified variety.

The same turned out to be true when he came to talk about the military communications satellites – the DSCS-2s; DSCS-3s; and the Fltsatcom systems for naval communications. There was also highly confidential material on the SDS – the Satellite Data Systems – which tracked, and monitored, all the hardware of space. The man, Bond could hear, knew exactly what he was talking about; and the bulk of it was considered highly secret, and sensitive, on both sides of the Atlantic.

After about an hour and a half of the session, Luxor announced that they would break for some light refreshment. Bond again heard the footsteps move above him and listened, with ears straining, as the audience left the hall.

For a while, he had thought SPECTRE's plan centred on the United States' progress with the Particle Beam Weapon, but this, he now guessed, was wrong. They were after the satellite systems already in operation. The primary targets in any conventional nuclear war – which would all be changed on the advent of the Particle Beam Weapon – had to be the communications and reconnaissance satellites, for they were the heart of military strength in an age of long-range warfare.

But where would SPECTRE wish to strike? How, and what, would be their target? Slowly, James Bond realised the full implications of HOUND. Of course, HOUND. Why had he not thought of it before? Hound? Wolf? The Space Wolves, as they were called. The United States was well ahead there. SPECTRE's target was the Space Wolves; but, before Bond could follow through this line of thought, there were sounds from the auditorium as people filed back. Then, within minutes, the complete target and plan of action were revealed.

Luxor quickly called the audience to order, and launched into the second part of his briefing in a brisk, concise manner.

'The long preamble during our first session,' he began, 'was necessary for us to come to the heart of our project. The control of space, ladies and gentlemen, means the ability to neutralise the enemy's eyes and ears in space. It has been thought, for a long time now, that the Soviets had a fair, if limited, capability for space control. They were able, in theory, to neutralise United States' satellites within a twenty-four hour time-scale. It was also thought that the United States had no such capability. In the past eighteen months, however, this has proved to be incorrect. The killersats, as they have been called, have now emerged as the current essential weapons. Powerful weapons. That power, my good colleagues, lies totally with the United States.

'It has, of course, been denied that any such satellites are in orbit. But there is no doubt that the United States has at least twenty laser-equipped killersats already in space, disguised as weather satellites. They also have the capability of launching over two hundred of these weapons in a matter of minutes.'

Luxor again paused. Bond felt the anxiety in his throat, and twanging, like a plectrum, at his nerve ends. Once more, he had seen the documentation and knew the truth.

'Our problem,' Luxor continued, 'or, I should say, our client's problem, is that these satellite craft are hidden under one of the most successful security schemes ever mounted by the United States. We know the satellites are laser-armed; that they have a superlative chase capability; and that these facts are held on computer tapes and microfilm – their numbers, place, present orbital patterns, position of silos, order of battle. All this information exists, and is, naturally, required by our clients.

'The full intelligence concerning these killersats is held in the Pentagon. But the Americans have been so careful to isolate each section of information that our two sources inside the Pentagon reported, some months ago, that theft was virtually impossible. In fact we have lost a great deal of time attempting to procure microfilm and other documentation in this manner. Each attempt has led to failure.

'However, there is another way. By the year 1985, these

weapons – known, in military jargon, as Space Wolves – will be controlled and operated through See-Sok, an abbreviation of the lengthy title North American Air Defence Command's Consolidation Space Operations Centre.'

There was polite laughter, which seemed to ease the tension in the hall. Luxor went on to say that See-Sok was already under construction. Vast modifications were being carried out at Peterson Air Force Base, not far from the existing NORAD – North American Defence Command – Headquarters, deep within the Cheyenne Mountains of Colorado.

'And, until See-Sok becomes operational,' Luxor's voice rose to its high pitch again, 'until Peterson Field is converted, the Space Wolves are controlled from NORAD Headquarters, in Cheyenne Mountain. That, fellow members of SPECTRE, is the weak link.

'Because NORAD HQ controls the Space Wolves, all information must be available to the Headquarters. And so it is. Where it has been hidden away, in segments, at the Pentagon, it lies open and collated, on the computer tapes in Cheyenne Mountain.'

It was all true enough, Bond could vouch for that. But the really big question still had to be answered. How did you walk into the well-screened NORAD HQ and lift computer tapes giving every detail of the Space Wolves? Bond had a feeling that, under Blofeld's instructions, Luxor was about to answer the question. At least, Bond thought, he now knew that Blofeld equalled Bismaquer. Luxor was the specialist in many fields, but the final planning would go to SPECTRE's leader: Markus Bismaquer, ice cream maker and squire of Rancho Bismaquer.

'Operation Heavenly Wolf,' Luxor intoned. 'That is the name for project HOUND. Object: to penetrate NORAD Headquarters, and bring out all the computer tapes carrying information on the US Space Wolves.

'Method? We have considered two possibilities, and rejected one, the obvious one: an assault using all SPECTRE's forces. That would be doomed from the start. However, our Leader, Blofeld, has come up with something positively brilliant.'

As Luxor began to explain Operation Heavenly Wolf, many of the dark pieces of the jig-saw fell into place.

'Simplicity,' Luxor maintained, 'is often the answer to all things. Here, at this very ranch, we have been doing two things which have now provided the key to Cheyenne Mountain. First, as you know, we have an ice cream manufacturing plant on the premises. We have also made many contacts, including distributors of foodstuffs to military bases. One such is the sole distributor to NORAD Headquarters.'

Luxor paused. Bond could almost see him smiling that ghastly gaping grin.

'Ladies and gentlemen, we have just sent that distributor four days' supply of ice cream. Apparently they consume a great deal of ice cream at NORAD – it must be the atmosphere within the mountain, and those long hours spent underground. We are told that over 90 per cent of the staff and technicians eat ice cream regularly.

'The very large consignment which we have just conveyed is not, however, a normal brand. We have also developed the ultimate in happiness – a mild narcotic, harmless and with no side effects. It produces a state of euphoria and well-being, an ability to operate normally but with a suspended moral sense of right or wrong. Anyone taking even a minimum dosage will obey, without question, the orders of a superior. He, or she, would even kill his best friend, or most loved wife or husband.'

Bond nodded to himself, thinking of the two men he had seen in the padded cell off the laboratory.

'What is more,' Luxor sounded highly pleased with himself, 'our most recent tests have proved that the effects of our happy cream last up to twelve hours. Tomorrow, at around noon, the shipment will go into Cheyenne Mountain. We are reliably informed that distribution will start tomorrow night. This means that Operation Heavenly Wolf begins after lunch on the day after tomorrow. We simply go in, ask for the Space Wolves computer tapes, and they will give them to us. They will also smile happily while they commit this gross act of treason.'

'Is it really as simple as that?' a voice called from the audience.

'Not quite.' Luxor's voice generated confidence. 'Naturally, there will be some officers, technicians, and enlisted men, who will spurn our dessert. Ten per cent, according to our latest information. We may well, therefore, encounter some slight unpleasantness. Also, you must remember, the drug works only if commands are given by somebody with authority and seniority. Therefore, we plan to give NORAD HQ a surprise inspection by a four-star general. In fact it will be the new Inspector-General of Air/Space Defence. I've arranged for the officer commanding NORAD HQ to be warned of his arrival roughly an hour before he makes an entrance – together with, say, twenty or thirty aides and military personnel. All will be armed, of course, and ready to handle the unlucky few who reject our ice cream. A sad prospect, I admit, to die for not liking such a delicious dessert.'

There were chuckles around the room, and one voice asked who was to wear the lucky four stars?

There followed a terrible silence. It was as though the questioner suddenly realised he had, in his jesting way, put his foot in it – making a most ghastly error by even asking.

Bismaquer, Bond thought – Blofeld himself – would be the four-star general. Nobody else would do. Then came Luxor's voice, chilling, like ice in the gullet.

'We have someone very special in mind for that job,' he rasped. 'Someone *very* special indeed. Poor fellow. I'm afraid he will not survive the ordeal. Now, we must decide on schedules, times, weapons and escape routes. Can I have the map, please?'

It was almost noon. In twelve hours, Bond thought, Cedar would be at the roadside tunnel entrance with the Saab. If her luck held. Meanwhile, Bond had twelve hours to remain hidden, listening under the stage, sorting the facts in his mind. Then, once the hall emptied, he must find somewhere to wait until he could safely negotiate the trek back down the tunnel. After that, assuming Cedar was on time, they would either have to fight their way out or find some way for Bond to draw the fire, priming Cedar with the bare information so that she could get help.

In any case, one of them had to make it. Until the real arms race for the Particle Beam Weapon was won or lost, the United States – possibly all the Western powers – needed the Space Wolf satellites, for they gave the real edge over any aggressor.

In the middle of the tension induced by these thoughts, 007 recognised a chilling prospect: the one person in all the West who might yet be able to avert disaster was James Bond.

18

SHOCK TACTICS

Bond had looked forward to emerging from the tunnel into a deep velvet blue night, with stars like diamonds. In fact, he came out through the roadside opening into a steambath of hot air, with the sky at war. Far away, great sheets of lightning sizzled and cracked, while distant thunder rolled – as though heaven had taken a pre-emptive strike into its own hands.

He drew a deep breath, hoping for fresh air and inhaled only the cloying damp scents of the jungle area. Muttering belligerently, Bond operated the lever, restoring the slab of stone to its proper place.

Hidden for so long under the conference hall stage, Bond had been forced to remain still and silent, breathing stale air, for the better part of nine hours. Now, he felt in need of a shower and, not least, a change of clothes.

The day's work had finally came to an end late in the afternoon, and, when the coast appeared to be clear, Bond had crept out – his head now crammed with details of Operation Heavenly Wolf: locations, method of transport, weapons, RV points, contingency plans. Now he had everything there was to know about the great, and dangerous, confidence trick to be played out at NORAD HQ in Cheyenne Mountain – everything except the vital role: who was to play the four-star general, the Inspector-General of US Air/Space Defence.

The hall was empty, and the urgency of Bond's mission preyed on his mind. The Space Wolves were, certainly, the most important link in the current Western defence system. Alone, they could hold off the threat of any nuclear conflagration. Any crucial emergency would bring the Space Wolves into play, as they roamed high above the world – a cover for all continents. Every NATO power was secretly alert to the situation, as well as to the capability of other Space Wolves, ready to be hurled into orbit, with their chase tracks controlled and monitored from the operations rooms deep within Cheyenne Mountain, Colorado.

Bond had known of the plan to change the operational control centre, but it made sense. Nobody had any doubts – within the secret corridors of power – that the next few years, before the perfection of the Particle Beam System, were as crucial to the world as those which had passed when the early cannon took over from the siege catapult and ballista.

In hiding by the roadside – eyes straining for any sign of the Saab and Cedar – Bond thought of the moves now being made: of the refrigerated trucks ready to take the deadly cargo of innocent-seeming ice cream into NORAD HQ, and of the Space Wolves themselves, circling the earth.

It was almost midnight, and still no sign of Cedar. Bond's agitation grew as he crouched close to the jungle edge. Then, at around ten minutes after midnight, he heard the growl of the Saab: the sidelights coming fast, from the direction of the wooded knoll.

Cedar's face showed the same kind of strain which Bond felt. Her eyes were red-rimmed, her reactions fast, nervous, and jumpy. Like Bond, she was dressed in dark jeans and a sweater. As he leaped for the Saab's door, Bond saw she had the revolver ready near the gear lever, easily within reach.

'They're looking for us. Everywhere,' she gasped. 'Do I go on driving?'

Bond told her to carry on and head for the mono-rail depot.

'It's no good saying that,' her voice cracked. 'They've got most of the roads blocked, and there are guards at the station.'

Bond unholstered the big automatic pistol. 'Then we'll just

have to blast our way out. If you spot roadblocks, turn away. They can't cover everything. If we have to shoot our way on to that mono-rail and then deal with the terrible twins at the other end, so be it. I've got the hottest information since the warnings about Pearl Harbor – only they'll listen this time. Look, I've got to share it with you, Cedar, in case only one of us gets out.'

He began to talk, giving her the bare, but most important facts. When he was done, Cedar repeated what Bond had told her, adding, 'Let's both try and make it, though, James. I don't feature doing it alone.'

She kept to side roads, sometimes slewing off tracks and roads, punishing the Saab on grass and rutted ground. Soon they were in sight of Tara. Great banks of floodlights were turned on all around the area, while the distant flashes of sheet lightning seemed to be slowly coming nearer. Even in the car they could hear the heavy, approaching thunder of the storm.

It was, in the end, the storm which helped them. Like most desert weather, the change was both extreme and spectacular. As they kept close to the boundary walls with their screens of trees, the thunder and lightning swept in on a raging wind – a massive thunderhead, like an anvil, hanging directly over Rancho Bismaquer. In its wake came torrential rain.

They could hardly see through the windscreen, even with the wipers going full speed; but the storm appeared to have driven the watchful guards to cover. Sitting it out, about half a mile from the mono-rail depot, Bond waited for the first break as rain lashed against them, buffeting the car like rifle fire on the armour plating.

Cedar said that, as far as she knew, the mono-rail was in place. 'They had some plan to take cars out early in the morning,' she told him, explaining that her own escape had been made more difficult by the advent of more men, and guards, at the house.

'In the end I screwed up my courage and went for a walk. Markus saw me and asked what I was doing. I just told him I needed some air. I took off like a jack rabbit after that. Haven't run so fast since I was a sophomore in college and the captain of the football team dated me.'

'Did he catch you?' Bond asked.

'Of course, James. I slowed down after a while. Why not? He was cute.'

At this point in the conversation, the rain appeared to ease slightly.

'This is it.' Bond spoke quickly, giving her instructions. 'Drive like the devil. Don't worry about any shooting; we can't be hurt in here. As long as you can see through the rain, go straight for the mono-rail ramp and drive right in.'

'Do you know how to run a mono-rail?' Cedar shouted, as they took off.

Bond said there was always a first time for everything.

They got within a couple of hundred yards of the rail depot without being spotted. Then, some security guard must have glimpsed them through the rain.

Bond saw the car pull out behind them, then lost it again as a squall drove a great wet shower between the two cars. Then another appeared, from the right, just as they were racing alongside the depot, Cedar's head pushed forward, almost on the windscreen, as she searched for the ramp.

The two sets of headlights – behind, and to the right – appeared and disappeared through the rain. Then the Saab rocked as a bullet struck the armour on Bond's side. Another two squashed into the thick, impenetrable, toughened glass of the driver's window.

But the weather saved them. The rain, which had eased for a moment, suddenly turned on a last downpour, as though giant buckets were being emptied from the skies.

'There,' Cedar shouted, realising they were practically alongside the ramp and overshooting it. Grimly peering through the windscreen, she backed up, changed into first, and smoothly set the Saab's wheels on the covered way leading to the mono-rail.

Bond wondered if the chase cars would find their way through the shield of rain, or even if they realised where the Saab was heading. Cedar had the headlights on now in the dark tunnel, and there appeared to be no one behind them.

A minute later, the Saab's lights picked up the big metal sliding doors, and they bounced into the transporter van, coming to a standstill right in place on the restraining rails.

Bond shouted for Cedar to get the doors closed as he sprang from the Saab, praying that the entrance to the driver's cabin was not locked. As he passed through into the cab, he heard the satisfying thud of the doors closing. Now it was a matter of using common sense and sorting out the controls.

The rain still lashed down, driving against the big windows of the cabin. A small fixed seat perched in front of a flat bank of levers and instruments. To Bond's relief, they all appeared to be marked. A red button, with two switches below it, was designated as Turbine: On/Off. He tripped the switches and pressed the button as he scanned the other controls. The throttle was a metal arm which swept in a half-circle across spaced terminals. The braking mechanism was near his feet, with a secondary device to the right of the throttle. He found the speed indicator, the windscreen wipers, the lights, and a series of buttons marked Doors: Automatic. Close/Open.

Pressing the red button brought a comforting throbbing whine as the turbine turned over. Bond slammed down all the automatic door buttons on the Close circuit, switched on the wipers and lights, released the brakes, and tentatively moved the throttle arm.

He did not expect such a sudden reaction. The train jerked, took the strain, then moved with oiled smoothness from the depot. Cedar was at his elbow now, peering out of the big forward windows, trying to see the track through the rain as the big headlight cut into the downpour.

Bond increased the power, then up another notch, watching the speed gauge rise to seventy miles per hour. At eighty, they seemed to be clearing the storm. It was dying away as fast as it had come, for the rain was now only a slight drizzle, and the long single track became visible in the bright cutting cone of light which arrowed from the train's nose.

On either side, the protective, electrified fencing rose intimid-atingly, prompting Cedar to ask what they would do at the far end.

'They'll be ready and waiting. Shotguns, the electrified fences, everything. Worry when we get there.'

Again Bond increased the power and then wondered aloud if the train could stand the shock of going right through the far station. 'If we were in the car there'd be protection.'

'Not if the whole thing capsized,' Cedar said. 'You'd telescope us all, James. There're bound to be bumpers at the other end.'

'And they'll be waiting,' Bond reflected.

The mono-rail sliced on, speed rising, as though they were floating on a soft cushion of air. There was no vibration, and now that the rain had cleared they had perfect forward vision.

Bond thought for a few moments. They had been travelling for roughly ten minutes. Gently he eased back on the throttle, then told Cedar to get her revolver and the Nitefinder glasses from the Saab.

While she was gone, he eased back even more on the throttle, feeling the train slowing in a gentle vibration.

'I'm going to switch the main lights off in a minute,' he told Cedar when she got back. 'There's only one way to do this. Use the Nitefinders, and stop well short. You'll hold the fort here while I go in: up the track.'

It was pitch black outside, beyond the beam of the great spotlight. In the far distance, the storm raged on and an occa-sional great sheet of lightning flared and faded.

Bond strapped on the glasses, took out the VP70, placed it on the instrument shelf, and continued to slow the turbine. Then he switched off the lights.

Now they slid along, slowly, in complete darkness. Cedar stood by Bond, one hand resting on his arm as he looked out through the Nitefinders. The track curved slightly, and he would have to judge how far they were from the desert depot. About a mile, he thought, bringing down the throttle another notch, then cutting it altogether and gently applying the brakes.

The driver's cabin had its own sliding door which would, presumably, unlock when the other doors were set to Automatic/Open. There should also be rungs from the cab that would take him down for part of the way at least. After that, it would be a long drop.

With his usual economy, Bond told Cedar exactly what he proposed. 'I have night eyes with these things,' touching the Nitefinders: 'After I've unlocked the doors, the turbine has to be switched off, and you'll be left alone here while I go quietly up the track.'

'James, be careful of those protective fences.' Cedar's voice betrayed her state of mind.

'Don't worry about that. Nothing'll concentrate my mind so well as that damned fence.'

In the darkness, Bond watched through the glasses for any movement in front of the train.

'If they're waiting – and I've no doubt they will be – I should imagine the Brothers Grimm will be intrigued by the fact that we've stopped short, and with no lights. If I'm lucky, at least one of them'll come looking, which is what I need. Once I've dealt with them, switched off the current and opened the gates, I'll be back fast. Your job is to stay here and kill – I mean *kill* – anyone who attempts to board. I'm the only one that you let back into this contraption. Okay?'

She agreed, with a very firm 'Yes'.

Bond activated the automatic door buttons and turned off the turbine. As he had hoped, the cabin door slid open easily. He peered down, spotting the rungs leading to the underside of the cabin.

'Okay, Cedar. Be as quick as possible.'

Adjusting the Nitefinders to their maximum brightness and

range, Bond swung himself from the cabin and started to descend.

At the bottom of the train itself, he paused, craning his neck to see along the track. He estimated the drop to be around fifteen feet. There was a good twelve feet between the great concrete pillars that held the track and the electrified fence.

Grasping the bottom rung, Bond allowed his body to fall free. He dangled in mid-air, swinging slightly, until he had controlled the oscillation of his body, then glanced down into the blur below, positioned himself and let go. The ground was flat and firm. Bond landed neatly, knees bent, not even staggering or rolling. As his feet touched the earth, so the automatic came out, and he froze, still and silent, peering through the goggles, ears straining.

The night seemed unnaturally quiet, and there was that particular clear, sweet smell of the desert after rain. No movement ahead. Holding the pistol against his thigh, Bond started forward, keeping close to the high, pillared concrete track supports, and noting, with some relief, that there were rungs – for maintenance he supposed – on every third pillar.

Every now and then Bond stopped, to listen and take a longer look. Despite being a big man, he could walk with that silent, stalking manner of a cat. Within ten minutes, the desert depot was clearly visible ahead.

They had turned the lights off, to make the train's approach difficult, and there was definitely movement ahead of him now. One tall figure slowly walked towards him, staying close to the pillars. The man carried a shotgun, not under his arm but at the ready, held professionally away from the body, the butt a few inches from the shoulder and the barrel pointing downwards.

Bond sidestepped, flattening behind a pillar. Soon the approaching man was clearly audible – an expert, Bond judged, for the sound came only from the man's low, controlled breathing.

The hunter must have instinctively sensed danger. About a

foot from Bond's pillar, he stopped, listening and turning. Then Bond saw the barrel of the shotgun come into view.

He waited until the man cleared the pillar before making a move – quick as a cobra, and just as deadly. Bond's heavy automatic was balanced firmly in the right hand. His arm came back, then shot forward with all the force that 007 could muster. As the punch came out of the darkness, the hunter sensed activity. Not soon enough, Bond's wrist turned so that the full force of the punch lay behind the barrel of the VP70 – the arm fully extended at the point of impact, which landed on target, just below the man's right ear.

There was a sudden hiss as the victim expelled air from his lungs, then a ghost of a groan before he fell backwards. Bond grabbed out at the unconscious man, but it was too late. The tightly-meshed protective fence danced with a flash of blue fire which, in turn, played around the man's body as he fell against the heavy wires, jerking and kicking as the massive voltage poured through him.

The smell of burning and singed flesh floated into Bond's nostrils, almost making him retch. But in a moment, it was over and the depot guard lay still, thrown away from the fencing, his gun – a Winchester pump – almost between Bond's feet on the earth.

Even through the Nitefinder glasses, the flash from the electrified fence left traces of light floating in Bond's vision. All thought of surprise had gone. Blinking to clear his eyes, Bond dropped to one knee, picked up the Winchester and replaced his automatic in its holster.

The pump-action Winchester was loaded and ready. As his hands touched the weapon, Bond heard a cry less than fifty yards up the track.

'Brother? You okay, brother? You git him?'

The other guard, twin giant to the dead man, was thumping along the little path between pillars and fence, flushed out by the flash and noise. Bond lifted the Winchester, holding the oncoming figure in the centre of the barrel, and called out, 'Stay where you are. Drop the gun. Your brother's had it. Stop now.'

The man did stop, but only to aim his own Winchester in the general direction of Bond's voice. Before the first shots came, Bond ducked behind the pillar, coming out at the other side and lining up the shotgun again.

The man charged on, firing at random, hoping, in rage, for a lucky shot. Bond fired once, low and accurate. The target's legs seemed to be pulled back from under him, the force of the shot dragging the whole body face down. There was a long shriek of pain, followed by a whimper; then silence.

Gently, Bond searched the body of the electrocuted guard. No sign of keys there, so he walked forward gingerly, not knowing what reinforcements Bismaquer might have ordered to man the desert depot.

The other guard was unconscious but would live. His legs, peppered with shot, bled badly, but there was no jetting from severed arteries.

Bond went over him thoroughly. No keys either. The guards, he decided, must have been caught off-balance and left the keys in their little blockhouse, which also controlled the electric protective fencing. It was either that, or there were others waiting, ready to trap Bond and Cedar.

He took his time approaching the end of the line, repumping the Winchester, crabbing sideways on, towards the low buildings.

Silence. Not a movement, as Bond reached the platforms, where the big motor ramp extended, ready to meet the monorail.

He stayed close to the buildings, well in the darkness, watching.

Nothing.

At last, Bond broke cover, walking quickly to the blockhouse, where lights still burned. It was deserted. There seemed to be no sign of life anywhere inside the fence or out on the desert track.

The keys lay on a table near the big fuse boxes and main switches that controlled the fences. In less than a minute, Bond had thrown the master switch, picked up the keys and – after hurling the Winchester at the fence to make certain it was no longer live with electricity – unlocked the main gates, pulling them back fully so that they could drive the Saab straight off the train and through.

If luck held, they would be in Amarillo and telephoning the people who mattered within an hour.

He ran, fast, all the way back. The injured guard was still not conscious but had begun to groan. His brother lay silent, reeking of burned clothing and flesh.

At last, Bond saw the train, ahead and above him. Its great curved sides hung over the edge of the platform, supported by the pillars. Without pausing, Bond swarmed up the nearest metal rungs. There was a space on the platform, about three or four feet of stressed steel with concrete overlay between the edge of the pillar and the big rail.

Standing upright, Bond crabbed his way along this catwalk until the front of the train towered over him. With just room to kneel, he could see around the long drooping side of the monorail. The cab door was still open, its rungs leading down to the point below him where he had swung and dropped before.

Now, the cab's rungs were just out of reach. Straightening up, Bond shuffled back a couple of steps, then leaned forward with his hands close together, as far to the left of the train's metal front as he could get without slipping.

The angle of his body was obviously too steep, so he gently edged his feet forward, flexing the knees, his eyes not leaving the line of rings – elongated D shapes – coming down from the cabin. If he let his hands slide now, Bond would simply fall headlong from the platform holding rail and train.

He needed a little more agility this time. Once his hands released their grip on the smooth metal, he would have to spring, trying to leap towards the cabin rungs, grabbing as he went in the hope of maintaining a firm hold.

A deep breath, flexed knees again, then a hard push away from the platform, using all his skill to place the weight of his body forward, near to the train's side. One hand touched a rung, one palm – but not quite firmly enough. He was falling, arms flailing and hands snatching at the rungs as they streaked by him. It only took a second, but the fall gave the impression of suspended time. Then his whole body jarred – an arm almost wrenched from its socket – as his left hand closed around the penultimate rung.

Bond remained swinging by one arm for a second or two, until at last he had a firm grip with both hands. He waited another second to catch his breath, and then began a steady ascent.

As his face came level with the cab door, Bond called out: 'It's okay, Cedar, I'm back. We're on our way.' He hoisted himself into the cab, a trifle breathless.

Cedar was not in the cabin. Nor did she answer when he called to her again.

Bond leaped towards the control panel, to activate the light switches. The whole train lit up, and as it did so, the cabin door slammed closed inexplicably. He reached across, hauling on the manual handle, but without result.

Turning, Bond once more called for Cedar. He had the pistol out again as he made his way back into the vehicle compartment. The Saab stood as they had left it. But still no trace of Cedar. Then, as he stood there, the door to the cabin – and the one at the far end – slammed shut.

'Cedar?' Bond yelled. 'Where are you? Have those bastards got you?'

A disembodied voice answered, making his flesh crawl. 'Oh yes, Mr Bond. Mrs Penbrunner will not get away any more than you. Why not relax, Mr Bond? Relax and have a rest.'

It was the voice of Walter Luxor, thin and strangled, from a loudspeaker system. It took Bond a few seconds to recognise the other phenomenon – an odour in the air, oddly pleasant but stinging to the nostrils. Then he saw the faint cloud, like thin smoke, rising from tiny grilles in the floor: gas; some form of gas; and he understood.

In an almost detached way, Bond became aware that he was functioning more slowly. His brain took longer to make decisions. Oxygen. Yes, that was it. He had oxygen. In the car: the oxygen kit which slid out from under the passenger seat.

Now he was moving in slow motion, his brain repeating 'Oxygen . . . Oxygen . . .' over and over again.

Bond's hand reached out for the Saab's door, wrenching it open, his body swerving, turning towards the interior. Then he felt himself sliding, going down a long gentle slope, a chute, which descended into greyness, growing darker and darker, until he seemed to hurtle into space and the world turned black, while all knowledge was blotted out.

19

FOUR-STAR GENERAL

There was one tiny moment, on regaining consciousness, when James Bond knew who he was: James Bond, a field agent for the SIS, holding the special double-O prefix. Number 007.

The knowledge lasted for a second or two and was accompanied by the sensation of floating in warm, pleasant water, as though suspended. He also heard a voice saying something about Haloperidol. He recognised the name – a drug, a tranquilliser, hypnotic in action. Then came the tiny prick, as a needle slid home. James Bond ceased to exist.

Lord, what time was it? He had been dreaming. Vivid dreams, nightmares almost, about his time at the academy. There were voices in the dream. Mum and Dad, God rest their souls. Friends, training, then his first appointment after he was commissioned.

General James A. Banker fumbled on the night table for his digital watch. Three in the morning. Shouldn't have had that last whiskey. Must give it up. Since the new promotion there had been too many nights like this.

He flopped back on to the pillows, sweating, and immediately fell asleep again.

Watching, through the infra-red glass, Walter Luxor turned to Blofeld. 'Going well,' he squeaked. 'There's plenty of time. I'll give him some war experience now.' He pulled the microphone towards him, and began to speak, quietly, soothingly.

Below them was a bedroom, very military in décor: an on-base senior officer's room, functional, with only a few personal photographs and mementos to break its austerity.

In the deep hypnotic sleep, General James A. Banker was not really aware of the whispering voice coming close to his ears, from the pillow.

'Now, General,' the voice said, 'you know exactly who you are. You know, and remember, things about your childhood, your training, and your rise through the service. I shall tell you more about that rise now. More about your active service; and a lot more about your present job.' The voice launched into a long, vivid description of the General's work up to the time of Vietnam, then of his special duties during that war. There were acts of bravery; fear; desperate times and the deaths of friends. Some of the incidents were almost entirely relived, complete with sound effects: the sound of weapons and other people speaking.

General James A. Banker muttered in his sleep, turned, then woke again. Lord, he felt terrible; and he had a job to do in the morning. Pretty important. He'd had more dreams. He could recall them as clearly as he knew his wife Adelle. Nam: he'd been dreaming about all the guts and blood and hell in Nam.

He desperately wanted to call Adelle, but she was off into dreamland as soon as her head touched the pillow. Adelle got kind of huffy with him if he called in the middle of the night.

The General wondered how long it would be before he found the right house for her. Was it this weekend she was coming down to have another look? He hoped he felt better than this by morning, otherwise he'd walk through that inspection like a zombie. Sleep. Must get more sleep. Another look at his watch. It was only four o'clock. Too early to get up. He'd try and grab a little more shut-eye.

Gently, the General slid back into his jumbled dreams, and just as gently Walter Luxor, in the window overlooking the bedroom, started to talk again.

He had only done this once before, and then he had more

time. Putting a hand over the microphone he said to Bismaquer, 'Not bad, you know. He really believes, deep down inside, that he is a four-star general. Very good for twenty-four hours' work. I'll reinforce it now.' As Luxor spoke, the door to the bedroom below opened, and the large figure of Mike Mazzard appeared. Looking up at the unseen hiding place, and making a twirling motion, Mazzard tiptoed towards the bed, picked up the clock and altered it, as he had been instructed.

Luxor began to talk again. He too felt tired. Usually, he knew, the technique took a lot longer than twenty-four hours, but as the subject only had to alter personality for a relatively short time, he was convinced it could be done with complete success.

They had started almost as soon as Bond had been brought back to the ranch. Injections of Haloperidol and other hypnotics; followed by short in-and-out sessions of audio-hypnotic implant, first to give the subject complete disorientation, then to put him back together – with new memories and a new identity.

The technique entailed small, frequent doses – implanting ideas and memories which would, they knew, be rejected within a day after the subject was brought around. But a day was long enough.

Bond had been a thorn from the start. Someone who had to be isolated and destroyed as quickly – and, if possible, naturally – as convenient. So Blofeld had first instructed. But Blofeld's mind could change, and with that flexibility, that mercurial brilliance, came great ideas.

Originally they had planned for another candidate to play the general. Indeed, Luxor had practised this very technique on the man in question, right to the breaking point. The FBI man had died as a result.

Then Blofeld had picked on Bond, having lured SPECTRE's old enemy to Texas and put him off balance, watching his every move. Now, with the minutes ticking away and a very definite need for the new general to have at least three hours' peaceful sleep, Luxor realised the wonderful irony of the whole scheme. Bond, as the general, would perish in Cheyenne Mountain, and many people would be highly embarrassed.

Luxor talked on for another fifteen minutes, then switched off the microphones. 'That's as far as I dare go. He'll be a little disoriented, but that'll be put down to a hard night's drinking. I've implanted that most firmly. At least you've got your four-star general. I would suggest, Blofeld, that you brief Mazzard personally. That man down there must die in the mountain, preferably while he still believes he is General James A. Banker.'

Blofeld smiled. 'The irony is complete. I'll see to it. Close down now, and let him sleep.'

General Banker at last got some rest. The dreams had gone, and he slept the sleep of the just. It was only as he became fully awake that he had another kind of dream, oddly erotic, about a woman with only one breast. He even thought she was leaning over him. At some point there was a voice too, though he could not make out if it was male or female. 'James,' the voice said, 'my dear James. Take these pills. Here . . .' A hand cradled his head, lifting, and he felt something in his mouth, then a glass to his lips. He was very thirsty and drank what was offered, without resistance. 'They'll take a few hours to work,' the voice said, 'but when they do, you'll be your proper self again. God help you; and God help me for doing this.'

When he was dragged fully out of sleep, by a sergeant serving his usual steaming black, sweet coffee, it was the only dream the General could remember. He was conscious that he had not slept well, but that was the wretched party last night.

His mouth felt terrible, his stomach queasy; but at least he was well enough to do his job.

The General shaved, showered, and began to dress. Sometimes, James, he thought. I don't recognise you in this outfit. It was always amazing, for the General, to think he had come so far in the Service. But here he was, a four-star general, with plenty of combat experience, a beautiful wife, and an exacting job. To be Inspector-General, US Air/ Space Defence, was quite something.

The tap at his door heralded the usual appearance of his adjutant, Major Mike Mazzard, who entered quietly to the General's call, saluting as he always did.

'Good morning, General. How're things today?'

'Terrible, Mike. I feel like I've been dragged through several swamps, infected with swine fever, and swallowed something out of the latrine.'

Mazzard laughed. 'With respect, General, you've only yourself to blame. That party was really too much.'

The General nodded. 'I know, I know. Don't tell me – and for heaven's sake don't tell my wife. I'm going to have to cut down, Mike.'

'You want breakfast, sir? We can . . .'

'Perish the thought, Mike. Perish the thought. Another good slug of coffee would help . . .'

'I'll fix it, sir. In here?'

'Why not? Then we can go through today's arrangements without interruption. I'm afraid you're going to have to carry me through most of it.'

'Tut-tut, General. A good Bostonian like you.' Mazzard paused by the door. 'You know something funny, sir?'

'You think I should hear it?'

'Well, it's the Boston thing again. I heard one of the other officers talking. He said you were true blue Boston, and anyone could tell that by the way you spoke . . .'

'Yes?'

'The funny thing, sir, was that he said, "Put General Banker in one of those bowler hats and a pinstripe, then give him an umbrella, and you'd think he'd walked straight out of a British bank." '

The General nodded. 'I get it all the time, Mike. Had a British journalist in Nam take me for one of their own. I'm not ashamed of it, though.' He put on a sly smirk. 'You want I should take lessons? Learn to say boid, and absoid, like in Brooklyn?'

Mazzard grinned back and went out for more coffee.

Outside the room, Luxor waited. 'Well?'

'Amazing.' Mazzard shook his head. 'I wouldn't have believed it. Will it last?'

'Long enough, *Major* Mazzard. Long enough. You have your orders from Blofeld?'

'I'll do it personally, and with pleasure. Don't worry. Now, what about the General's coffee?'

About two hours earlier, a young Captain who worked in the Pentagon's Space Intelligence Department had come on duty early. The skeleton night staff were still around but nobody took much notice of the Captain. He was known as an eager beaver.

At this time in the morning, however, the main communications teletype machine – personal to his superior officer, the General in charge of Air and Space Defence Administration – was not in use. The young Captain held a set of keys, not only to his General's office but also to the teletype machine.

The little suite of offices was empty when the Captain let himself in, quietly locking the door behind him. He then unlocked the teletype and began to transmit.

The first message was to the Officer Commanding Movements, US Air Force Base, Peterson Field, Colorado. The text read:

BE PREPARED ONE SMALL ARMED CONTINGENT CONSISTING APPROX TWO OFFICERS FOUR SERGEANTS AND THIRTY ENLISTED MEN AT AIR SPACE ADMIN STAFF ARRIVE BY ROAD THIS MORNING STOP TWO GENERAL JAMES A BANKER INSPECTOR AIR SPACE DEFENSE ARRIVE BY HELICOPTER FLIGHT CLEARANCE FOUR-ONE-TWO TO RV WITH THIS GROUP AND PROCEED NORAD HQ STOP REQUEST YOU

AFFORD ALL COURTESIES AND ASSISTANCE STOP ACKNOW-
LEDGE AND DESTROY STOP

He signed the communication in the name and rank of his
superior.

Within ten minutes the acknowledge and wilco signal came
back.

The second message was addressed to the Officer Commanding NORAD HQ, Cheyenne Mountain, Colorado. It read:

AS FAVOR I ADVISE YOU MY INSPECTOR-GENERAL – GEN-
ERAL JAMES A BANKER – WILL VISIT YOU TODAY FOR NON-
SCHEDULED INSPECTION STOP PLEASE GIVE HIM EVERY
COURTESY STOP DO NOT REPEAT NOR INFORM HIM OF
THIS PREVIOUS WARNING STOP ACKNOWLEDGE AND DES-
TROY STOP

This was also signed with the Captain's superior's name and
rank. The acknowledge and wilco signal came back with one
rider:

REGRET OFFICER COMMANDING ON LEAVE FOR ONE DAY
THIS DAY STOP I SHALL PERSONALLY SEE ALL IS IN ORDER
STOP

It was signed by a Colonel as acting commanding officer. The
Captain smiled, shredded all his copies, then picked up the
telephone to dial a number with a Texas prefix. When the
number answered he asked if Captain Blake was there.

'I'm sorry, sir, I think you have a wrong number.' The voice on
the line was thin, reedy, with a slight squeak.

'I'm sorry as well, but no harm's done, sir. I must have mis-
dialled. I hope I haven't disturbed you.'

'Not at all,' replied Walter Luxor. 'Goodbye, sir.' General
Banker and his adjutant, Major Mike Mazzard, walked out of

the officers' mess, receiving smart salutes from the two private soldiers on guard duty. They had been greeted by a number of other officers as they left. At least two of them had remarked to the General: 'Quite a party last night, Sir.'

'And I'm getting quite a reputation,' the General grunted. 'Nothing tonight, Mike, see to it. Early night. All right?'

'As you say, sir.'

The Kiowa helicopter was already sitting on the pad in front of the officers' mess, its rotor turning idly.

'Oh no,' the General groaned. 'We doing the whole trip in that, Mike?'

'I'm afraid so, sir.'

'Well, I just hope the flying weather's good. I don't think I'm well enough to stand too much bumping around today.'

'Weather report's excellent, sir.'

They had sat together over a large jug of coffee while the General's adjutant went over the day's schedule.

'Fly direct from here to Peterson Air Base, where there should be two trucks with around thirty enlisted men, some NCOs, and a couple of officers – Captain Luxor and another one. They'll be there for show, unless you decide the main security of the NORAD Combat Operations Centre needs testing. Your car and the driver'll be waiting as well, sir.'

'Good. And we go straight to Cheyenne Mountain?'

'We go to the Number Two Entrance. That is the best way, takes us straight to the main command post levels. You said in your memo that the object was to test readiness and examine the command post structure. That was the priority.'

'Yes, I seem to remember . . .'

'. . . that we were going to pull a fast one?' Mazzard finished for him. 'That's right. The Space Wolf question.'

The General frowned. 'The memory's going, Mike. Yes, wasn't I going to ask them point blank to hand over the computer tapes to me for personal keeping?'

'That was the idea. There's a regulation regarding the SW

tapes. They're closed, restricted, and on the Most Secret list. Nobody down there has the right to hand them over, or even let you see them. The idea was to test reaction to an order from a very senior officer.'

'Okay, we'll see if it works.' They were still talking about it as the General swung himself into the Kiowa helicopter, greeted the pilot and strapped himself in. Mazzard climbed aboard, after the General, and took the seat next to him.

A few moments later, the rotor turned, and the small chopper lifted off, nose down, circling, then climbing – heading north-west towards Colorado.

20

CHEYENNE MOUNTAIN

The General dozed a little during the flight and seemed less hung over by the time the pilot turned in his seat, pointing down. They were high in the clear, endless blue skies over Colorado. In the distance the mountain peaks reached up: serrated and sharp jags of rock.

A few minutes later they descended towards Peterson Field and the General's waiting convoy. Mazzard helped General Banker from the helicopter, asking if he wanted to inspect the men who were drawn up in front of their vehicles. The General took a perfunctory look, nodded and walked over, to be greeted by a painfully thin Captain whose face looked like a skull.

'Captain Luxor, sir.' The officer saluted, and led the General along the ranks.

'Did I meet you before, Captain?' The General stared hard at Luxor.

'No, sir.'

As they went towards the staff car, with Luxor just out of ear-shot, General Banker muttered to Mazzard, 'That Captain. I'm sure I've seen him before, Mike.'

'You saw his picture, General.' The Major spoke in an equally low voice. 'In all the papers. Some hot-shot plastic surgeon did one hell of a job on him. Poor guy had his face burned off in Nam.'

'Bastards,' spat the General.

The convoy was impressive: two motorcycle outriders, followed by an M113 Armoured Personnel Carrier, fully loaded with its two-man crew and section of combat troops, the heavy 12.7mm Browning manned at its curved swivel mounting.

General Banker's staff car rode behind the 113, while another APC boxed the car in from the rear.

The staff car driver was not known to the General, who thought the man had probably been built from the leftovers of the Mount Rushmore carvings. Certainly his sergeant's uniform appeared to be very tight on him, but he drove smoothly enough and showed all the correct courtesies. The General would have preferred his own regular driver, whose name eluded him at this moment.

Major Mazzard sat in the rear with the General, while the hideously scarred Captain took his seat up front, next to the driver. The small convoy moved slowly away from the helipad towards the main gates of Peterson Field, the General's pennant bright and flying from the offside wing matched, on the other side, by the stars and stripes.

The barriers were raised without question, the guard turning out to present arms as the staff car swept through, while other officers and enlisted men came to attention, saluting as befitted the exalted rank of a four-star general.

Within the hour they were travelling at a steady rate through the foothills, on restricted military roads. The area was well-policed by both air force and army, but nobody made any attempt to stop them or ask for documentation. The small police detachments simply came to attention as the convoy passed by. The General was impressed – two men on motorcycles, two more crewing each of the APCs. He also counted twelve or thirteen combat troops to each APC, including one young officer. Thirty-two men – possibly more. With his driver, Mazzard and the Captain, the force was at least thirty-five strong. Very good, and all armed with M16s and hand guns. Mike Mazzard, the Captain, and his driver also carried side arms. What General could have wanted for better protection?

'You've got it sewn up nicely, Mike,' said the General, beaming. 'Very good organisation. Well done.'

'I only pick up a telephone, General. You know that, sir.'

They were climbing into the mountains now, passing a side road marked with a military arrow sign: NORAD HQ.

'That's the way up to the main entrance, sir,' Mazzard told him. 'We go some five miles up here and turn back to come in at the side. It's like a kind of service entrance for the control rooms. I figure someone from Peterson'll have tipped them off by now. They'll probably all be on edge around the main entrance buildings.'

'They'll know at this end too,' the General grunted. 'Not fools, these people. They'll all know. Be expecting us exactly where we're going in.'

Ten minutes or so passed before the convoy reached the next slip road, duly marked NORAD 2. 'Here we go, then, sir. You really feeling better?' Mazzard craned forward to take a good look at the General, and the skull-faced Captain turned in the front seat.

'Is the General not well?'

'Captain,' General Banker growled, 'when a man's just given a new, and highly-responsible posting, parted from his wife while the house gets fixed up, and living on base, he sometimes makes a fool of himself. No, I am not ill; but I used up a lot of cleaning fluid last night.'

The Captain made a sound which the General took to be humorous.

'I feel', the General continued, 'a shade like a puppet.' Turning to Mazzard: 'You walk me through it, okay? I'll be fine if you simply guide me.'

'Don't worry, sir, we've done it all before.'

'Sure have,' said the General. From above came the clatter of a helicopter, flying low, as though following the convoy.

They were in a gap now, hewn through solid rock, the great slanting sides closing them in. Then out of the gap into a left turn, and the grey road widened, white dust falling around them, like a fine lawn spray as they came on to a clean mountain stretch.

The mountain reached up above them, and there – a mile ahead – stood a solid pair of gates, with a great high circle of cyclone fencing reaching out on each side. Large steel girders were set at intervals in the fencing, each topped by constantly moving cameras. Behind the fence, a cluster of buildings stretched back to the rockface of Cheyenne Mountain.

There were two GIs out in front of the gates. As the convoy appeared, one of them turned to shout towards the blockhouse on the right of the gates. Before they came within a hundred yards of the barriers, an officer appeared, through a smaller gateway by the blockhouse.

The convoy slowed, the motorcycle escort wheeling off, left and right, to come in close to the staff car. The first APC also turned, moving right, then circling on its own axis to point inwards. Precise and very military. The General was, once more, most impressed. These people knew what they were doing.

Turning towards Mazzard, he said, 'You do the introductions, Mike, will you? As usual. No fuss. I'll stay slightly aloof.'

Major Mazzard looked very pleased, as the electric windows slid down and the NORAD officer – a young Captain – approached the staff car.

Yes, thought the General, they were well-prepared here too. Looking forward through the cyclone fencing, he could see that an honour guard had already turned out, forming up on the flat area immediately inside the gates.

The young NORAD officer saluted as though his life depended upon it, and Mazzard spoke to him, clipped humourless: 'General Banker – Inspector-General United States Air/Space – to officially inspect your base, Captain.' He handed over an impressive-looking document, at which the Captain merely glanced. He knew top brass when he met it.

'Very good, sir.' The NORAD Captain smiled and turned his head, ordering the gates to be opened. 'We're delighted to see you, General, sir. The base is open to you. If there's anything we can do to make your trip more pleasant . . .'

'It's not meant to be pleasant, Captain,' the General snapped. 'I'm here to look at your operations rooms and ask a few questions. You follow me, Captain?'

The NORAD officer's smile did not fade. 'Whatever you say, sir. Anything we can do for you, anything at all. Please drive right in.'

'The General's anxious to go inside the mountain as soon as possible,' Mazzard interpolated.

'Right, sir. Our acting CO is already waiting for you in Operations. It won't take you long to get there.'

The gates had opened, and they drove through, followed by one of the APCs. The other stayed outside the perimeter, turning to point back, down the road, its cargo of troops disembarking and taking up defensive positions. In minutes the General's team had NORAD No. 2 HQ entrance neatly sealed off.

As the car came to a halt, the honour guard snapped to attention and presented arms. 'That young officer seemed a hair casual, Mike,' the General muttered, climbing from the car.

'Yes. I'll get his name. Probably hasn't had many dealings with Inspector-Generals before, sir, and thought the friendly approach would be best.'

'Get his name.' The General had begun to sound crusty.

'You don't want to inspect that honour guard, do you, sir?' Mazzard asked. But the General, in spite of his hangover, appeared intent on doing everything correctly. Slowly he passed down the ranks of men, stopping to ask questions of every third soldier.

At the end of the last rank, the General dismissed the guard commander, returning his sharp salute, then looked at the young NORAD Captain who had met them. 'Right,' he snapped. 'I want you, Captain, to take me, with my adjutant and the Captain here . . .'

'Luxor,' the thin, damaged officer prompted, 'Captain Luxor.'

'Yes.' The General shot Luxor an unfriendly look. 'Yes, you; Major Mazzard, and Captain Luxor. Nobody else, just the four of us, will go in; and I wish to meet your Commandinng Officer.'

Mazzard, at the General's elbow, quickly asked, 'Sir, don't you think half a dozen of the men should . . . ?'

'No. Major.' The General was very firm. 'They don't need to see any of this. Don't really know why we bothered with an escort of this size. No, *we* go and have a look. Now let's move. I don't want to hang around here all day. Just the four of us.' Before he had even stopped speaking, the General began to walk purposefully, his back as straight as a ramrod, towards the buildings huddled close to the rockface.

He was well ahead of Mazzard and Luxor, when the NORAD Captain came up fast, trotting at the General's heels. 'The Commanding Officer, sir . . .'

'Yes?'

'Well, sir. As I said, we have a full Colonel on duty, waiting for you. The Commanding Officer's away on leave today sir. I think you should've been informed.'

The General nodded. 'That's nothing to bother about. Your Colonel'll do as well as anybody.'

The buildings, set against the rockface, were purely a defensive camouflage for the entrance. Solidly built, reinforced with steel, and housing a few small administrative offices their main purpose was to block the tunnel which led into the mountain.

The young Captain was still speaking. 'At the main entrance – around the other side – we have an underground park for vehicles and other facilities,' he chattered. 'This is really a kind of back door.' They passed through a pair of steel doors, which swung open when the Captain pressed his hand against a small screen.

Behind the steel doors, the world changed. The passage narrowed into a short metal-lined alley, only wide enough to accommodate one man at a time. This led to a small command post, occupied by four sturdy marines who stood guard over the next entrance of sliding steel panels.

The marines, for all their immaculate appearance, were co-operative and unquestioning. After a word from the NORAD Captain, one spoke into a white intercom, then they stood aside as the blast-proof panels slid noiselessly back.

The General and his entourage did not really know what to expect within the mountain. The General, himself, supposed that his mental picture would be coloured by other similar installations he had visited, though they all had seemed some-what like movie sets. He expected large elevators, taking staff deep below the earth, or open railcars, like a modern coal mine.

There turned out to be no such devices. Once through the doors they were already inside the mountain and standing in a great circular chamber, a reception area, fashioned from inside the bare rock. Air conditioning kept a pleasant, comfortable temperature, and there were carpets underfoot, though the place was, basically, a refurbished cavern.

Four large desks were manned by strangely uninterested staff, in charge of electronic sniffers for bugs, weapons, and explos-ives. The General insisted on checking each of these desks before turning to meet a tall, bronzed Colonel, who wore pilot's wings and a plethora of medal ribbons. The Colonel was backed up by a team of some four officers, most of whom wore the rank of major. All seemed to be around the same age – late thirties, or early forties.

The Colonel saluted, introduced himself and his staff, apolo-gised for the absence of his Commanding Officer, and offered the General what he called, 'every possible facility'.

General Banker nodded, noting that the Colonel and his men wore side arms. He then introduced his own two staff members.

The Colonel, who felt in strangely benign spirits that morn-ing, had noticed immediately that General Banker was in his dress uniform while his staff officers wore combat dress and carried side arms. It struck him as unusual, but not sinister.

Before coming up from the control room, he had also received a bizarre message – from the main gate – that the General's detachment of troops had sealed off the No. 2 mountain entrance, taking up positions both within and outside the perimeter fence. Now, the General was oddly uncommunicative, so the Colonel explained that the four officers with him had volunteered to stay on duty.

'By rights they should be just coming off shift,' the Colonel said, smiling proudly. 'But they all offered to stay on so you could be well briefed, General.' He continued to explain that, when on duty, these officers supervised the various command posts, the Main Control Room, and the monitors. 'When you're on duty here, it's a full-time six hours of concentration.' He appeared to be exceptionally serious when talking about the work. 'The officers on duty at this moment are not in a situation where they could be certain of answering all your questions, sir.'

The General thanked the Colonel for his officers' thoughtfulness, and deferred to him, asking what he should see first.

'Oh, whatever you like, General. We're at your service here. Look at anything, take over if you want to. Nobody will mind. We're serious people, doing a very special job; but we have to let you see everything, and give you any information you need.'

For a serious officer, the General considered that the Colonel had suddenly taken leave of his senses. A bit casual for a man in charge, he thought. Then Major Mazzard stepped in. 'I think the General's particularly interested in seeing how you control the Space Wolves, sir.'

The General held up a hand. 'Now don't let us rush into anything, Major. The Colonel knows how this outfit works. After all, this is one of the most important bases in the entire country . . .'

'Well.' The Colonel had a pleasant, slow drawl. 'Well, we'd certainly be the first to know if anything went sour, if that's what you mean, sir. I'd recommend we look at the Main Operations Control first.'

'Whatever you say,' General Banker agreed.

The Colonel gestured towards another pair of anti-blast doors, set in the centre of the half-circle wall behind the security desks.

'After you, sir.'

The General followed the NORAD Colonel across the soft carpet and through the doors, the other officers, including Mazzard and Luxor, at their heels.

On the other side of the doors, a wide passage led to a T-junction corridor. Looking to left and right, the General saw large swing doors set at intervals along the cross-stroke passage. Straight ahead were similar doors, marked in bold white lettering Gallery: Main Operations.

The Colonel stepped to one side, allowing General Banker to be the first through, the other officers following respectfully.

They were on a wide viewing platform, fitted with chairs and a high, angled, thick glass screen. The view from this gallery was both impressive and virtually unique.

Below them lay a vast amphitheatre in which the audience consisted of about a hundred men and women, each seated behind a bank of computer and electronic instruments – keyboards, scanners, and other complex hardware. Each person on duty appeared to be completely wrapped up in his or her work, making occasional entries on keyboards or speaking into headsets.

Above them – on the far, huge, curved wall – were three massive electronic Mercator projections, each mapping the world. All three projections were topped by rows of digital clocks, showing the accurate time along the earth's varied zones. But most important, each of the projections was crisscrossed by slow-moving, coloured lines – blues and greens; brilliant whites; blacks, orange; even lines which broke up into different, segmented, hues.

The General let out a slow whistle. He remembered seeing smaller versions of things like this, but never anything on such a scale. 'I'd be grateful, Colonel, if you'd come over by me and tell us about this amazing display.'

The Colonel started to speak, his voice a strange monotone as he explained the use, and purpose, of the Main Control.

The three projections showed the exact number of known satellites and other space hardware in orbit – the left-hand projection being all non-USA satellites; the one to the far right showing American equipment; while the centre projection monitored all new indications.

At the same time, this centre screen could be programmed, in an instant, to show everything – both American and non-American: even down to the juxtaposition of satellites.

'That is also the so-called Early Warning projection,' the Colonel told them. 'Anything new thrown into space by a foreign power will be spotted on the central screen.'

All three of these great electronic maps were monitored and operated by the technicians seated in the amphitheatre, while they, in turn, were passed information from a number of sources. 'Anything new would come from one of our tracking stations: ground-based or satellite. Our own hardware is passed on through individual Command Posts, within this complex.' As the Colonel described it, the whole display sounded very simple, yet nobody seeing it could fail to be awed.

The Colonel was still speaking. 'For instance, the Big Bird and Keyhole II reconnaissance satellites, are shown on the right-hand projection, but their work is monitored by their own Command Post, which is just along the passage outside this gallery. Of course, all the information those particular satellites send back goes to other stations.

'Now, if we get something new from, let us say, the Soviet Union, this is immediately picked up on the trace. Within seconds, our SDS – Satellite Data System – relays details. We would take action before knowing exactly what the new object is; but it's all very fast when it happens, which it does quite often.'

He went on to explain how each satellite system had its own headquarters, working independently. The weather satellites, for instance, passed their data directly to meteorological centres, and the same applied to the reconnaissance eyes in the sky.

'In a way, we're like police patrols.' The Colonel spoke directly to General Banker. 'We can see what's up there, check it out, pass on information, and take action. But we're not responsible for the individual tasks.'

'Except for the Space Wolves,' Major Mazzard, on the General's right, said.

The Colonel nodded. 'That's a very special project,' he said. 'Would the General like to see their Command Post? It's possibly the largest we have here.'

Major Mazzard and Captain Luxor both answered for General Banker. Yes, the General would very much like to see the SW Command Post.

'Anything you want, sir.' The Colonel led them out of the Main Operations Gallery and along the corridor to their left until they came to one of the sets of swing doors, marked KS Control. 'Killersat,' the Colonel explained, leading the way into a large chamber.

Inside there was semi-darkness. Against the far wall, a smaller version of one of the electronic Mercator projections glowed with light – creeping red lines sweeping above the world – while three men, an officer and two Master-Sergeants, tended the computers and controls.

'There it is.' The Colonel waved a hand. Then he spoke louder, for the benefit of the three men controlling the Space Wolves Command Post. 'Gentlemen, General Banker, the Inspector-General Air/Space Defence. Just taking a look.'

Mazzard was close to the General now. 'I think the General wants to take more than a look,' he said loudly.

General Banker turned towards Mazzard, a question forming on his lips.

'You remember, sir,' Mazzard prompted. 'You're the senior officer here.'

Banker's brow creased and he looked around. The Colonel stood next to him, while the rest of the staff crowded in the doorway. Captain Luxor stood behind the Colonel's staff, out in the corridor.

'Sir, the computer tapes and printouts,' Mazzard prompted, close at his right elbow.

'Of course. Sorry, Mike.' The General smiled, then raised his voice. 'I don't wish to bother you, gentlemen, but who's in charge of this Command Post?'

The officer seated in front of the central bank of controls raised a hand. 'Sir.'

'Would you be good enough to unhook your computer tapes and box up all available printouts, please? I need to take them away for study,' the General said calmly.

The officer in command slowly stood up. 'Very well, sir,' he muttered and began to move around to the rear of the large console. Within a few minutes he had the big spools of tape in containers, on top of which he placed a number of flat metal boxes, containing the computer printouts. 'Anything else the General requires?' the officer asked.

'No, that'll be all,' Mazzard answered for his General. 'Just bring them over here.'

The Space Wolves Command Post officer started coming towards them in the dim light.

Then, with speed and complete surprise, General Banker moved, his body pivoting in front of the Colonel, one hand reaching out to wrench the Colonel's pistol from its holster.

Even as he turned, the General let out a yell: 'Stop! Don't hand those over! The rest of you, grab the two officers with me. They're not what they seem. Now! Get them *now*!'

It had all happened that morning, during the helicopter ride to Peterson Field.

The General, feeling decidedly queasy from the previous night's party, had closed his eyes, intending to doze. But as soon as he relaxed, General Banker began to suffer a light-headedness, followed by strange mental experiences.

At first he thought it was something very serious, like a heart attack. He felt faint, and images began to flash through his mind.

It was like a film running backwards, at great speed, intercut with odd details he could not properly identify. There were memories from recent days, just after his promotion; scenes from his time in Vietnam; and moments before that – as though the reel was taking him back to childhood.

The intercut images were very odd. A woman, with one breast had come to give him pills. At least he thought it was her, for he smelled her hair. Nena. Tara. Cedar. Bond. James Bond. 007.

The General opened his eyes and realised that he was not General James A. Banker at all. While he was still feeling light-headed, the truth flooded into him, as though through an open window to his mind.

She had come and given him pills for this very purpose. Then and there, in the helicopter, Bond had not even attempted to work out how he had been drugged, and hypnotised, into another personality. All he could think of was how to keep in character until the best possible moment.

That moment was here, and now.

As he swung around, grasping the Colonel's big Colt .45, Bond realised that Mazzard was reaching for his gun, yelling as he did so: 'Don't listen to the General! Don't listen to him! The man's crazy! Take no orders from him!'

Mazzard's pistol came out of its holster a second too late. Bond's arm was up, and the roar from his two shots came as gigantic, echoing explosions in the chamber.

Mazzard was lifted off his feet. His body hung aloft for a second, blood beginning to spout from his chest, then slammed back against the wall. Immediately, Bond turned, looking for Luxor.

The skeleton man appeared to have vanished.

With every ounce of authority he could muster, Bond shouted for the computer tapes to be returned. 'Colonel, get your men into action, and fast. Those troops who came with me mean business. See to your defences.'

The Colonel hesitated for a moment. The Command Post reeked of cordite and death. Two of the other officers had drawn their weapons but seemed uncertain about what to do. From the moment of his arrival, Bond had recognised the workings of Bismaquer's sinister drug. They had been within an ace of actually handing over the tapes. Now it was a question of making sure they were not taken by force.

Bond shouted orders again, this time demanding to know what had happened to Luxor.

'He went . . . After you shot at . . . he walked away . . .' one of the NORAD officers stammered.

'Colonel, your defences. Get on to the nearest base. You'll need help,' Bond commanded, his voice sharp as a whip.

As though to underline the order, the entire chamber shook with the dull thud of an explosion from the direction of the main entrance.

A marine appeared in the doorway. 'Anti-tank rockets being fired at the entrance block, sir,' he shouted at the Colonel, who had already leaped to the nearest telephone.

There was another whoomp, sending a tremor through the mountain complex.

Bond looked at the marine. 'The officer who came in with me?'

'Sir?'

'The one with a face like a skull . . .'

'There were shots from here, and he ran past us, sir, saying he had to get help.'

The complex shook again, to another rocket burst.

'That's the help he was going for,' said Bond. 'Muster everyone you can. The Colonel's getting word out. This base is under attack. It's not a drill. It's the real thing.'

By this time, they had all realised the danger. Bond turned to the Colonel. 'They'll try for a quick break-in,' he said, willing himself to remain calm. 'Blast their way through with anti-tank rockets . . .'

'M72s by the sound of them.' The Colonel looked ashen. 'I don't understand this. We nearly handed over . . .'

'Don't worry, Colonel, that's not your fault. The point is that those bastards'll smash their way in, hacking with knives if they have to. If that skull-face is out there, they'll be even more determined. What've we got in the way of defence?'

The Colonel gave a couple of quick orders to his officers, who hesitated until Bond – realising the problem with Bismaquer's drug – told them to carry on.

'The guard out front is fighting back,' said the Colonel, swallowing. 'Doing quite well, I'd guess. We've got reinforcements coming in, but the problem is here. Within the mountain. They've blasted through the first doors, and the section into the reception area's now catching it. I gather they're close to the doors . . .'

'And when those doors are down, the force that's left'll come piling through that narrow entrance. What've we got?'

'A few grenades, the side arms, and a pair of AR18s.'

'Get the Armalites, then. Quickly!'

The AR18, as Bond knew it, was the latest commercial Armalite weapon. It was fully automatic with a fire rate of 800 rpm, and magazines holding twenty rounds. He was at the Colonel's heels as the two men made their way to the arms locker, set into the wall near the Main Operations Gallery doors.

The weapon felt good in Bond's hands, and he grabbed magazines from the Colonel, stuffing them into his uniform jacket and slamming one into position on the gun.

As they turned away from the locker, a larger explosion ripped from the reception area, and several soldiers staggered back through the entrance to the main complex. One was the marine Bond had spoken to earlier.

'They've broken through, blown the doors into reception,' the man gasped, and Bond saw he was clutching a jagged tear in his shoulder, the blood trickling through his fingers.

As he reached the doors to the big, circular reception area, Bond briefly took in the carnage. The neat desks were shattered and bodies lay everywhere, some dead, others crying with pain from their wounds. From the main entrance directly opposite him, smoke poured into the reception area.

The assault would come down the narrow passage, one man at a time, Bond thought. He braced himself against the wall, gripping the weapon against his hip. From the corner of his eye, he saw the Colonel taking up a similar stance. One of the officers who had been with them in the Space Wolves Command Post was sprawled on his back within a few feet of them, a slash where his throat had been. It crossed Bond's mind that Bismaquer already had a great deal to pay for.

Then, through the smoke, SPECTRE's men started to enter the reception area.

The Colonel and Bond opened up at the same moment, sending a double spray of bullets into the hole which had once been a pair of sliding steel doors.

'Like shooting fish in a barrel, General,' shouted the Colonel, for SPECTRE's troops came pounding down the narrow passageway and into the reception area like sheep being penned into an abattoir.

Their AR18s rattling, the Colonel and Bond scythed through the attackers as they appeared through the smoke. The bullets hurled them back, threw them aside, cut through them, until suddenly there was an unearthly silence.

Finally the smoke began to clear, and even Bond winced to see the damage they had done. Then he reloaded, bracing himself. From outside there came yet another explosion, then a shout.

'Colonel? Colonel, sir? Any NORAD officer in there . . . ?'

'Yes,' the Colonel shouted back. 'State your name and rank. What is it?'

'They're finished out here, sir. The other APC's pinned down on the road by forces from the main entrance. It's Sergeant Carter here.'

The Colonel nodded at Bond. 'It's okay, General. I know Carter.'

Bond thought it best that he remain a four-star general for the time being. At least that would stave off awkward questions. His main concern, now that Heavenly Wolf had been foiled, was Cedar Leiter. Then, once he knew what had happened to her, he would hunt down Bismaquer.

Outside, there was more carnage. Medical teams worked on the wounded and carried away the dead. The one APC was still burning, and there were great gaps in the cyclone fencing.

From down the road, out of sight, came occasional bursts of rifle and automatic fire.

'How's it going?' The Colonel shouted to a three-man team crouched over a field communications radio. A sergeant answered him. More aid was on the way, and the other APC was now almost put out of action, the troops on their last legs.

'Still can't understand why we nearly gave the stuff away,' the Colonel muttered almost to himself. 'I don't feel good about any of this.'

'You will – eventually. Not your doing, Colonel. They had me as a sitting duck as well . . .'

The sergeant with the radio called to the Colonel that there was a civilian helicopter a mile away. 'A woman. Keeps making calls, asking permission to put down. Wants to know if we've got a Mr Bond with us, sir.'

'Let her down,' Bond ordered, still pulling rank. 'I know what that's all about. Bring her in here.'

It could easily be Bismaquer, holding a pistol to either Cedar's or Nena's head. But this was his only quick route out. Alternatively, it could be a fast lead to Bismaquer, and Bond could not resist that. He remembered there had been a helicopter following the convoy on the way in.

'That okay, sir?' the radio man called to the Colonel.

'If the General says so. Yes.'

Bond went over to the radio sergeant. 'You don't like ice cream, do you, sergeant?' he asked, having just witnessed the man clear a four-star general's order with his immediate, known superior.

Reaching for the hand mike, the communications man shook his head. 'Hate the muck, sir. I can't even look at it.' He gave Bond a puzzled look as he started to call in the helicopter.

Bond quickly explained to the Colonel that he must get away, saying he would contact him as soon as possible. 'Any problems, call the White House. Say you ran into a Mr Bond. They'll clear it, I think.'

The Colonel was obviously dazed as he watched the little white metal insect dropping gently into the compound, neatly sliding to one side at the last moment in order to avoid the burned out APC – a final memorial to Bismaquer's ruined attempt on the security of Cheyenne Mountain.

The small helicopter was a faithful model – a modern twin-seater version of the old Bell 47. Bond could see only one figure seated within its perspex bulb. It was certainly not Bismaquer. This figure was slim, in white overalls and helmet.

She already had the door open and was swinging herself down as Bond reached the machine.

'Oh James. Thank God. Oh, thank God you're safe.'

Nena Bismaquer wrapped her arms around Bond's neck, clinging to him, as though she could never bear to let him out of her sight again.

Tired as he was, worried about Cedar's safety, and anxious to discover if Luxor had escaped, and where Bismaquer had hidden himself, James Bond still felt it might be a good thing never to let go of Nena.

21

BLOFELD

It was already growing dark as the helicopter flew in low over the Louisiana swampland. Nena craned forward at the controls, trying to spot the landmark she said would be there.

They had stayed for only a few minutes in the compound of the NORAD base while Bond shot questions at her. What had happened? How did she manage to get there? Did she know what had become of Cedar?

Flushed and excited, Nena gave him the answers as quickly as he fired the questions. In the early days at the Rancho Bismaquer, her husband had given her lessons in the helicopter. She had taken her pilot's licence a year ago. It had been her personal salvation.

Wakening in the night – a good forty-eight hours ago – she heard noises. Bismaquer was nowhere upstairs, so she crept down and saw Luxor with some other men. They had Cedar with them.

Then her husband arrived; orders were given. She had no idea what was going on but heard talk about Bond being taken away in the other helicopter. She also heard Bismaquer tell them where they were to rendezvous when it was all over. 'I still don't know when *what* was all over. They talked about Cheyenne Mountain, that's all. Lord, you look so dashing in that uniform, James. Now, I need to know what's been going on.'

He would tell her later. Now he needed the urgent facts. Where was Bismaquer? What happened to Cedar?

'He's taking her to Louisiana. I know exactly where – and Luxor'll head for the same place.' Her face, glowing with pleasure until then, suddenly darkened. 'It's horrible, James. I know what they'll do to her. Markus took me there once. I never thought I'd go again. The people know me there, and – if we hurry – we should make it well before Markus arrives with Cedar. They're going by road. It was always she they wanted dead, James. I know that. He wanted you alive, but Cedar was to die. I just hope to God we're in time, because I can guess what he'll do to her now.'

A few minutes later they were airborne, and now, after a long steady flight, the swamps and *bayous* slid by in the dusk beneath them.

Bond was pleasantly surprised by Nena's standard as a pilot. She handled the helicopter with skill and great flair, as though she was used to flying it every day.

'Oh, I take it out when I can,' she said with a laugh. 'It's always been a way of getting clear of Markus for a while. Funny, I always knew that, when I finally left him, it would be in the chopper.'

She had switched on the main landing lights, slowing almost to a hover, peering down, then, suddenly, exclaiming, 'There! That's the place. On that spit of land, right between the two *bayous*.'

Bond thought that, even allowing for the light, the house seemed pretty run down.

'Just wait.' She laughed again. 'Markus keeps a couple of people there to look after it. The outside's only a shell – like some conjurer's box that fits over the real thing. It's a palace inside.'

She tilted the little Bell, to come in low, telling Bond that she thought there was a place on the far side of the *bayou* where she could put down. 'Markus keeps a number of marsh hoppers around; only I don't want to take the one nearest the road. It'd be best if he doesn't know we're here.'

Bond went along with that. The one thing he needed was total surprise, for the final confrontation with Bismaquer, the new Blofeld. He wondered what would happen to SPECTRE now that the expensive, and ingenious, attempt on the Space Wolf secrets had collapsed on them.

'I haven't thanked you yet.' He turned to look towards Nena, who was concentrating on the ground below.

'For pulling you out of Cheyenne Mountain?' The helicopter faltered, then gently let down. Nena clicked off the switches. The engine died, and they sat there, the rotor cleaving the air, making its whupping noise as it slowed to a stop.

'No, Nena, for what you did after they'd gone over me with the drugs and hypnotism. How did you get in to give me the antidote?'

She paused, 'Oh, that? Well, I had to do something. It was clear they had you doped up to the eyeballs. I just had to pray I'd chosen the right stuff.'

'Well you did – and it worked. Very quickly really. You saved the day, Nena. *You* really stopped it all from working, stopped Markus's and Luxor's plans.'

The darkness closed in on them, like a wall. Nena had to switch the lights on again.

'You'll tell me what it was all about, James, won't you? Everything. I only heard parts of it. It seemed very complicated to me – difficult and daring. Would they really have got a lot of money for whatever they were after?'

'Billions.' Bond closed the subject. 'Now, let's find this marsh hopper. I'm ravenous, need a bath and could do with a rest before I come face to face with your venomous husband.'

'Yes,' she said, unbuckling her straps. 'Yes, he is pretty venomous, isn't he?'

They found the marsh hopper exactly where she said it would be. A small, narrow-beam spotlight was fitted to the front, and Nena switched it on after the motor fired.

As they reached the water surrounding the old rotting house, a light flashed out from what appeared to be the porch. Bond went for the .45, but Nena put out a restraining hand.

'It's okay, James. Only a deaf mute Markus keeps on the place. Named Criton.'

'Admirable,' muttered Bond.

'Criton, or the woman, Tic – she's a first-rate cook. You won't have to worry about food, James. Yes, I can see him now. It's Criton guiding us in.'

The marsh hopper came alongside a small pier, the sullen-looking deaf mute nimbly stepping down to help tie the craft to the pier. Criton gave Nena a little bow but took no notice of Bond, who kept the .45 at the ready, to be on the safe side.

She had been right about the house. Going up the crumbling and rotten wooden steps to the main door, Bond kept his reservations, but, once inside, it was a different matter. You immediately forgot the camouflage, for the interior was beautiful: expensively immaculate.

Nena spoke to Criton, facing him and enunciating carefully, while Bond looked around at the heavy silk wall coverings, the antiques and the fresh flowers which seemed to have been gathered only a few hours ago.

'Has Mr Bismaquer been here?' Nena asked.

Criton shook his head.

'Understand me, now, Criton,' she continued. 'You take the marsh hopper, and you put it out of sight. Okay?'

He nodded.

'Then tell Tic we need food and drink. In the main bedroom.'

Criton nodded vigorously, grinning broadly.

'Now, most important. You understand? *Most* important. Mr Bismaquer is coming. As soon as he is on the way – in a marsh hopper – you come wake us up. Right away. You watch all night. You do that, and I give you a good present. Okay?'

The deaf mute nodded as though trying to dislocate his neck.

'He'll do it.' Nena locked eyes with Bond. 'We're safe, James.

We can relax. Criton'll warn us when Markus shows up; then we'll be ready for him.'

'You sure?'

'Certain.'

She took hold of his hand, tugging gently, leading him up the stairs.

The master bedroom was huge, with carpet so thick you could roll up in it and go to sleep without recourse to sheets. The bed itself was typical of Bismaquer's style: a huge, gilded four-poster, with a headboard carved and glinting with gold leaf— a large B displayed prominently among the scrollwork.

The bathroom had bath, shower, and jacuzzi. It was, Bond decided, only half the size of the bedroom.

They only heard Tic leave food in the bedroom, calling to them with a creole intonation. Nena and Bond were enjoying themselves far too much, naked in the jacuzzi.

Later, wrapped in towelling robes, they sat on the bed to eat a delicious crab and okra gumbo, which, Nena maintained, was reckoned among the locals, to be a great aphrodisiac.

Bond, who had felt near exhaustion on arrival, did not know whether to thank the gumbo, or Nena's natural feminine powers. But they made love several times – with concentrated power, and increasing mutual delight – before switching the lights off and cradling each other into sleep.

At first, Bond thought he was dreaming; that the shot was simply part of some immediately-forgotten nightmare. His eyes snapped open, and he lay still for a second, listening in the dark.

The next moment, though, he knew it was the real thing. There were two more heavy reports. He reached out for Nena, but she was not there.

He switched the light on, grabbing for the towelling robe and the .45 as his feet touched the carpet.

The robe was there, but the big automatic – which he had so carefully left by the bed – had disappeared.

Once in the robe, he turned the light off again and felt his way to the door. The house still seemed to echo from the shots. Downstairs, he thought, moving knees bent, his bare feet silent on the carpet.

He stopped, to listen again, at the top of the staircase. He thought he heard sounds from behind a door adjacent to the big carved newel post at their stair foot. A thin sliver of light showed under the door. Nena, he thought, his heart thudding. Bismaquer had arrived and the deaf mute had given no warning. Either that, or she had tried to go it alone.

He moved more quickly down the stairs, pausing for a moment just outside the door, listening to the muffled sounds coming from the other side. Gradually the noises took form – a whimpering, pleading babble. Without waiting another second, Bond kicked the door open, just in time to see the last act of Bismaquer's drama being played out.

It was a long room. Most of the space was taken up by a polished oak table, the chairs pushed neatly in around it. The far wall appeared to be made of glass. But it was the tableau close to this huge window that stopped Bond, as in a kind of paralysis, in the doorway.

It was a grotesque scene. Slumped against the wall lay the big pink-faced Markus Bismaquer, one shoulder and both his legs covered in blood where the three bullets had chewed their way into kneecaps and arm. The cherubic face was changed – a child in pain and terror.

Standing over him, stark naked, her one magnificent breast caught as though by a spotlight, was Nena. She held the Colt .45, pointing directly at Bismaquer's head as he pleaded through his pain, begging her to stop. The bear, finally overcome and helpless.

She seemed not to see – or even notice – that Bond was there. In turn, he was so shaken by the sight that he stood, rooted, mesmerised, for too long.

'I always knew your heart wasn't in it, Markus.' The glissando laugh had changed to a harsh crow, while the endearing French accent was now guttural and rough.

'No, Markus. I might just have spared you; but you didn't cover your tracks. The Britisher, Bond, gave it all away. When we had him set up – with the new personality well implanted in him – you crept in, from my bed no doubt, because he told me that he smelled my hair.

'You went to him and filled his mouth full of wake-up pills, didn't you? Another of your loves, Markus? Did you fall for him? Like you fell for that Leiter bitch? Anything that moves, eh? Luxor, me, Leiter, Bond. Well, there's no reason to keep you any longer – husband.'

Bond actually jumped as she pulled the trigger, and Bismaquer's head disintegrated like a burst blood-filled bladder, the gore splattering Nena's naked body.

'My God. You bitch.'

For a single beat in time, Bond thought he had not said it aloud. But Nena Bismaquer turned quickly, with the deadly eye of the Colt steady, and pointing directly at Bond's chest.

Her face had changed, and in the clear light Bond could see that she appeared older. The hair was tousled, and the black fire now burned a hatred in her eyes. It was the eyes which brought the whole thing into perspective. No matter how he had tried to cover it, even with the use of contact lenses, Ernst Stavro Blofeld's eyes had been black: black as the Prince of Darkness himself.

Nena smiled, lopsided, and in the smile revealed her paranoia.

'Well, James Bond. At last. I'm sorry you had to watch this nasty business. I really *was* thinking of sparing him, until you thanked me for feeding you wake-up pills. Then I knew he had to die. It's a pity. He was quite brilliant in his way. My organisation can always make room for chemists who have a streak of genius – like Markus Bismaquer. But his stomach wasn't up to it, I'm afraid.'

She took a step towards Bond, then changed her mind.

'In spite of everything – and I have to admit you have prowess in some areas – I don't think we've really met. My name is Nena Blofeld.' She laughed. 'I might say, your name is James Bond and I claim my reward.'

'His daughter?' Bond's voice was barely audible.

'My reward,' she continued. 'I've had a price on your head, ready to be claimed for some time. Are you surprised? Surprised that I managed to fool your people and the Americans? We knew you would be called in – Mr James Bond, the expert on SPECTRE. Yes, from a distance I enticed you, James. And you fell for it.

'Now, I can claim my reward myself. You killed my father, I think. He warned me, even as a child, about you.'

'And your mother?' Bond played for time.

She made a dismissive, retchy sound from the back of her throat. 'I'm illegitimate, though I know who she was. A French whore, who lived with him for a couple of years. I did not, knowingly, meet her. I loved my father, Mr James Bond. He taught me all I know. He also willed the organisation to me – SPECTRE. That's all you really have to be told. Markus has gone. Now it's your turn.'

She raised the Colt just as Bond dived towards the side of the table, and at that same moment, the dusty, frail figure of Walter Luxor came hurtling through the door, shouting:

'The place is surrounded, Blofeld. They're here – police, everywhere!'

She fired, and Bond saw part of the table splinter about a foot from his head. Twisting his body, he grabbed at the legs of the nearest heavy chair, hauling it out as Walter Luxor made a lunge for him, throwing himself directly into the path of Nena Blofeld's next shot.

The bullet gouged into the left side of Luxor's chest, spinning him like a top against the wall. He seemed to be pinned there for a second, before sliding down, a collapsed skeleton, leaving a crimson trail behind him.

Bond heard Blofeld gasp, cursing, and in that moment when

she was still off-balance, he summoned all his energy, heaving at the big chair with every ounce of strength, making a supreme effort to fling it, at Nena Blofeld.

The chair appeared to hang, in mid-air, as she tried to duck it. But the combination of need for survival, hatred for any member of the Blofeld family and some hidden well of strength, served Bond's purpose well.

The bottom of the chair's seat hit her full in the chest. The four legs neatly pinioned her arms and the full force of the impact hurled her back against the window.

There was the sickening noise of cracking glass, then a terrible screaming. Nena Blofeld was thrown out on to the hard earth, which sloped down to the dense reeds and the water of the *bayou*.

The screaming continued, and Bond stood, transfixed by what happened next. As Blofeld hit the ground, so a metal cage, protected by tight wire mesh, dropped from the darkness above. At the same time, the area immediately outside the broken window became alive. The cage, Bond could see, had a roof and three sides, being open at the front, and reaching down to the reeds.

As the cage descended, so the lights dimmed in the room, but it was still bright enough to give a reasonable view of the reptiles which came squirming in. At least two of them – though Bond had the distinct impression there were others near by – were huge, fat, lethal pythons, thirty feet or more in length.

As the creatures slid over the screaming and kicking body, Bond heard the chair crack like thin plywood. Then the screams stopped. He was conscious of other people coming into the room, of a back he recognised as his old friend Felix Leiter.

Leiter limped towards the window, black gloves covering both his own and the artificial hand. Bond saw the arms being raised and Leiter's hands come together. He turned his eyes away after the third explosion, as Felix put a bullet into the brains of each python, and – in case she was crushed, but not yet quite dead – gave the *coup de grâce* to Nena Blofeld.

'Come on, James.' It was Cedar, by his side, who guided him out of the corpse-strewn room.

A few minutes later, in the hall of the *bayou* house, she told him, simply, what had happened to her on the mono-rail.

'I couldn't kill them all. You told me to kill anybody who tried to get in. There were at least a dozen: Maybe they were already on board when we left the ranch. I just got out fast. Sorry, James. I tried to catch up with you, give some kind of warning, but it was all over too quickly. I didn't dare shout – they seemed to be everywhere. I couldn't see. We must have missed each other by inches. The only thing I bumped into was a body.'

'How . . . ?' he began.

'I walked. Straight out through the gate and into the night. By the time I finally made Amarillo, it was too late to do anything. There *really* is nothing between that depot and the city.

'Then things opened up, and reports started to come in from Cheyenne Mountain. By that time, Daddy had arrived, and a lot of other people. They finally got a trace on Madame Bismaquer's helicopter. That's how they tracked you down here. I always told you she was no good.'

Bond merely shook his head. It had not yet quite sunk in.

Felix Leiter came into the hall. 'Nice to see you again, James, old buddy.' His grin still had that sense of fun and impetuosity that Bond had always warmed to, trusted and admired. 'You do realise that my daughter's in love with you, James.' Another quick grin. 'As her father, I hope you're going to make an honest woman of her – or a dishonest one. Either one will do, just to keep her quiet.'

'Daddy!' said Cedar, in a shocked voice that fooled nobody.

22

TO JAMES BOND:
THE GIFT OF A DAUGHTER

Cedar Leiter and James Bond stood on the balcony of his room at the Maison de Ville, New Orleans, looking out at the view. Somewhere near at hand, below them, a pianist was trying to recreate Art Tatum playing 'Aunt Hagar's Blues'. Cedar and James were arguing.

'But you've said it *would* be different if I wasn't your old friend's daughter, James. Can't you forget about that?'

'Difficult.' Bond had turned monosyllabic, particularly since talking, long distance, to M, who had sounded exceptionally cheerful and told him to take a couple of weeks' leave. 'No, 007, make that a month. You really have deserved it this time. Very good show indeed.'

'What do you mean, difficult?' Cedar became petulant. 'You have said it all, James. You'd take me to bed like a shot if . . .'

'If it wasn't for your father, yes. And there's an end to it.'

'It's *not* incest!'

'But it wouldn't seem right.' Bond knew very well that it *would* seem very right if it happened. But . . .

'Look. I've got time to kill. So have you. At least let's go off and have a vacation together. She held her hands up, palms facing outwards. 'No strings, James. I promise, no strings.'

Cedar immediately put her hands behind her neck, crossing her fingers in the old childhood ritual which allowed you to lie.

Bond sighed. 'Okay. Just to keep you quiet. But I warn you, Cedar, you try anything and heaven save me – I'm just about old enough to be your father anyway – I'll warm that pretty little backside for you.'

'Oh. Promises,' Cedar giggled.

They stood in silence for a while, and she groped for his hand. 'Isn't it fantastic out there? That sky, all velvet, and the stars?'

They were not to know it, but at that very moment, a rocket blasted off from Russia's Northern Cosmodrome, near Plesetsk, to the south of Archangel. A very few minutes later, a bleep showed on the centre projection in the Main Control Room of the NORAD centre, in Cheyenne Mountain.

Within seconds, the Space Wolves Command Post, just along the passageway from Main Control, was setting one of its laser-armed platforms in a similar orbit, to close on the unidentified new object.

The Space Wolf was held off, within range, for the next thirty minutes, until the Satellite Data System recognised the newly launched arrival as another Meteor weather satellite. Only then was the Space Wolf quietly withdrawn and placed back into its normal orbit.

But Cedar and James Bond knew nothing of this. They simply stood there, looking out at the stars, with Bond's hand gradually gripping Cedar's palm. He gave it a little squeeze.

'Okay, daughter,' he asked, 'where do you want to go?'

'Well . . .' Cedar's answer was cut short by the telephone.

'Hi, James.' Felix Leiter's voice made Bond feel oddly guilty. 'I'm in the bar, and there's a package for you, old friend,' Felix told him.

'Down in a couple of minutes.' Bond cradled the telephone. 'Your father. With a horse whip I should think.' He told Cedar to wait for him, then they would go out to dinner.

Felix was not in the bar, however, nor could he be found in any of the hotel's public rooms. But the barman told Bond that a man with a limp had been in. There was a package, and a note, for Mr Bond at Reception.

Sure enough, a heavy package, beautifully wrapped, waited for him, together with a neatly typed envelope. Bond tore open the envelope. Inside there was another sealed envelope, and a note. *Open the package first,* it read. *It's from someone really important. Then try the envelope. Felix.*

Bond took the package into the bar, ordered a vodka martini, lit one of his specially made H. Simmons cigarettes, and carefully unwrapped the parcel. Inside was a large box, similar to those made for expensive jewellery. This one carried the Presidential seal embossed on the lid.

Slowly Bond undid the clasp, and lifted the lid. Lying in a specially-moulded bed of silk was a silver-plated Police Positive .38 revolver. Engraved along the barrel were the words *To James Bond. For Special Services.* There followed the signature, and title, of the President of the United States of America.

Bond closed the box, tearing open the other envelope. A single card, handwritten with great care. It read: *To James Bond: The Gift of a Daughter – or whatever you want her to be.*

It was signed, *Felix Leiter,* and, as Bond read it, he knew that the planned holiday with Cedar was going to be laughter, fun, and a purely platonic relationship right down the line.

Waiting for Bond upstairs, Cedar had other ideas, and they were both stubborn as mules.

In his cab heading for the airport, Felix Leiter chuckled to himself.

AFTERWORD

In 1941 Fleming accompanied Admiral Godfrey to the United States for the purpose of establishing relations with the American secret service organisations. In New York Fleming met Sir William Stephenson, 'the quiet Canadian', who became a lifelong friend. Stephenson allowed Fleming to take part in a clandestine operation against a Japanese cipher expert who had an office in Rockefeller Center. Fleming later embellished this story and used it in his first James Bond novel, *Casino Royale* (1953). Stephenson also introduced Fleming to General William Donovan, who had just been appointed Coordinator of Information, a post which eventually evolved into the chairmanship of the Office of Strategic Services and then of the Central Intelligence Agency. At Donovan's request Fleming wrote a lengthy memorandum describing the structure and functions of a secret service organisation. This memorandum later became part of the charter of the OSS and, thus, of the CIA In appreciation Donovan presented Fleming with a .38 Police Positive Colt revolver inscribed 'For Special Services'.

JOAN DELFATTORE,
University of Delaware
(from a dictionary of
literary biography)